Marek was hiding something.

Tahra didn't know how she knew, just that she did—Marek wouldn't sit back and wait for someone else to solve the mystery and bring the perpetrators to justice. Even if she wasn't involved, even if she wasn't still a potential target, Marek was too über-alpha, too much of a take-charge man, to sit quietly on the sidelines while someone else ran the ball.

"What exactly are you doing?" Tahra asked.

"What makes you think I'm doing anything?" he parried.

Tahra knew he was keeping something from her...again.

Again?

Tahra stiffened. Where had that thought come from? What would make her think Marek had deceived her about something in the past? The past she couldn't remember.

She'd ask him, but if he told her too much about her past, how would she know if she ever really regained her memory or just thought she had?

There's another reason, too, a little voice in the back of her mind taunted her. *You're afraid to know*.

Because despite the strikes Marek had against him, he was drawing her under his spell, like a fragile moth to a far-too-tempting flame.

Be sure to check out the previous volumes in the Man on a Mission miniseries!
Man on a Mission: These heroes, working at home and overseas, will do anything for justice, honor...and love

* * *

If you're on Twitter, tell us what you think of Harlequin Romantic Suspense!
#harlequinromsuspense

Dear Reader,

“Oh, what a tangled web we weave. When first we practice to deceive!” Sir Walter Scott wrote those lines centuries ago, but they still hold true today. One lie begets another, and another, and soon the lies take on a life of their own.

When I wrote *King’s Ransom*, part of my Man on a Mission miniseries, Captain Marek Zale played a pivotal role, providing secret protection for the woman who would become Zakhar’s queen. And in *Alec’s Royal Assignment*, he (and we) met Tahra Edwards, administrative assistant to the hero of that book at the US embassy in Zakhar. Marek and Tahra were such compelling characters, I knew I’d have to write their story.

In many ways Tahra reminds me of the heroines I loved in romances years ago. But just as I have grown and changed over the years, Tahra is also very different from those long-ago heroines. She knows what she wants, and she won’t settle for anything less than an equal partnership with the man she loves, despite being “an old-fashioned girl.”

And Marek? Zakhar is fifty years behind the times, and über-alpha hero Marek is a product of his environment. But he has already learned a few home truths about women and their role in society in *Alec’s Royal Assignment*. Now, in *The Bodyguard’s Bride-to-Be*, he’s about to be brought into the twenty-first century in the way only Tahra can do it. But first Marek must explain away a tangled web of lies and deception... begun with the best of intentions.

I love hearing from my readers. Please email me at AmeliaAutin@aol.com and let me know what you think.

Amelia Autin

THE BODYGUARD'S BRIDE-TO-BE

Amelia Autin

Recycling programs
for this product may
not exist in your area.

ISBN-13: 978-0-373-28203-6

The Bodyguard's Bride-to-Be

This edition published by arrangement with Harlequin Books S.A.

For questions and comments about the quality of this book, please contact us at CustomerService@Harlequin.com.

Printed in U.S.A.

Award-winning author **Amelia Autin** is an inveterate reader who can't bear to put a good book down... or part with it. She's a longtime member of Romance Writers of America and served three years as its treasurer. Amelia resides with her PhD engineer husband in quiet Vail, Arizona, where they can see the stars at night and have a "million-dollar view" of the Rincon Mountains from their backyard.

Books by Amelia Autin

Harlequin Romantic Suspense

Man on a Mission

Cody Walker's Woman
McKinnon's Royal Mission
King's Ransom
Alec's Royal Assignment
Liam's Witness Protection
A Father's Desperate Rescue
Killer Countdown
The Bodyguard's Bride-to-Be

The Coltons of Texas

Her Colton P.I.

Silhouette Intimate Moments

Gideon's Bride
Reilly's Return

Visit the Author Profile page at Harlequin.com.

For my sister, Peggie Autin Schommer, who encouraged me in the early days of my writing career...as well as when I decided to jump back into the fray after many years. For a real-life hero, Shannon Johnson, who shielded a coworker with his body during the San Bernardino massacre, saying, "I got you." Not every man has it in him to be a hero, but Shannon Johnson's action that day is the very definition of bravery—conquering your fear and doing what you have to do in the instant you have to do it...even at the cost of your own life.
Requiescat in pace, Mr. Johnson.
And for Vincent...always.

Chapter 1

Tahra Edwards grabbed her lunch bag from the refrigerator in the break room and headed for the elevator. It was too nice a day not to eat lunch outside, and the park across from the United States embassy in the heart of Drago was the perfect place. She ate there a lot, joining the native Zakharians, young and old, who also found the park the perfect midday escape.

She settled on her favorite bench in the shade of a massive oak tree, not too far from the preschool that bordered the park on its eastern side. She loved watching the children at play, even though the sight of them had been bittersweet for the past two weeks…ever since she'd turned down the marriage proposal she'd once prayed to receive. Knowing the children she'd dreamed of having with the man she loved would never be. Knowing she'd never watch her own children this way.

She was early—the playground was empty. But she'd deliberately come early to make sure her favorite spot wasn't taken, as it had been on occasion. That wasn't a problem today.

Tahra had finished her sandwich—the Zakharian bread from the bakery two doors down from her apartment building was worth the extra calories—and was just starting on her apple when the children poured out the door into the preschool's fenced yard. Happy, high-pitched voices came to her as the children swarmed onto the playground equipment—swings set in motion, bodies whizzing down the slide, the more intrepid climbing to the top of the jungle gym.

She smiled to herself with a sense of nostalgia. Her older sister, Carly, had been the intrepid one growing up, daring anything. Tahra had always been the fearful one, afraid to climb so high, afraid of falling. But not when Carly was there. Somehow, when Carly was there, Tahra had found the courage to clamber until they reached the top, pretending she was as fearless as her sister. But Carly had known. And she'd understood. Carly had always understood.

Sighing a little, and missing her globe-trotting big sister a lot, Tahra stood up and walked over to the discreetly placed trash container, the motion taking her closer to the preschool and the children. She watched them for a moment from where she stood, wishing the world at large could see this playground and take a lesson from the blond, fair-skinned Zakharian children—no more than four or five years old—clutching the hands of the newest arrivals to their nation, urging them to join in their play.

Zakhar, like other countries within the European

Union, was taking in as many of the refugees streaming over its borders as it could accommodate…at the express invitation of the king who could do no wrong in the eyes of most of his subjects. These dark-skinned children of refugees from war-torn countries in northern Africa and the Middle East had experienced things no child should ever experience, Tahra knew. Had seen things no child should ever see. But the open hand of friendship from the children in this preschool would go a long way toward helping those terror-filled memories fade with time. And though she wasn't Zakharian, Tahra couldn't help feel a tiny thrill of pride in the country she'd once thought would be her adopted homeland… if the man she loved hadn't…

Tahra had just thrown away her trash when her attention was caught by a lone man standing next to the fenced playground, a knapsack at his feet. One hand clenched the metal fence, and he was staring at the children, who played on, completely oblivious. Something in his intent gaze made Tahra hesitate and made the hair on the back of her neck stand up. Something wasn't right. She couldn't put her finger on it at first, but then she realized the man was too old and too well dressed to be carrying a student's knapsack.

The man turned suddenly and strode in the opposite direction, and Tahra started forward. "Sir!" she called in her rudimentary Zakharan. "Sir, you forgot your knapsack!"

The stranger cast one long look backward. Their eyes met across the short distance, and Tahra knew she'd never forget those eyes. Never forget that face. Then he turned away and continued walking, faster now. Almost running. Tahra watched him for a couple of seconds, then her gaze moved to the knapsack, sitting at the base of the preschool fence, and she knew. "Oh, my God!"

She darted toward the bag, only one thing in her mind. Away. She had to get it away from the children. She grabbed one of the straps and hefted the knapsack into her arms. It was heavy. Heavier than it looked. At first she ran away from the playground as fast as she could, until she realized how risky that was. She put both hands on the strap and swung backward, then heaved the knapsack as far away as possible. She turned toward the playground and screamed to the children at the top of her lungs, "Run! Run!"

She'd taken only two steps toward the fence when the world exploded behind her.

Captain Marek Zale was driving toward the base of the mountain where he liked to hike on his day off, when his pager went off at the same time his cell phone pinged for an incoming text message. He pulled over, checked the number on his pager, then looked at the text message, both from the same sender. He cursed long and low before hitting speed dial. "On my way," he told the man who answered. He glanced at the clock on the dash. "Twelve minutes at the most." He hung up, made an abrupt U-turn and headed for the royal palace.

He made it in ten minutes, then hurried inside to the palace's security command post. "What do we know?" he asked the room. "Where is the royal family?"

"Safe," Major Damon Kostya replied. "The king was just about to leave with Colonel Marianescu for a tour of the air force base outside Timon when we got the news. Major Branko is with him now in the king's private office."

Captain Angelina Mateja-Jones—head of the queen's security detail, who'd just recently returned from maternity leave—answered next. "The queen was with the crown prince in the Royal Garden, but they are now safely inside, with the king. Reports are coming in from all over Zakhar. Four bombs have exploded so far in Drago. Six elsewhere."

Marek closed his eyes briefly, trying but failing to suppress his anger at the cowardly terrorists who would do something like this, who would kill innocent victims to make their political statement—whatever that statement was. "Where?" he rasped. "Has any group claimed responsibility?"

"Not yet," Major Kostya stated, answering the second question first. "All four bombs in Drago appear to be the same type—explosives packed densely inside a loose shell of fléchettes for maximum mortality. Reports from elsewhere in the country are still unconfirmed, but preliminary reports seem to indicate the same. So the working theory is this is a coordinated attack."

Marek nodded.

"As for where," Major Kostya continued, "here in Drago, one bomb exploded on a train from the eastern border, just as it was pulling into the main station in the center of the city. Twenty-three people are dead, more than a hundred fifty wounded, both inside and outside the train. Another bomb went off at the refugee processing center downtown. The death toll there is lower... for now. Nineteen dead for sure, but that number could rise. And there are roughly two hundred wounded."

"Suicide bombers?"

Angelina shook her head. She was Angelina to Marek

now that she no longer reported to him, now that they were captains together and he'd become friends with Angelina and her husband, the US embassy's regional security officer. "Not to the best of our knowledge," she said. "A third bomb detonated at a Zakharian National Forces training facility on the outskirts of Drago. Two training officers are dead and seventeen enlisted personnel—all new recruits. Twenty-nine are in the hospital."

Major Kostya cleared his throat. "One of the dead and two of the injured were women recruits. But they do not appear to have been specific targets."

Marek glanced at Angelina. "What about the fourth bomb?"

"A preschool near the US embassy."

"My God," Marek whispered. "Children?"

Major Kostya answered him. "Miraculously, no. Eyewitnesses in the park say someone spotted the bomb and got it away from the playground before it exploded. Only one person was wounded—the woman who saved the children. Apparently she saw the man leave the bomb, which was hidden in a knapsack. Then she—"

Angelina's cell phone chirped, and she moved away to take the call. The two men watched her stiffen. "Yes, Alec," she said in a husky voice. "Yes. He is here. I will tell him."

She put her phone away, drew a deep breath, then turned to Marek, sympathy on her face. "There is no way to tell you except straight-out. It is Tahra. Tahra is the woman who saw the terrorist leave the bomb. She is the one who saved the children."

Not dead, Marek pleaded with God in his mind as he steeled himself to hear the worst. *Please, God, not dead.*

"Alec just called me," she explained, referring to her husband, who was Tahra's boss at the US embassy. "Tahra is in surgery."

"Where?" Marek was surprised at how calm his voice sounded. As if his world hadn't just nearly ended.

"Saint Anne's Hospital, near the cathedral." He nodded as he took the information in, although his brain wasn't really functioning. "Do you want someone to drive you there?"

"No, I… My duty is here," he said automatically.

Angelina grabbed Marek's arm and pulled him out of earshot of Major Kostya. "Admirable," she said fiercely. "But stupid. Do you think I will let you anywhere near the crown prince in this state? Do you think that is what the king would wish? You are not capable of functioning as a bodyguard at this moment, and no one expects you to, least of all the king."

She waited for that to sink in, then added, "You are not even supposed to be working today. Go to the hospital. Go be with Tahra. If the crown prince's own father is not enough to protect him along with the men who *are* on duty, then I will personally make sure he is safe. *Your* duty is with Tahra. Go!"

Marek arrived at the hospital to find that Tahra was still in surgery. And the waiting room receptionist would tell him nothing of how she was doing. Even when he claimed this was a matter of national security and tried to invoke his authority as head of the crown prince's security detail, she steadfastly refused to disclose anything until he lied. "She is my fiancée."

The lie helped a little, but there wasn't much the receptionist *could* tell him, except that Tahra hadn't yet come out of surgery. "But the surgeons here—they are the best," she reassured him. "She is in good hands—the surgeons' and God's."

Marek collapsed into the nearest chair, abruptly aware his muscles were trembling. Relief flooded him, and he realized he'd been steeling himself to hear the worst. The worst that could still happen, but hadn't yet. He glanced around the waiting room and was surprised—yet not really surprised—to see Alec Jones sitting across the room. He wasn't sure if that was a good sign or not. Was Alec waiting for a dying declaration, the way a policeman would be? When that thought occurred to him, that was when he saw the two other men in the waiting room. *Plainclothes policemen for sure*, he thought. *Detectives.* Which only made sense—perhaps they were hoping Tahra had seen something more than the knapsack she'd managed to get rid of before it exploded and killed the children the bomb had been intended for.

That brought it all down on him again—Tahra could be dying. His darling Tahra…who'd been right to accuse him of not trusting her with the truth. Why hadn't he told her at some point during the past eighteen months, especially once they became constant companions? Because of Zorina, of course. As if Tahra could ever do what Zorina had done.

"Marek?" Suddenly Alec was standing in front of him, and he looked up at the other man. "The police wouldn't tell me much about what happened," Alec said, taking a seat next to Marek. "Other than to let me know Tahra was in the hospital here because she'd been wounded in a bombing. And the receptionist won't divulge anything," he added, inclining his head toward the same woman who'd guarded Tahra's privacy from Marek. "Do you know anything more?"

Marek shook his head in automatic denial, then realized that wasn't fair to the American. Tahra *did* work for him. Not only that, but Alec was also the principal security attaché and adviser to the US ambassador. Which meant he was entitled to know of any threat to the embassy's security. "All I know is what the eyewitnesses in the park told the police. They saw Tahra grab something from the fence next to the preschool and throw it as far away as she could before yelling to the children to run. But she was not able to escape herself before the bomb—"

He couldn't finish because the idea of a blast anywhere near Tahra threatened his composure. Zakharian men never cried. Hadn't he been taught that since childhood? And yet...without that emotional release he needed something else. Vengeance. An eye for an eye. But right now there was no one on whom to wreak vengeance. No terrorist organization had come forward to claim responsibility for the attacks. That could change at any time, but for now...

Alec glanced away for a moment, as if to give Marek time to get his emotions under control. Then he said, "I heard you tell the receptionist Tahra's your fiancée. Probably not the best time to say it, but congratulations—Tahra's one in a million, and you're a lucky man." Alec and Angelina were the only ones who knew how Marek felt about Tahra. Not that he'd ever actually come right out and told either of them, but anyone who'd seen Marek and Tahra together—which Alec and Angelina had—would know...

Alec added, "Tahra didn't mention the two of you

were engaged, but I've been pretty busy lately. Guess she didn't have a chance to tell me." Something in Alec's steady gaze told Marek the other man suspected he'd lied about being Tahra's fiancé, but wasn't going to call him on it. Yet. Not when the lie had garnered information about Tahra's condition.

He opened his mouth—to say what, he wasn't quite sure—when a man in medical garb walked into the waiting room, spoke to the receptionist, then came over to where Alec and Marek were seated. Both men stood quickly.

"You are waiting to hear about Tahra Edwards?" the surgeon asked in Zakharan.

Alec spoke first. "Tahra works for me at the US embassy."

"She is my fiancée," Marek threw in, not even waiting for Alec to finish.

The surgeon nodded. "She is in recovery. Her wounds are serious, but not life threatening. There was internal bleeding, but no major damage to any vital organs. We were easily able to effect repairs without complications via a minimally invasive technique called a laparoscopy. She has a broken right wrist, but it was clean and we set it without difficulty. There will be some scarring, of course, from the fléchette rounds that pierced her body." His lips tightened as if merely the *idea* of fléchettes angered him. "But she was turned away from the bomb when it detonated, so her face is fortunately untouched."

He hesitated. "The only thing that concerns me is the head injury she received. Severe concussion. Apparently the force of the bomb blast threw her into a park bench, and her head took a terrific blow. There is some swelling of the brain, but there does not appear to be any internal bleeding inside her skull. We have induced a medical coma to allow her body to heal without the distraction of pain. We are monitoring her closely, however, and will deal appropriately with any cause for alarm." He smiled reassuringly at Marek. "Your fiancée was a healthy young woman before this happened, and the prognosis for a complete recovery is excellent."

How Marek was able to hang on to his stoic expression, he never knew. "Thank you," he told the surgeon in a voice wiped clean of emotion. He shook the man's hand. "Thank you."

"Always glad to deliver good news," the surgeon replied with a smile. "You can see her as soon as they bring her up to her room. She will not be able to respond, of course, but remain positive—it is always possible she can hear you even in a coma." He glanced at Alec and switched to English. "You may also see her as soon as she is conscious, but she will not be returning to work any time soon."

"She saw my face," Sergeant Thimo Vasska reported to his superior officer in the headquarters of the Zakharian Liberation Front. "It is possible she could identify me."

Before the lieutenant could reply, another man entered the room so quietly he was there before either man was aware. Sergeant Vasska stiffened, then nervously saluted the supreme commander of their revolutionary force.

"That is unfortunate," Colonel Damek Borka said in his flat, emotionless voice. It wasn't his real name, of course. Everyone in the Zakharian Liberation Front went by a pseudonym because the danger of disclosure was great...although more for some than for others. "Unfortunate...for her and for you." The colonel said nothing more, but his face conveyed how badly the sergeant had screwed up.

Failure was unacceptable, the man knew. If the witness could not be silenced, the Zakharian Liberation Front would have no choice but to remove the link between the botched attack today and their secret organization. Sergeant Vasska nodded his understanding. "Yes, sir," he said, saluting again. "It will be dealt with immediately."

Marek stared down at the unconscious woman in the hospital bed, his emotions churning. Tahra, his darling Tahra, could have died today. And he wouldn't have been able to do a damn thing to prevent it.

He took her unbandaged left hand in his and raised it to his lips. *Forgive me*, he told her silently, aware that the nurse attending Tahra and setting things up could hear every word he said. *But until you are conscious, I have no choice. I must protect you the only way I know how.*

He waited until the nurse turned away, adjusting something on one of the machines monitoring Tahra's condition, then reached into his pocket and pulled out the little ring box he'd been carrying for weeks. Tahra had declined his proposal, but that had changed nothing. She was still his *mariskya* and always would be. He had drawn back, wanting to give her time to see what a mistake she was making, but he'd had to repeat the lie he'd told the receptionist to hospital staff, that Tahra was his fiancée, or else he would have been shut out of her sickroom. And that he couldn't have borne.

He surreptitiously slid the engagement ring onto her finger, then kissed her hand again. "Sleep well, my darling," he whispered in Zakharan. "I will keep you safe from this moment forward."

Tahra slept on, oblivious, but he took comfort in the slight rise and fall of her chest.

Marek caught the nurse's eye. "I have left my phone numbers with the main desk. Call me immediately, please, if there is any change in my fiancée's condition."

The nurse nodded, and Marek walked out, passing the two soldiers from the Zakharian National Forces posted right on either side of the door, returning their salutes automatically. He hadn't even had to ask Colonel Marianescu to post guards, although he would have if necessary. The colonel was too smart not to realize the attacks today *had* to all be related and were a threat to national security. Which meant Tahra—a witness to the attack on the school—was also vital to national security. No one else had been close enough to the man who'd left the knapsack to identify him, but several witnesses in the area had indicated Tahra had been much closer to the terrorist. Anything she could tell them about the attack would be crucial. Which meant it was very possible her life was still in danger…and *not* from the injuries she'd received.

Chapter 2

Tahra floated in a sea of disjointed memories. Carly was there, and her parents. Then her parents were gone, and seventeen-year-old Carly was kneeling in front of ten-year-old Tahra, saying gently, "They're not coming back, honey. They're never coming back. But I'm here. And I'll take care of you, I promise."

Tears and years.

There was Carly, fiercely confronting the secretary of state. "You think you can sweep this under the rug? Hell, no. That's not going to happen. The State Department is going to come up with a better solution, and this had better not impact Tahra's career in *any* way, you hear me? Not in any way. Believe me, you don't even want to be *thinking* along those lines, understand? Because I'll blow the lid off this scandal so fast it'll make your head spin. And you won't be the only one affected by the fallout. You got that?"

Carly, so protective of her baby sister, who, Tahra was ashamed to admit, had always had trouble standing up for herself in any confrontational situation. She'd fought off the foreign diplomat who'd attacked her—at least she wasn't *that* much of a coward—and had saved herself from being savagely raped by stabbing him repeatedly. But when the State Department had tried to blame everything on her and throw her to the wolves, Tahra had called Carly from jail as her world crashed in around her. And Carly had come charging to the rescue again, bailing her out, then storming the secretary of state's office. Carly, who wasn't afraid of anyone or anything…except losing those she loved.

In the way of dreams, Tahra was a little girl again, watching from the sidelines as most of the kids in her kindergarten class played Red Rover during recess. She knew she would be good at it. She could run like the wind and she was stronger than she looked—the locked hands could never hold *her* in Red Rover, she'd break through the line in a heartbeat. But the other kids never asked her to join in the game, and she was too shy to force her way into their charmed circle the way Carly would have had no trouble doing.

Then, through the murky depths of her dreams, she heard a voice. A masculine voice. Deep. Strong. Just a hint of an accent that made the English words sound unbelievably sexy. A voice she knew she should recognize…but didn't. What was he saying? At first she couldn't quite force her brain to comprehend, but then…

"I am back, Tahra. I promised you I would be, and here I am. I will always keep my promises, *mariskya*.

Just as I will always honor and cherish you. Just as I will protect you with my life."

The words floated in the ether surrounding Tahra, but there was something incredibly appealing about them. About the simple way they were uttered, too. There was also something about the voice she responded to instinctively. And she knew he spoke the truth. Whoever he was, she was safe with him, the same way she was safe when Carly was there.

She didn't recognize the foreign word, though. *Mariskya.* Didn't know what it meant. But she wanted to. The way he said it, she knew the word was important. She also desperately wanted to know who he was. Because—like the word—the man who'd spoken it was important, too. She just didn't know why.

"The Zakharian Liberation Front," Colonel Marianescu announced in Zakharan to the seven other men and one woman sitting around the conference table in the War Room inside the royal palace. "They have claimed responsibility for yesterday's bombings. What do we know about it?"

Marek exchanged a rueful glance with Angelina because he knew the answer was "Nothing." The Zakharian Liberation Front had never popped up on anyone's radar until yesterday. And while technically this wasn't an indictment of Angelina or him because she was responsible for the queen's security and he was responsible for the crown prince's, any threat to national security could be a danger to the royals, and they both knew it.

The silence in the room was deafening. "I see," said the colonel. His lips thinned. "Needless to say, the king is *not* pleased."

His last five words were a lash against the pride of all his listeners, but especially Marek. Until he'd met Tahra, nothing had been more important to him than the king he was proud to serve. Keeping the queen safe—and subsequently the crown prince when the king had personally asked him to take over protection of his son—had been especially important to him because those things were of paramount importance *to the king*. The king had made it abundantly clear that in any life-and-death situation, the safety of the queen and the crown prince came first. *Then* the king. That had required an adjustment in thinking, but everyone on the three security details had eventually come to accept it.

But from the moment Marek had met Tahra, the royal family had slid one notch in his personal priority hierarchy. Had he somehow overlooked a threat to them because of that? He didn't know, and the uncertainty ate at his gut. Because duty was *everything* to him. Or at least it had been…until Tahra.

Marek dragged his attention back to Colonel Marianescu with difficulty. The colonel was saying, "It is fairly obvious from the one-sentence credo stated in their press release that the Zakharian Liberation Front's political agenda is in opposition to the refugees Zakhar has recently welcomed inside its borders. 'Zakhar for Zakharians' leaves no room for any other interpretation. And all the targets of yesterday's bombings were—"

The door to the War Room opened, and King Andre Alexei IV strode in. Everyone scrambled to their feet, but the king said quickly, "As you were, gentlemen. I apologize for being late—I had intended to be here from the beginning, but I was detained by the Privy Council." He spoke softly with his cousin, Colonel Marianescu, then nodded and faced the room again, standing. "What I have to say will not take long."

Marek had rarely seen the king like this—cold anger was coming off him in palpable waves. "I will not speak the name of this organization because its very name is an affront to every decent Zakharian. Nor will I repeat their credo for the same reason. All I will say is that this organization's actions are unacceptable. *Unacceptable!*" The king paused and clenched his jaw against the anger that obviously threatened to get away from him.

When he had himself under control again, the king continued. His voice was soft, but no one in the room took his words as anything other than a direct order. "I want three things. First, I want the refugees who are here *at my invitation* to be protected at all costs. Second, I want the individuals involved in these murderous and cowardly acts caught and brought to justice. Third, I want this organization rooted out and destroyed. It is one thing to espouse this credo—every man is entitled to his own thoughts. It is another thing entirely to take violent action to force that on others, and it will *not* be tolerated. Is that understood?"

A chorus of "Yes, Sire" echoed through the room.

The king nodded with satisfaction. "Very good, gentlemen. I will leave you and Colonel Marianescu to work out the details. Thank you." He turned and spoke privately with his cousin for a moment, then they headed for the door together. As they had when the king had entered the room, everyone stood and remained at attention until he was gone.

Angelina caught Marek's eye. "Have you ever seen him this angry?" she whispered as they took their seats again. "Not even the assassination attempt on his son generated this kind of reaction as I recall."

"I did not witness it myself, you understand," Marek replied in an undertone that couldn't be heard by the others sitting around them. "But he nearly killed Prince Nikolai for attempting to kill the queen. That was before she was the queen," he clarified. "The man who *did* witness it said the king's anger was awesome to behold—similar to his reaction today, I would imagine. I do not know how the queen convinced the king otherwise, but somehow she did, and Prince Nikolai lived that night—he went on to stand his trial before being convicted."

Angelina nodded her understanding. Prince Nikolai was dead now, which they both knew, but *not* at the king's hand. Then quickly, as Colonel Marianescu returned to the head of the table, she asked, "What is the word on Tahra? Has she regained consciousness yet?"

Marek shook his head, fighting off his own surge of anger at what had nearly happened to her. "She is still in a medically induced coma. Until they bring her out of it, she will not… That is, she is still—"

"Shh," whispered the man on Marek's left. "Colonel Marianescu is speaking."

"Suggestions?" the colonel was saying.

No one spoke, and once again Marek and Angelina exchanged speaking glances. They were the only two captains in the room, included in this high-level meeting because they headed the security details for the crown prince and the queen, and neither felt comfortable speaking up first. But when the silence dragged on, Marek asked, "Do forensics on all the bombs confirm it *was* the action of one group? Yes, the Zakharian

Liberation Front has taken public credit, but before we rule anything else out..."

"Good point, Captain Zale." The colonel's gaze swept the room. "Forensic analysis is not complete, but yes, the preliminary assessment supports the theory that the bombs were all the work of one group. In fact, that they were all the work of one man."

"*That* tells us something," Angelina pointed out. "If all ten bombs were assembled by the same man, we may be looking at a relatively small organization."

The colonel nodded. "Possible, of course. A good working theory."

"Especially since the organization has managed to fly under the radar until now," Marek added. His eyes sought out those of Major Stesha, the head of the secret intelligence service, who had sat himself at the far end of the conference table that could seat many more than the nine who had congregated there, and who—up until now—had avoided catching anyone's eye. As if he felt the shame of failure more keenly than anyone else. "It is also probable the Zakharian Liberation Front has only recently come into existence," Marek continued, welcoming the change his words wrought in the expression on Major Stesha's face. "'Zakhar for Zakharians'? As Colonel Marianescu said, that credo can only refer to opposition to the influx of refugees who have settled here over the past two years, and in even greater numbers in the past six months."

"Confirmed by the targets of yesterday's bombings, at least here in Drago," Angelina threw in. "A train from the eastern border, carrying mostly émigrés. The refugee processing center in downtown Drago. The Zakharian National Forces facility where new recruits were training—almost seventy percent of whom were male refugees eighteen and older who had joined pursuant to Zakharian law."

Marek, along with every other man in the room, knew what Angelina was referring to. All Zakharian men were required to join the military when they turned eighteen and serve for at least four years. Service in the military would be part of the émigrés' path to Zakharian citizenship.

"And the preschool that was targeted but was miraculously spared due to one woman's bravery?" Angelina reminded them all. "When the king decreed that as many refugee children as possible be placed in the same schools to keep friends together and ease their assimilation into Zakharian life, that preschool was one of the magnet schools chosen for placement. Nearly half the children in that yard yesterday were émigrés."

Pain slashed through Marek as Angelina spoke, reminding him of how close Tahra had come to dying. But while he fought to retain his stoic demeanor, this time the pain was accompanied by an intense wave of pride. From the moment he'd heard the news about Tahra, all he'd focused on was how much she was suffering and how he'd nearly lost her. Now he realized just how courageous she was, risking her life without hesitation to save those children. If he hadn't already loved her to the last drop of his blood, he would have for that selfless act alone.

He'd slept in her hospital room last night. And he had every intention of doing the same tonight and every night until she regained consciousness and was able to tell the nurses herself that Marek was *not* her fiancé and had no business being there. Some men might not have been able to sleep slouching in a chair, but Marek was not one of them. He was a soldier—he could sleep anywhere. And where he chose to sleep was at Tahra's side.

He couldn't guard her 24/7—there were soldiers posted outside the door to her hospital room to do that. And besides, it would be unthinkable to request leave during this national crisis, despite his desperate worry over Tahra.

But he could guard her when he wasn't on duty. He could sit beside her. Sleep beside her. Express his love—the love she didn't believe in—the only way he could while she was unconscious. He would do this because he couldn't *not* do this.

And when Tahra came out of her coma? When she banished him from her side the way she'd done when she'd rejected his marriage proposal just over two weeks ago? *I will cross that bridge when I come to it*, Marek thought, his eyes narrowing with determination. *For now, she is mine to protect.*

Marek abruptly halted on the threshold of Tahra's hospital room when he saw a strange woman sitting in *his* chair beside the bed. The woman looked up, and though he'd never met her, he recognized her from a picture Tahra had shown him, and from his own research into Tahra's family. Carly Edwards. Tahra's famous older sister.

Someone must have called her, he realized. Guilt stabbed through him because he should have called Tahra's sister himself, as soon as he learned Tahra was in the hospital. But the idea had never occurred to him—too many other things to worry about. *Alec*, he thought. *Alec must have called her.*

His supposition was confirmed when Tahra's sister stood and walked toward him, then took his arm and led him out of the room, saying softly, "The embassy notified me immediately because I'm Tahra's next of kin. I'm Carly Edwards, and you're Marek, right? Captain Marek Zale? I want to talk with you, but I don't want to do it where Tahra might hear."

She dropped his arm once they were outside, and she headed down the wide hospital corridor, not even looking to see if Marek was following her. He smiled a little to himself, remembering the bits and pieces Tahra had mentioned to him about her older sister...and Carly's formidable reputation in the world of journalism. "Tiger Shark" was her nickname—a well-deserved one—and his smile faded as he followed her to the waiting room on that floor. Alec hadn't called him on it when Marek had declared Tahra was his fiancée, but he didn't think Carly would afford him the same consideration. Which meant he'd better come up with a story—in the next sixty seconds. One that would satisfy Carly. Or else his little fiction was going to be blown out of the water.

She stopped when she reached a quiet corner of the waiting room, then turned to confront him. "Imagine my surprise," she drawled in the soft Virginia accent that reminded him of Tahra, but at the same time held a note of steel Tahra's voice never had, "when my fiancé's brother called me to say Tahra was in the hospital...but *her* fiancé was keeping close tabs on her and could keep me apprised of her condition."

Marek had forgotten. Tahra had mentioned her sister had recently become engaged to Senator Shane Jones, who—in one of those quirks of reality—was Alec's oldest brother.

"I can explain."

"I hope you can, Captain. Because I'm *this* close—" she held her thumb and forefinger up to show him exactly what she meant "—to having you thrown out of this hospital, and arrested if I can swing it." When Marek didn't immediately speak, she pounced. "You are *not* Tahra's fiancé. She told me all about your proposal, and why she turned it down. So you have no business being here."

His face hardened. "Whatever Tahra may have told you about that fiasco is meaningless. She loves me. If she confided anything to you, she would have confided that. Yes?"

"That's neither here nor there," Carly countered quickly.

"If you know that much, you know I love her, too." The words poured out of him, the words he hadn't been able to say to Tahra herself, but which she'd known were true when he proposed.

"Again, not germane to the situation."

He didn't know what *germane* meant—he prided himself on his English, but it wasn't perfect. He could infer the meaning by the context, however, and there was even more steel in his voice than in Carly's when he answered her. "The hospital would give me no information on Tahra's condition until I said I was her fiancé. Have you never told a lie for the purest of reasons, Miss Edwards?"

A flash of something that might have been guilt crossed her face, but she raised her chin and said, "Ms. Edwards. Not 'miss.'"

"I apologize, Ms. Edwards," Marek said stiffly. "We do not have that distinction in Zakhar, and Tahra never—" He chopped that sentence off before he could finish it, then returned to his initial point. "I would tell any lie I had to in that situation. I would do it again, no matter the consequences. In my heart Tahra is mine to cherish, and I could not bear—"

He broke off as emotion threatened to swamp him. When he had himself under control, he said, "My deception has harmed no one, least of all Tahra. Ask yourself what you would have done under the circumstances, Ms. Edwards."

Her eyes searched his face for a full minute before they softened. "Okay, I'll buy that. But what are you going to do when Tahra regains consciousness?"

"That will be up to Tahra. If she asks me to leave, I will leave." He hesitated, then added, "I pray she will not, but that is in God's hands."

"Okay," Carly repeated, and the confrontational tone in her voice was noticeably absent. "So what can you tell me about how Tahra was injured? Alec wasn't all that specific when we talked on the phone, and I came directly to the hospital from the airport." She gave a delicate snort. "And though the guards on the door let me pass—*after* I showed them my passport and they checked with their commanding officer, who consulted with the US embassy—they either wouldn't or couldn't give me any details."

"I can tell you what I know...but only as Tahra's sister." He gave her an apologetic smile. "This information cannot be broadcast because these attacks are a breach of national security, and an investigation is underway. You are a journalist, and—"

She cut him off. "You have my word. Anything you tell me as Tahra's sister will be in strictest confidence."

Marek quickly relayed the facts he knew. "So you see, Tahra could still be in danger. We do not *know* this, but it is very likely. If the terrorist who left the bomb at the preschool thinks she can identify him, he will likely stop at nothing to silence her." Marek let that sink in before adding in a low voice, "There are guards protecting her, but I…I slept in her room last night because I could not stay away. Because I had to protect her *myself.* I will do the same every night until she regains consciousness. Until she personally rejects my protection. Can you understand this?"

"I understand." A tiny smile flickered over Carly's lips and spread to her eyes. "I understand something else, too. You really *do* love her."

It wasn't a question, but Marek answered anyway. "But of course."

"There's no 'of course' about it."

Marek shook his head. "To know Tahra is to love her," he said simply. "I had no choice."

"There is always a choice," she insisted.

"Not with Tahra."

Tahra was tired of swimming through the murky waters of her memories. She swam and swam, but no matter how hard she tried there was something just out of reach. It was important—she knew it was important—but her head ached dreadfully whenever she tried to force herself to remember.

Giving up for now, she latched onto the memory of her sister, so fresh and crisp in her mind. There was Carly at Tahra's high school graduation. So proud. So happy. Tahra hadn't known it at the time, but Carly had passed on an exclusive interview to be there for her little sister. Carly had done something similar when Tahra had graduated from college. *"Don't sweat it,"* Carly had told her. *"You're more important than the senior commander of the US forces in Afghanistan."* Tahra hadn't really believed it, but it had made her love Carly even more…if that were at all possible.

Love. That was it. The thing she couldn't remember had something to do with love. Not the love of sisters for each other, but someone else. And though she couldn't remember the details, she knew one thing for sure. Whatever it was—*whoever it was*—she'd wept bitter tears. Then she'd picked up the shattered remnants of her life and forged ahead. Just like Carly.

The room was shrouded in darkness when Tahra groggily opened her eyes. She didn't know where she was—this wasn't her bedroom in the quaint apartment she'd just moved into a half mile away from her job at the US embassy. She liked her new apartment better than her old one, even if it was farther away from work. And she liked her new boss, too, a lot more than her old one. She hadn't worked for Alec Jones very long—less than a week. And he wasn't an easy man to work for unless you were a perfectionist like him—which she was. The previous regional security officer had done a slipshod job, in Tahra's estimation, and she'd been glad when Alec had replaced him with almost no notice.

Tahra gave herself a little mental shake as she suddenly realized she'd allowed her thoughts to wander. *Where am I?* she wondered now. She wasn't in her bedroom. She wasn't in her bed. *Where am I?*

She blinked at the darkness and turned her head, then caught her breath at the pain that throbbed behind her eyes when the side of her head touched the pillow.

She hadn't realized there was anyone else in the room, but someone had heard her gasp, because a dim light over the bed was suddenly switched on and adjusted so it wasn't shining directly into her eyes. A strong hand curved beneath her neck and lifted her head, turning it until the damaged area was no longer in contact with anything.

Tahra sighed with thankfulness and smiled up at the stranger at her bedside. Then her eyes widened because this man was so handsome he took her breath away. His close-cropped golden-brown hair and deep blue eyes adorned a face that—even without a smile—could have been the model for Adonis. Her heart skipped a beat, and she blinked. Then her gaze took in all the equipment surrounding her bed, some of it faintly beeping. The IV connected to the back of her left hand. The cast on her right wrist. And though she didn't remember coming here, she felt she was on solid ground asking, "Am I in the hospital?"

"Yes." There was just the slightest trace of an accent to this man's English, and it seemed familiar somehow.

She frowned. "I could have sworn I heard Carly talking earlier, but—"

"Your sister *was* here. She left around midnight." He darted a glance at his watch. "That was almost three hours ago. She will return in the morning."

"Oh." So she hadn't imagined it. "I'm in Zakhar, right?"

"Yes, Tahra." The back of his hand brushed her cheek in a way that seemed too intimate for a doctor or nurse, and she shrank away from it.

"Please don't," she whispered. She'd once let a man touch her this way without voicing an objection, not wanting to cause a public scene. That had eventually led to a nightmare she'd only recently recovered from, and she'd learned a hard lesson about speaking up for herself. "I don't know you, and I—"

The stranger froze. "You do not know me?"

Chapter 3

Of all the things Marek had envisioned happening when Tahra came out of the coma, he'd never imagined she wouldn't recognize him. For just a moment his mind went blank. Then, before he could calmly and rationally consider what he should do, he heard himself saying, "I am your fiancé, Tahra."

He gently raised her left hand so she could see the old-fashioned engagement ring he'd placed there, a large pearl surrounded by diamonds in an antique setting, a ring that had been in his family for more than two hundred years. The ring she'd first accepted…then returned. "We are engaged."

"We are?" Her eyes squeezed shut and her lips moved silently. When she finally looked at him again, there was a bewildered expression on her face. "I don't remember. Why don't I remember?" When he just shook his head at her, unable to answer, she pleaded, "Your name. Tell me your name."

"Marek. Marek Zale. Captain in the Zakharian National Forces, on detached status. I am the head of security for the crown prince." He watched closely for a sign that his name or occupation might mean something to her, but they didn't.

"Marek." His name on Tahra's lips was soft and sweet, and Marek's heart ached for all the times she'd uttered it before in exactly the same way. Her chest rose and fell as she breathed deeply. "I'm sorry," she said after a minute. "I don't remember you." And he could tell by the poignant catch in her voice that she really *was* sorry. Then to his amazement her eyes fluttered closed. "Marek," she whispered, "I'm so sorry." Her breathing slowed until he knew without a doubt she was asleep again.

"Oh, Tahra." Her name was torn from his throat, and he touched her cheek with fingers that trembled.

Marek was waiting outside Tahra's door when her sister showed up punctually at seven, the exact time she'd told him last night she would arrive. "We need to talk," he told Carly urgently. He glanced at the two guards standing at attention on either side of the door, who were due to be relieved at eight. "Privately."

"We can't talk in there?" Carly asked, pointing toward Tahra's room. He shook his head. "Well, can I at least go in and see her first?"

"She is sleeping, but she is no longer in a coma. She woke around three this morning, and we spoke for a few minutes. That is what I must discuss with you."

"Tahra's no longer in a coma?" she asked eagerly. "That's great news! Why didn't you call me immediately?"

He held out his hand, indicating the waiting room at the end of the corridor they'd used last night for their private conversation. "Please."

They'd no sooner seated themselves in a secluded corner when Carly said, "Something's wrong. Hemorrhage? Stroke?" Her lips tightened. "Just tell me straight-out—I won't fall apart, I promise you." Her quickened breathing was the only indication she wasn't as calm as she appeared.

"No, nothing like that," Marek assured her. "But I spoke with Tahra's doctors an hour ago. They examined her again and questioned her minutely. Physically she is fine. Still in great pain, of course, but nothing that will not heal."

"Then what? She doesn't remember the explosion, is that it?" Carly shot at him. "It's not all that unusual, you know. People's brains often block out traumatic events, and—"

Marek cut her off. "It is not just that," he said vehemently. "Tahra remembers nothing of the past eighteen months…including me."

Sergeant Thimo Vasska saluted his superior officer, and when told to stand at ease he did so. "What news do you have to report, Sergeant?" the lieutenant asked.

"She is being closely guarded. She had not regained consciousness as of last night, but the nurse's aide I bribed for information said the doctors had lessened her morphine dosage, preparatory to bringing her out of the medically induced coma. So—"

"So she could wake up at any time," said Colonel Damek Borka from the doorway.

The sergeant and the lieutenant both jumped, then turned and saluted the founder and supreme commander of the Zakharian Liberation Front.

The sergeant cleared his throat. "I have taken steps to ensure she will never awaken."

"How, if she is being closely guarded?"

"There will be an unfortunate mix-up with her morphine drip," the sergeant explained. "It was not cheap—the aide was greedy and time was short. But the money will come out of my own pocket," he rushed to add.

"Since it was your mistake to begin with," the colonel said in icy tones, "I never assumed otherwise."

"You did *what*?" Carly demanded, and Marek couldn't really blame her. He could hardly believe it himself.

"I told Tahra we are engaged," he repeated. "I cannot tell you why I said it, unless subconsciously I believed it. But I must ask you not to contradict my statement."

Carly stared at him as if he'd lost his mind. "You can't possibly think I'm going to lie to my sister."

"Not lie. Just do not disabuse her mind of the notion that I have the right to look after her, both here in the hospital and once she is discharged."

"You're crazy if you think—"

"To protect *her*. That is all I am asking."

She made a gesture of frustration. "I can take Tahra back to the States. She'd be safe there."

He shook his head. "Even the United States is not immune to acts of terrorism—you of all people must know this. We know almost nothing of the organization that set the bombs. Ergo, one or more of these men could easily slip into the US, kill Tahra and slip out again before anyone was aware." Icy determination speared through him. "That is *not* going to happen to Tahra, even if I die for it. I give you my word, I will not take advantage of the situation. Tahra will be as safe with me as—" He broke off, then finished, "As you could wish her to be."

"Protecting Tahra doesn't require lying to her."

"No," Marek agreed. "But only I know the memories she is missing. For the past year and a half she and I… That is, I know what her life has been here in Zakhar. I know who she knows, I know who her friends are. Can you say the same?"

Carly shook her head.

"It is also possible that being in close proximity to me will trigger something and those missing memories will return. We were nearly inseparable for most of the past eighteen months, and despite what you might think, Ms. Edwards, the fact that Tahra and I are *not* truly engaged is a mistake I had every intention of rectifying. When I first proposed, she accepted. Did she tell you that?" He didn't wait for a response. "It was only later, when I revealed—"

"She told me."

He continued with barely a pause. "Then you know why she returned my engagement ring. But you cannot think I would leave it at that. I was merely giving Tahra time to come to terms with it. But then this terrorist attack occurred, and I…"

He writhed internally as Carly just stood there for a moment without saying a word, but years of the stoicism demanded of a soldier allowed him to stand calmly under her piercing gaze. Finally she said, "I'll probably live to regret it, but okay. You've convinced me for now not to tell her the truth. But if anything happens to Tahra," she added fiercely, "I will hold you personally responsible, Captain. That is not a threat—merely a statement of fact."

"If anything happens to Tahra," Marek replied, "you will have no target for your vengeance, Ms. Edwards, because I will already be dead. That is also a statement of fact."

Marek headed back toward Tahra's room with Carly at his side keeping pace with his longer stride. He saw a nurse's aide approach the door carrying something and noted with approval that she was challenged by one of the guards stationed there. He was too far away to hear what was said, but the aide showed the guard something she wore on a lanyard around her neck—*hospital badge*, Marek guessed, since it was perused intently before she was allowed to pass inside. A minute later Marek quietly pushed open the door and entered the room himself, Carly right behind him.

The aide had already disconnected the drip tube from the half-empty saline bag hanging from the IV stand beside Tahra's bed and was attempting to insert the tube into another fluid-filled bag, smaller than the first one. She jumped when the door opened, and dropped the full bag she was holding.

"Here," Marek said, moving quickly to retrieve it from the floor, "let me help you."

"No. No. I need no help, thank you," the woman blurted out, grabbing at the bag in Marek's hands.

Her strange behavior set off warning bells in his head, and he refused to let go. He quickly read the label and went cold all over as he realized exactly what he'd barely managed to prevent. "This is not saline," he accused the aide. "This is intravenous morphine."

The woman yanked the bag from Marek's hands and tried to make a break for it. But he snagged her arm and deftly jerked it behind her back, incapacitating her and making her whimper in pain as she tried ineffectively to free herself.

Carly had swiftly moved to block the door to prevent the aide from escaping but stepped aside when Marek bellowed, "Guard!" and both soldiers on duty burst into the room, guns drawn.

The guards were followed closely by a nurse, and Marek realized someone must have pressed the call button. He shot a look at the bed and saw Tahra—pale and obviously in pain—clutching it in her left hand. Their eyes met for a moment, and another flash of pride in her ripped through him. His Tahra wouldn't let herself be a victim if she could help it.

"Retrograde amnesia," the neuropsychologist explained to Tahra later that morning, long after the aide who'd tried to kill her had been hauled off, under arrest by the Drago police. "Most likely a result of the head trauma you received."

Tahra glanced from Carly standing on one side of her bed to Marek standing on the other, and with her left hand lightly touched the right side of her head, which was still bandaged. They hadn't shaved it, the surgeon had explained when he'd visited earlier; they didn't do that much anymore because of the increased risk of infection. And they hadn't even had to clip it. She had a deep contusion from where her head had made contact with a park bench, but no laceration, which meant no stitches, no staples, nothing of that nature.

Just a headache, and—oh, yes—the loss of eighteen months out of her life.

"At this stage, I would not worry too much about it," the neuropsychologist reassured her. "Your motor reflexes are excellent. There is no loss of auditory sensation or perception. Your sight is unaffected, and your grasp of language is unimpaired. More than likely your memory will return slowly over the next few days… possibly even a week or two. But," he said, holding up a cautionary hand, "do not be surprised if your recollection of the actual incident and the moments leading up to it never return. That is very common in trauma of any kind. The brain…" He smiled. "We do not know everything about the brain, you understand, but this much we do know."

The specialist continued listing what Tahra could reasonably expect in the coming days and weeks, and she tried to stay focused. But running through her mind was a thread of panic and fear—that her memory would never return. *There is nothing more frightening than not remembering*, she acknowledged now.

Especially when the not remembering included a terrorist attack…and a fiancé.

Her gaze slid surreptitiously to the man standing so reassuringly beside her. A fiancé who was as obviously unforgettable as Marek Zale.

Tahra was discharged from the hospital three days later. She no longer sported the bandage on her head that made her look like a freak in her own eyes, although she still retained the cast on her right wrist that made it difficult to do something as simple as brushing her teeth. And the open wounds wrought by the fléchettes that had pierced her body from behind had already been replaced with newly formed pink scar tissue. No woman could look at scars on her body with complacence, but Carly had assured Tahra they weren't that bad, and the doctor had said they would fade with time.

The only thing that wasn't on the mend was Tahra's memory. Either the concussion had been worse than the doctors had realized up front, or they'd been too optimistic in their prognosis. Regardless of the reason, eighteen months of her life had been erased, including any memory of the man who had spent every night at her bedside. Who had treated her as gently as if she were made of crystal. Who had gazed at her with the kind of love most women yearned for…although he'd never spoken a word about it. Who'd made no attempt even to kiss her.

Carly had left the day before, at Tahra's insistence. "I'm fine," she'd asserted. "You have a job and a fiancé who both need you more than I do now." Inside Tahra had been afraid of the gaping unknowns in her life, but she hadn't revealed that to her sister.

"You're in good hands," Carly had whispered as she kissed Tahra goodbye. "Let him look after you until you're completely recovered." She'd hesitated, then added enigmatically, "Be kind to him."

Him could only refer to Marek Zale, the man who had solicitously helped her out of the wheelchair the nurse had wheeled her out in as she was being discharged, and then into the waiting limousine, before going around to the other side to sit beside her in the back.

"Where are we going?" she asked.

"Your apartment first, to pack whatever you need for an extended stay in the royal palace."

"What? Why would I—"

"The nurse's aide who tried to kill you has talked," Marek replied. "She was bribed to switch the IV bags, which tells us you *are* in danger. Imminent danger. So the king has decreed you are to be housed in the palace for the time being." He took a deep breath. "Safer for you, and the US ambassador has agreed. You are on short-term disability leave from your job until such time as your memory returns."

She voiced her secret fear. "But what if it never returns?"

Marek took her left hand and held it in his much larger one, squeezing gently, and the gesture was more reassuring than Tahra could have imagined. "Let us not think that way, *mariskya*. Let us remain positive."

Mariskya. For some reason the word was vaguely familiar, but its meaning was tantalizingly just out of reach. And yet it seemed *right* for him to call her that, as if he'd used it before. Many times. There was a glass barricade between the driver and them, ensuring privacy, so Tahra had no hesitation asking Marek, "What does that mean, *mariskya*?"

He smiled faintly. "There is no direct translation. It is a Zakharian endearment along the lines of 'my dearest one,' although it is much more comprehensive."

"You can't expect me to be content with that." Her brow wrinkled, and she asked hesitantly, "Should I know what it means? Did you tell me before?"

His answer was slow in coming. "Yes. The first time I called you *mariskya* you asked me. But I would not tell you because you would not have understood. Not then. Only later, after I… That is, after we…"

He seemed to be heading down a path he found difficult to speak about, and Tahra made an educated guess. "After we became lovers?" Her words hung in the air between them, and though he didn't respond immediately, Tahra knew somehow she'd guessed wrong—that was *not* what he'd been trying to say.

After a long silence, Marek finally said in a low voice, "We have never been lovers."

Chapter 4

"Why not?" Tahra's question seemed to take her by surprise as much as Marek, because warm color rose in her cheeks and she gave a little embarrassed laugh. "I'm sorry, I don't know why I said that. Please forget I asked." She tried to pull her hand away from his, but he held tight.

"But I want to answer that question." His thumb brushed the engagement ring on her finger. "I have said this to you before…when I asked you to marry me."

Her eyes sought his, and she said softly, almost shyly, "Please tell me again."

"It was harder than you know leaving you at the door to your apartment," he confessed in a low voice. "Holding you…kissing you…" He shook his head. "Letting you go every night took every ounce of determination I have."

"Why did you?"

He smiled faintly. "Because you are the first woman I have ever envisioned as my wife. And in Zakhar a man does not… That is, we are taught…"

To his amazement, Tahra's cheeks whitened and she jerked her hand away from his. "In other words, you have a double standard where women are concerned." Her voice was cool, but he heard a thread of anger running through it. "I thought that went out of fashion fifty years ago."

"That was not what I meant."

"Isn't it?" She gave a scornful snort. "Virgin brides are the exception nowadays, Marek, not the rule. Are *you* a virgin?"

He couldn't believe she was asking him, but his answer was automatic and immediate. "Of course not. I am thirty-three and I am a ma—"

She cut him off. "*Man.* You're a man, and therefore it's expected that a thirty-three-year-old *man* wouldn't be a virgin."

He tried to possess himself of her hand again, but she refused to let him. At a loss to understand what was happening, he asked, "Why are we arguing about this?"

"So what you're saying is that if you knew I wasn't a virgin, we would have been lovers long ago…but you wouldn't have asked me to be your wife." She tugged furiously on his engagement ring, which wasn't easy with the cast on her right wrist. When it was finally free, she grabbed his hand and slapped the ring in it, then forcefully closed his fingers around it. "You don't have to worry. I won't hold you to an engagement entered into under false pretenses."

"Tahra!"

"I can't believe you told me this before, and I agreed to marry you," she said under her breath. "I *don't* believe it."

"I did not tell you that part." He opened his fingers and stared at the ring it contained…the second time Tahra had returned it to him. The second time she'd turned him down. "That is not why—" He broke off when he realized what he'd almost said.

She wasn't listening to him, and Marek could only thank God. "How could I?" she was saying to herself. "How could I possibly… Especially since…"

Then he focused on what she'd said earlier, and a savage pain slashed through his heart. *"…if you knew I wasn't a virgin, we would have been lovers long ago… but you wouldn't have asked me to be your wife."*

Was Tahra telling him she *wasn't* a virgin? Could it be possible his sweet, shy Tahra hadn't waited for him? Had…slept with other men?

Just as swiftly her scornful question leaped to mind. *"Are* you *a virgin?"*

A two-word litany began repeating in his brain—*double standard, double standard, double standard*—and shock sent icy shards everywhere. Tahra was right. *He* had slept with other women. Women he'd desired but hadn't loved. *He* had not waited for Tahra. Why had he automatically expected she would have waited for him?

This new thought struggled with the Zakharian concepts with which he'd been raised, a culture clash of momentous proportions. Out of the maelstrom, only one thought emerged—he loved Tahra. That hadn't changed. *Could* never change. No matter what, she was still his darling to cherish. To protect. And that meant maintaining the fiction they were still engaged so long as she needed his protection.

"No," he told her firmly, capturing her left hand and sliding the engagement ring back on her finger. "Do *not*." His voice was as implacable as his words when she opened her mouth to protest. "Do not fight me on this, *mariskya*. Your accusation is untrue. Whether you believe it or not, I would have asked you to marry me no matter what."

Tahra stopped resisting, but her eyes searched his face, as if needing confirmation of his words. Finally she nodded. "Okay. I believe you." Then she smiled and he could breathe again. "They told me in my pre-assignment briefing that Zakharians are a little...shall we say...behind the times where women are concerned. Not like some other countries where women have to go around covered head to toe and aren't even allowed to drive a car, but..."

His fingers tightened on hers. "I am a product of my upbringing, yes," he admitted. "But I am not wedded to my ignorance. You know I have already learned a few home truths about women and their role in society from Angelina, and I—" He stopped when confusion spread across her face. "Captain Angelina Mateja-Jones," he explained patiently. "Head of the queen's security detail, a post I held until the king asked me to take over the security for the crown prince. She is married to the man you work for at the US embassy, Alec Jones." He paused for a moment, then stated flatly, "None of this strikes a chord in your memory, does it?"

She shook her head, a shadow creeping into her eyes. "No, it doesn't. I wish it did."

"We are friends with them," he continued after a

moment. "Alec is the regional security officer—RSO, you call it—at the embassy, and you are his administrative assistant. That created a slight problem at first, because Alec and I are friends, as are Angelina and I. But we all agreed that when you are at work, you and Alec act as professionally as if that is all there is to your relationship. When we are together as friends…that is a different story."

"I see." There was a tinge of doubt in her voice, but she didn't add anything.

"As I started to say, Angelina has taught me much about women and their place in society." His voice dropped a notch. "As have you, *mariskya*. You must believe me. I am not the man I was two years ago. I am not even the man I was two *weeks* ago." That was getting dangerously close to revealing too much he was concealing from Tahra, and he gratefully changed topics when he saw they had arrived at Tahra's apartment building. "Ahh, here we are."

He came around and held the door for her before she could get out, but then she paused on the sidewalk, staring in confusion. "I live *here*?"

His heart ached for the touch of panic in her voice. *Everything* from the past eighteen months was unknown to her. Everything was strange and…yes…potentially frightening. "You moved here six months ago, when your lease expired and the owner raised the rent on your old apartment. You had only lived there a year, and you loved it, but you were adamant about moving."

"Why would I do that?" she murmured to herself. "I'm not dependent on my salary." She glanced at Marek, almost as if embarrassed to admit, "Carly and I…we inherited money from our parents. Not a fortune, but enough so that we never had to worry about where the money would come from for college and…well… other things."

He cleared his throat. "Perhaps I had something to do with your decision to move." When she gave him a questioning look, he added, "I live around the corner."

"Oh." Her smile returned. "I guess that explains it."

"She is not dead." Colonel Borka's voice was always chilling, but now it sent fear trickling down Sergeant Vasska's spine. "The woman who interfered in our plans is not dead. Worse, the aide you bribed is in custody. And she is talking."

Sergeant Vasska was surprised into asking, "How do you—"

"I know. Let us leave it at that." The colonel looked the sergeant up and down. "If you were me in this situation, what would you do, Sergeant?"

The fear moved to his bowels, but Sergeant Vasska forced himself to ignore it. "I would…eliminate the man who had failed to carry out his assignment." He snatched at a breath. "I would eliminate…me."

Colonel Borka smiled, but there was no humor in it. In fact, there was not the slightest shred of any human emotion in that smile. "That is why you are merely a sergeant," Colonel Borka said. "I do not waste men… even men who fail. I do not even demote them—I give them a chance to redeem themselves. But…" He held up one hand. "I do not think it serves our cause to have you here in Drago at this time, where you might be spotted. I am sending you to the eastern border…for now. You will go there directly and await orders. Is that clear?"

Sergeant Vasska saluted. "Yes, *sir*!"

* * *

"I must leave you here," Marek told Tahra after he'd seen her comfortably ensconced in her suite in the royal palace. He touched her cheek briefly. "I have work waiting for me."

He didn't say it, but Tahra filled in the blanks. He'd neglected his duty for her. She barely knew him, but she knew this much—duty was *everything* to Marek. "I'll be fine," she hurriedly assured him.

"Your luggage will be here shortly," he told her. "The master of the household has assigned a maid for your use. She will arrive at the same time as your luggage to unpack for you and provide anything else you might require."

"I don't need a maid."

"Nevertheless, one has been assigned." He unbent enough to add with a hint of a smile, "Please do not make the maid feel she is unnecessary. You would take away her face, wound her pride. And that, I know, your heart is too tender to do, *mariskya*."

"No. Oh, no," she rushed to say. "Of course I wouldn't want to hurt her feelings."

"And even though you have been discharged from the hospital, that does not mean you are completely healed. The doctors told you to resume normal activities slowly, yes?"

"Yes, but..." He headed for the door and she trailed after him, suppressing a tiny dart of panic. So she was in a strange place. So what? So she didn't know anyone in the palace. Was that really important? So Marek was abandoning her here. *He's not abandoning you*, she quickly chastised herself. *He has a job to do, and he has already spent the entire morning on you.*

She was so lost in her thoughts that when Marek turned around and pulled her into his arms she didn't resist. Then he kissed her, and—*oh, God!*—could he kiss. Being kissed by Marek was so much more intense than anything she'd ever experienced. Her breasts swelled, her nipples tightened, her stomach quivered. And that was just in the first ten seconds. He deepened the kiss, and sparks flew everywhere, melting her with incredible heat from the inside out. He wasn't even touching her between her thighs, but she felt him there and she trembled.

When he finally broke contact, both of them were short of breath. She stared up at him, dazed. Wondering if another bomb had just exploded, knocking her senseless.

"You will let the maid do her job, yes?"

One word was all she could manage. "Okay."

Only after Tahra closed the door behind Marek did she realize she just might have been had. That his little smile had deepened when she'd agreed to accept the maid's services. That very possibly she'd been manipulated into doing exactly what he wanted her to do.

"And that is *not* going to continue," she muttered to herself, despite acknowledging there was some truth to Marek's statement; the doctors *had* told her to take it easy, to not overdo anything. But still… "Maybe I'm not as assertive as Carly, but I'm no pushover, either. He's not going to walk all over me."

But if he kissed her that way again? Could she stand up to him then? "Doubtful," she whispered, touching a finger to her lips, reliving the kiss that had turned her entire body into a quivering mass of jelly. "Highly doubtful."

* * *

Marek checked on the crown prince and the men guarding him in the royal nursery on the second floor—something he did on a regularly irregular basis. Not that he didn't trust his men. He did. But showing up from time to time accomplished two goals: it kept his men on their toes, since they never knew when he might appear, and it ensured the little prince knew Marek, which could be important if it was ever necessary for Marek to guard Raoul personally. Not likely, but as a belt-and-suspenders man he always wanted to be prepared for any contingency.

There was another reason why Marek wanted to retain a personal connection with the crown prince... something he didn't like to think about but was always there in the back of his mind. The succession.

Should anything happen to the king—*God forbid!* Marek always told himself whenever he thought of it—Crown Prince Raoul would ascend the throne. That transition would be difficult enough for an adult, much less a child of tender years, and Marek would do anything in his power to smooth the way. It was his duty, yes, but it was also his honor. The men of the king's security detail would assume responsibility for their new monarch, but Raoul wouldn't be familiar with any of them the way he would be familiar with the men who'd guarded him in the past. It would be Marek's job to facilitate that transfer.

During Raoul's minority, the king had named his cousin, Prince Xavier, and his wife, Queen Juliana, as regents...something the queen had vehemently protested. Marek had been an unwitting witness to the ensuing argument when *that* issue had arisen...almost a flaming row, in fact. *Not* that the queen wanted sole control; that wasn't it at all. She just refused to accept the king might die and objected to any plan that meant she would have to go on without him.

A smile touched his lips. The timeless bond shared by the king and queen was becoming legendary, rivaling the love story of the first king and queen of Zakhar more than five hundred years ago. *Two hearts as one, forever and a day.* Words carved in Latin on the tomb of the first King Andre Alexei and Queen Eleonora. Words etched in his heart. Were they also etched in Tahra's heart? He'd thought they were...until she'd rejected his marriage proposal three weeks ago. Until she'd tugged his ring from her finger—the same way she'd done today—and whispered in a voice that shook, *"I can't marry a man who doesn't trust me. I can't. I won't."*

He'd told himself when Tahra had been in surgery that she'd been right to accuse him of not trusting her. But now a little voice of doubt whispered in the back of his head. *If she really loved you as she said she did, would she have returned your ring?* He would never know...until Tahra regained her memory. *If* she regained her memory.

Unless...

Unless he could make her fall in love with him all over again.

When the thought flashed through his mind as he descended the back stairway on his way to his office on the ground floor, he stopped so abruptly one foot was suspended in midair, and he almost missed the step.

Was it possible? Could he do it? Could he accomplish in a few weeks what had previously taken eighteen months...winning Tahra's trust? Winning her heart?

Gaining Tahra's trust hadn't been easy. He'd wanted her from the first moment he'd spotted her in the reference section of the library, and he'd pretended to bump into her just so he could have an excuse to apologize… and start a conversation. But her reaction had been totally unexpected. He hadn't missed the flash of fear in her eyes, quickly masked. And from the way she'd drawn back, her stammered apology, the color that had come and gone in her cheeks, he'd known instantly she wasn't pretending—she really was afraid of him.

All of which had intrigued him and immediately aroused his protective instincts. And awakened the wolf inside him at the same time. He'd exerted himself to put her at ease, initiating friendly yet casual conversation, but making sure he kept a physical distance between them to make her feel safe. And eventually she'd rewarded him with a tentative smile.

He'd vowed in that moment that someday she would trust him enough for a real smile. One without the shadows in her eyes.

Within a month of knowing her, he'd known she was The One. As he'd told Alec Jones, a man would have to look far and wide to find someone like Tahra. Sweet without being cloying, with a tender, loving heart that made him determined to win her for his own. So he'd sat down, and with the deliberateness with which he'd planned his whole life after Zorina, he'd charted a course to accomplish his goal—Tahra as his wife.

It had taken him almost seventeen months, but he'd persevered. And three weeks ago he'd been the happiest man on earth when Tahra had agreed to marry him. Only to have his dreams come crashing down around his ears.

But he hadn't given up hope. He hadn't been lying when he'd told Tahra's sister he was merely giving Tahra time to come to terms with what he'd disclosed right after his proposal. Time for her to remember they shared a bond that could not be broken—especially not for so insignificant a reason.

Marek walked into his office just as the phone was ringing, and he answered it with his name as he always did. "Captain Zale."

He listened to the voice on the other end without saying a word, his eyes growing hard and cold. Then he asked one question. "How could that happen when she was in custody?"

Chapter 5

Tahra took a book from the sitting room to the daybed in her bedroom, thinking to read for a bit until her luggage arrived. But the novel, one of an eclectic collection that seemed to have been placed in her suite to appeal to a wide variety of readers, couldn't hold her interest…because her eyelids fluttered, then suddenly became too heavy. She laid the book facedown on her lap, intending only to rest her eyes for a couple of minutes. But before she knew it, she'd dozed off.

She floated dreamlessly at first. Then things changed, and faces flashed through her mind. Faces she knew she should recognize…but she didn't. The only man whose name she knew was the man who'd kissed her senseless earlier—and she only knew him because he'd been a nearly constant companion since she'd woken in the hospital. *I should remember you*, she confessed to Marek in her dream, *but I don't.* Then pleaded, *Please don't be upset with me.*

A knock on the door to Tahra's suite startled her awake, and with the dream still vividly in her mind, her first thought was that Marek *hadn't* been upset. He'd been understanding. *Too* understanding? Shouldn't he be more upset she didn't remember him?

The knock sounded again, and Tahra hurried to answer the door. *I guess Marek is right*, she thought, although she'd never tell him that. *I'm not completely recovered.* She'd never fallen asleep in the middle of the morning before. *Well, not since I was a toddler*, she added with a dart of humor. *I must have been more exhausted than I thought.*

The knock at the door turned out to be the delivery of her luggage…and the arrival of the maid, just as Marek had predicted. Tahra made only a token protest, then allowed the fresh-faced maid—who'd introduced herself as Ani, and looked to be somewhere in her late teens—free rein. But Ani had barely begun unpacking when there was another knock.

Ani said something in Zakharan when Tahra headed to the door to answer it, then bustled past her and switched to English. "No, miss, I will do that. You are to rest and take it easy—that is what Captain Zale said." Ani shooed Tahra back into the bedroom, then returned two minutes later, a cream-colored envelope in her hand, excitement bubbling over. "An invitation from the queen," she said in reverent tones, handing it to Tahra.

Ani's excitement quickly transferred itself to Tahra. Like many Americans, she was fascinated by royalty—other countries' royalty. Especially *this* queen, who was as American as Tahra was, a film actress who'd reigned as queen of Hollywood for years before she became a queen in real life by marrying the king of Zakhar.

"Open it, miss," Ani pleaded.

Tahra was able to restrain herself just enough to keep from ripping the envelope open, forcing a calm she was far from feeling. Then read aloud the handwritten note card with rising excitement.

Dear Ms. Edwards, the note said. *Thank you for accepting my husband's invitation to stay in the palace until such time as it is safe for you to return to your home. I realize your memory is temporarily impaired, but I would love to renew our acquaintance. I would also appreciate the opportunity to thank you in person for saving the lives of all those schoolchildren. Would you do me the honor of lunching privately with me today? If that's convenient for you, I'll send a footman to bring you to my private dining room at noon. Sincerely, Juliana Marianescu.*

"Lunch with the queen!" Ani breathed. "What will you wear?"

Tahra laughed a little at that, because Ani's question had been the first thing she'd thought of, too. She mentally reviewed the clothes she'd packed. Most were utilitarian—the slacks, blouses and blazers she usually wore to work, and more casual clothes. "There's a flowered dress," she began, remembering the one dress she'd thrown in at the last moment with Marek in mind. Most of her dressier clothes were unwearable…until the scars had time to fade, so she hadn't bothered to bring them. The flowered dress was different. It was deliciously feminine, yet had long sleeves and a cowl neck. Beneath the taupe nylons she'd also packed, those pinkish scars would be completely hidden. "But it may have gotten wrinkled when I—"

Ani interrupted her. "Leave it to me." Her eyes twinkled suddenly. "The queen's beauty is beyond compare—but you are beautiful, too, miss." Tahra couldn't help but blush a little at the compliment. Ani nodded to herself and added with a touch of self-importance, "When I am done, you will see."

Tahra followed the footman who'd been sent to fetch her through a maze of corridors, unsure if she'd be able to find her way back unaided. They passed priceless objets d'art displayed in glass cases as well as out in the open on massive mahogany side tables. And what were obviously masterpieces hung in splendor from the walls, rivaling a museum. She recognized two famous Rembrandts, a Botticelli, several Sheridans and dozens of paintings whose artists she couldn't name for sure but which she guessed. She would have stopped to confirm the signatures…if she wasn't being led to lunch with the queen.

Finally the footman stopped and rapped on a closed door, which was almost immediately opened by another impassive footman, who bowed, ushered Tahra into the relatively small but exquisitely appointed dining room, then…surprisingly…left with the first footman, closing the door behind them. A tiny, dark-haired woman she recognized as Queen Juliana rose impulsively from the table and hurried toward her.

"Don't you do that, too," she laughingly chided when Tahra attempted a curtsy. "It's bad enough I have to accept it from every Zakharian around me," she confided. "But I don't expect it from my own countrywomen."

She took Tahra's left hand in a friendly way and led her to the table already laid for two. "I thought it would be more comfortable for both of us if we dispensed with service and just helped ourselves from the buffet. Oh, I forgot," she added as an afterthought. "I'm Juliana. We met last year, but you probably don't remember me, Tahra."

"I know who you *are*, Your Majesty," Tahra said shyly. "You were one of my screen idols before you married the king."

"Oh dear, such a lowering thought—being someone's screen idol makes me feel quite old." But the queen's smile conveyed she wasn't really bothered by it. "And please call me Juliana. We're not that far apart in age, you know. I'm thirty-two and you're…twenty-eight, right?" When Tahra nodded, the queen explained, "We've actually had this conversation before, when we first met. Your boss at the embassy and my husband are friends, and we were first introduced at a reception here in the palace." She was serving herself from the tempting variety of dainty dishes on the sideboard as she spoke, and Tahra made haste to follow suit, albeit a little awkwardly with her left hand. "I've also met your older sister, Carly," the queen continued.

"You have?"

Juliana nodded. "A couple of months ago. Another reception." Her barely perceptible sigh informed Tahra the queen was *not* a fan of formal receptions, although they were a mandatory duty in her life now. "This one was at the Zakharian embassy in DC. She accompanied the man who's now her fiancé, Senator Jones."

"Carly told me about him…when she was here while I was in the hospital," Tahra volunteered hesitantly. "And she said I flew home to meet him when they became engaged a couple of weeks ago. But I don't remember him." She rushed to add, "I know who he *is*, of course, the same way I know who you are." She couldn't help the bleakness in her voice when she added under her breath, "But I don't remember him any more than I remember Marek."

The queen set her plate down and took a seat at the table, then darted a quick glance at Tahra's face and changed the subject. "You resemble her, you know."

Tahra seated herself and shook her head. "Carly's beautiful."

"So are you." She was as discomfited by the queen's unexpected compliment as she had been by Ani's. "Oh, I know you weren't fishing." Juliana laughed softly. "I know you well enough to know you don't see yourself in the same league as your sister."

"Carly is famous. Deservedly so."

"Yes, and unlike me, she's famous for much more than her beauty."

"That's not true!" Tahra said, putting her fork down and leaping to the queen's defense. "You're a wonderful actress." Then she paused. "Or rather, you were before you retired. Two best actress Oscars and those Golden Globe awards," she reminded Juliana, as if the queen needed reminding. "And you were fabulous in *King's Ransom*."

An expression Tahra couldn't quite decipher flitted over the queen's face. "We had this conversation before, too," Juliana said softly, and Tahra realized what she was seeing was sadness on the queen's part for her lost memory. "Almost verbatim."

"Oh." She couldn't think of anything to add to that,

so she picked up her fork with her left hand and resumed eating.

"That brings me to one of the reasons I wanted to lunch with you today. Andre," she said, referring to her husband, the king, "and I are awed by your courage in saving those children. He expressed his own gratitude and appreciation via an official letter sent to the president, the State Department and the ambassador at the embassy." She picked up a long white envelope that had been sitting beside her plate, with the official seal of Zakhar embossed in one corner, and handed it to Tahra. "This is a copy for your records. And when you're fully recovered, Andre plans to hold a reception in your honor."

Tahra stared at the envelope without opening it, then raised her eyes to Juliana's. "I…I don't really remember doing it."

"But you did—do you know how many witnesses came forward to say what they saw you do with that knapsack?—and we can never thank you enough. Every parent would feel the same—that could have been *my* child in that schoolyard." She touched a hand to her abdomen in an unconscious gesture, and Tahra's eyes widened.

"Are you…? That is…" She fumbled for words to a question she wasn't sure she should ask, and the queen nodded.

"We haven't announced it yet—we wanted to wait until after I pass my first trimester—so please keep the news to yourself. But yes, by this time next year your fiancé will be heading the security detail for two royal children, not just one."

"Oh, how wonderful," Tahra gushed. Then shook her

head. "I don't mean for Marek, I mean for you and the king." A smile curved her lips. "Another baby. That's so exciting!"

"You love babies, I take it?"

Tahra glanced down at her plate, then back up at the queen. "I know it's terribly old-fashioned. I know I *should* want a challenging career as my sister has in order to feel fulfilled," she confided. "But all I ever wanted was to be a wife and mother."

"There's nothing more fulfilling than being a mother, Tahra," the queen said gently. "Nothing." Her unusual violet eyes glowed for a moment before turning mischievous. "And being a wife is pretty darn fantastic, too... with the right husband." Her expression conveyed that her husband was the right husband for her...and Tahra immediately thought of Marek. She could *so* envision him as her husband. Not perfect. No man was perfect—no woman, either—but even though she couldn't remember anything about him from before the explosion, his stellar qualities shone clear and bright. Not to mention the way he'd kissed her this morning. If that was the way he always kissed, she had no idea how it was remotely possible they'd never been lovers, because her body had ached in secret places, and her mind had surrendered completely to the—

"So what are your plans?"

She blushed, as if the queen knew where her thoughts had wandered. "I don't really have any. I'm just following doctors' orders and taking things one day at a time."

The queen nodded her understanding and sipped at her water, which she was drinking in place of the excellent Montrachet that had been poured for Tahra. "That's probably wise. Not easy for your fiancé, of course. Zakharian men are…" She cleared her throat. "A *tad* on the alpha side," she said, tongue in cheek. "If you haven't already discovered that for yourself."

"A tad?" Tahra forgot for a moment she was chatting with the queen of Zakhar and answered the way she would have answered with one of her girlfriends. "Marek is über-alpha, not just a tad." She snorted delicately. "And controlling. He thinks he knows best in everything."

Juliana's laughter pealed out. "Oh, tell me about it. Andre is just the same. It must be something in the blood. Zakharian men like to see themselves as masters of their fate, and Viscount Saint-Yves is no exception."

A little chill ran down Tahra's back, as if the name should mean something to her…but it didn't. "Viscount Saint-Yves?" she repeated slowly, feeling as if something was right there on the outskirts of her memory, but try though she might, it wouldn't appear. She shook her head in puzzlement. "Who's he?"

Juliana's mouth formed an O. After a pregnant pause she said, "I forgot you don't remember."

Tahra could add two and two. "Is Marek…Captain Zale…Viscount Saint-Yves? Why didn't he tell me?"

Juliana cleared her throat. "That's another thing about Zakharian men…most of them, anyway," she explained. "Andre was that way when he was in the Zakharian National Forces, and woe betide anyone who addressed him as anything other than Lieutenant Marianescu when he was on duty! Zax, too. Prince Xavier," she clarified. "Andre's cousin, the head of internal security. He prefers his military title, Colonel Marianescu. So I'm not surprised Marek—Captain Zale—hasn't mentioned it to you. Military service is a particular source of pride to Marianescus."

Tahra gave up trying to eat with her left hand and laid her fork on her plate. "Wait," she said with a mixture of bewilderment and denial. "What do you mean, military service is a particular source of pride to Marianescus? Marek isn't a Marianescu."

The queen hesitated. "Well…actually…he is. He has the Marianescu fingers, you know, and that's a dead giveaway."

Tahra just stared blankly. "The Marianescu fingers?"

"Hadn't you noticed? It's a slight genetic defect that marks many of the Marianescus—a crook in the pinkies of both hands. Andre has it. Zax, too. And my son inherited it from Andre."

"But…"

"Apparently it's a dominant gene, because it has come down through the centuries from the first Andre Alexei right through to the present day. Not every Marianescu inherits it. Princess Mara didn't—her pinkies are perfectly straight. But Marek did."

"But…" Tahra couldn't seem to process that the man she thought was merely a captain in the Zakharian National Forces, and the head of the crown prince's security detail, was in fact a viscount *and* related to the king.

"Marek's grandmother on his father's side and Andre's grandfather on his father's side were brother and sister. She married the Count of Mortagne, whose family name is Zale. Which makes Marek… Let me think." The queen touched a finger to her lips as she tried to figure the exact degree of relationship. "If Andre's father and Marek's father were first cousins, that makes

Andre and Marek second cousins? I think that's right, because they share great-grandparents."

"You mean I'm engaged to...royalty?"

Juliana shook her head. "Not exactly. Royalty doesn't follow the female line, not in Zakhar. So Andre's sister, Mara, bears the courtesy title of princess, but her son and daughter aren't considered royalty and aren't in the line of succession. The same goes for Marek. While one of his grandmothers was a royal princess, he inherited no title from her and he's not in line to the throne."

"But he is a...a viscount, you said. Right?"

"Right. He's the oldest son of the current Count of Mortagne, and as such bears the title Viscount Saint-Yves." Tahra's confusion obviously showed on her face, because the queen smiled. "You'll get the hang of it eventually. Who married whom, the role Zakhar's nobility played in its history, et cetera."

"You mean—"

"When you marry Marek, of course. But don't worry about it now, just remember what I said. His military title is more important to him than his inherited title. The first one he *earned.* The other was merely a gift of fate."

Tahra couldn't take it all in. Had Marek told her all this before? Was that what he'd been referring to when he said he'd explained what *mariskya* meant at some point during the missing eighteen months of her life? His words replayed in her mind. *"The first time I called you* mariskya *you asked me. But I would not tell you because you would not have understood. Not then. Only later, after I... That is, after we..."*

It suddenly became exceedingly important to know. "What does *mariskya* mean?"

The change of subject didn't seem to faze the queen,

and a faint smile touched her lips. "It's a Zakharian endearment, but there's actually no direct translation."

"That's what Marek said," Tahra whispered, almost to herself. Then her eyes focused on Juliana. "But it does mean something. Literally. Please tell me."

"If that's what he calls you, he should be the one to explain."

"Please."

Juliana appeared torn for a moment, then decisively shook her head. "Ask Marek. I will tell you this, though—Marianescus love once, then never again. It's something in their blood, I think. In their DNA. If you're his *mariskya*, you're his once-in-a-lifetime love." The breathtaking smile that wreathed Juliana's face was the loveliest Tahra had ever seen. "And let me tell you from personal experience, that makes you a *very* fortunate woman."

Tahra retreated to her suite after lunch to consider everything she'd learned from the queen. Especially the things Marek—her *fiancé*, the man she should know better than anyone—should have told her about who he was. She changed out of her dress into jeans and a sweater, then curled up on the daybed again, one hand tucked beneath her cheek…to ponder.

She *hated* that she couldn't remember anything about Marek. She especially hated not knowing how he'd managed to win her trust, how he'd managed to break through the barrier she'd erected against all men after the attack that had devastated her. And what he'd done to make her fall in love with him.

Even more than that, though, she hated not remembering loving him. That wound cut deep. How could she forget the man she'd loved so much she'd agreed to marry him? It made no sense. And for a woman who rarely took risks, who always tried to play it safe, the loss of eighteen months of her life and the memory of the man who loved her so much he'd slept at her bedside in the hospital was devastating.

Her heartbeat jumped at the thought that maybe she would *never* remember, and a new ache stabbed through her. Not so much for herself, but for Marek. How heartbreaking for him to know himself forgotten. To know the woman he loved—who'd claimed to love him—had relegated him to a corner of her mind…and then lost him.

A rapping on the sturdy oak door again woke her. Unlike this morning, however, she hadn't merely been dozing, she'd been fast asleep. And this time it took her longer to figure out where she was.

She opened the door and found Marek standing there, one arm propped against the door frame, drawing her attention to a physique that just begged for a woman's hands to find out if he was as rock hard as he appeared. Everywhere.

She was so disconcerted by the thought that she blurted out the question foremost in her mind. "Why didn't you tell me who you really are?"

Chapter 6

Marek froze. Had Tahra recovered her memory? Had she remembered he wasn't really her fiancé, that she'd first accepted then rejected his proposal, all in the space of ten minutes...because he'd finally revealed the truth she was now accusing him of not having revealed when they'd first met?

He temporized, reaching out and tucking a strand of hair behind her ear in a deliberately intimate move. "What do you mean, *mariskya*?"

She impatiently shook his hand away. "And don't call me *mariskya*."

That didn't bode well. He knew he should be thrilled Tahra had regained her memory. But he would have to think of something—*fast*—to keep himself in her life.

Then she added, "Unless you tell me what it means," and Marek could breathe again. His conscience severely chastised him. *How can you be happy she still does not remember? Just how selfish is that?*

He ruthlessly suppressed the voice in his head and the questions it raised to consider another time. Then, because he couldn't help it, he slid his arm around Tahra's waist and pulled her closer for a kiss…on the cheek. But when she made that tiny, inarticulate sound he'd heard many times before—a sound that always accompanied her arousal—he lost his head and kissed her as he had this morning.

This time she kissed him back. Marek didn't know if her body subconsciously recognized him and accepted she was safe with him, that he wouldn't let things go too far, or if she was reacting to the here and now. Then he pushed those questions aside, too, and deepened the kiss, losing himself in the wonder of holding her this way.

When he finally released her, her rosy lips, flushed cheeks and erratic breathing gave him the satisfaction of knowing she was as aroused as he was. *Perhaps her mind does not remember me...but her body does.*

"How do you do that?" she whispered, her eyes still closed.

"Do what?"

Her eyes opened slowly, and she blinked at him as if she were drugged. "Make me forget where I am. *Who* I am."

His voice dropped a notch. "Do not worry, *mariskya.* I never forget those things, so you can always rely on me to tell you. *Where* you are is in my arms. *Who* you are is the woman I love."

The expression on her face softened, but she didn't

smile. "Please tell me what *mariskya* means. I need to know."

Marek laughed under his breath, then kissed Tahra again, but lightly, briefly this time. "Let us sit and I will explain," he said, putting his arm around her shoulders and leading her to the sitting room sofa. When they settled, he was startled at first when Tahra automatically laid her head on his shoulder the way he loved. Then he realized this was another good sign. Her *conscious* memory might not know him, but her subconscious did. That knowledge thrilled him and also gave him courage.

"Before I tell you, you must understand this is an ancient Zakharan word. It is *never* used in the literal sense, not for…oh…at least three hundred years."

"Okay, I get that."

"It is *always* used in the figurative sense," he added, stalling. "In essence, it means something a man cannot live without."

Tahra raised her head to gaze at him, a smile in her eyes. "Now I *really* want to know."

Marek cleared his throat, praying Tahra wouldn't laugh or be offended or… Praying her reaction this time would be the same as last time. "It…ah…literally means…a man's vital organs. Heart, liver, kidneys and such. Things he cannot live without."

She didn't laugh. And he could tell she wasn't offended. But she didn't say, *"That's so sweet, Marek,"* as she'd said the first time he'd told her. Instead, the smile faded from her eyes and was replaced with a film of tears.

"What have I said to make you cry?" She shook her head and swallowed visibly as first one tear, then another escaped its banks and trickled down her cheeks.

Each tear was like a dagger in his heart. "Please do not," he pleaded, brushing her tears away with his thumb. "I cannot bear it."

Her face crumpled and she buried it against his shoulder, weeping quietly. As if her heart was breaking. He gathered her close and did the only thing he could think of—he stroked her dark hair and pressed his lips against it, his own heart breaking for her pain that was also his. He didn't know why she was crying, just that she was. And somehow he'd been the unwitting cause.

Words of comfort flowed out of him in a disjointed stream, followed by entreaties that she tell him what was wrong. "Hush now, Tahra. Whatever it is, please tell me so I can make it right. I cannot bear to see you cry this way."

He might as well have saved his breath, because it was as if she couldn't even hear him. But she clung to him in her misery, and that helped him immeasurably, knowing that whatever was making her weep, even if he was the proximate cause, she still sought comfort in his arms.

When her tears finally ceased, she murmured something into his shoulder he had to ask her to repeat. "I'm so sorry," she whispered again, still on the edge of tears.

"For what, my darling?" he whispered back, his arms tightening infinitesimally.

She gulped and drew a sobbing breath. "Because you love me so much, and I…I don't remember."

Relief flooded him. "Oh, Tahra." He couldn't think of anything to say other than her name.

"I want to remember so badly. I've tried and tried, but I—"

"Your memory will return in its own good time." The

lie came easily to his lips because he knew it was what she needed to hear right now. Maybe she'd never recover those lost eighteen months, as he'd already begun to fear in the deepest recesses of his soul, but he would never tell her that. "Just relax and let yourself recover. Perhaps when your body is completely healed, your mind will be, too."

"You really think so?"

"You almost died, Tahra. If that had happened, I would also have died. I would have gone on breathing, but…"

"I understand." Her hand clutched his lapel. "Because I am your *mariskya*."

The word was infinitely sweet on her lips. "Yes," he affirmed. "I cannot live without you." He sighed deeply. "Please do not misunderstand. There is fierce pride in me for what you did. Your bravery still astounds me. And yet…if I could have taken that risk for you, I would have. I never want to live through anything like that again. Hearing the news…praying in the hospital while you were in surgery…sleeping at your bedside, waiting for you to come out of the coma."

He sighed again and was silent for a moment, trying to think of some way to lighten the mood. Eventually he teased gently, "You may apologize now for putting me through that torture," lifting her face to his with one finger beneath her chin. He deliberately raised and lowered his eyebrows suggestively a couple of times, and Tahra laughed the way he'd intended, albeit a little shakily.

"I'll think about it." But almost immediately she brushed her lips against his. "I'm so sorry," she murmured.

One kiss led to two. Then to kisses beyond count.

Marek was hard and aching long before he forced himself to let Tahra go. "You are hell on my good intentions," he told her firmly, setting her to one side and putting distance between them. "I did not come here for this."

"Why *did* you come here?" Her tears had long since vanished, but her breathing was as labored as his was. And the alpha male in him couldn't help but smile. Wolfishly. The gentleman he was on the surface was just that—camouflage. Scratch the surface and the wolf emerged. But he'd caged the beast for Tahra's sake.

For now.

"Would you believe I came merely to invite you to a picnic dinner? Here in the palace grounds?"

Refugees were still pouring over Zakhar's eastern border. Desperate, hollow-eyed men and women, often with ragged children in tow. Most were headed for Germany, but some—*far too many*, Sergeant Vasska and the other members of the Zakharian Liberation Front firmly believed—were intending to make Zakhar their new home. That could not be allowed to continue, despite the king's active support for the humanitarian effort.

The group's public credo—*Zakhar for Zakharians*—played well…to a small minority within the general populace. But most Zakharians stoutly held that the king knew best, so whatever he believed in, they believed in, too. Which meant most Zakharians supported taking in however many refugees their country could accommodate, financially and otherwise.

To counter that, the Zakharian Liberation Front was also trumpeting that these new immigrants would take jobs from decent, hardworking Zakharians—despite the fact that Zakhar had a chronic labor *shortage* these refugees would fill.

As he rode the train to the eastern border, where he'd been banished for now, Sergeant Vasska couldn't help but brood over this dichotomy. Most men in his situation would merely be grateful they were still alive, not wonder about the motivation behind it. And yet, something didn't sit right with him. Colonel Borka had spared his life. Why?

The sergeant knew he'd failed. Both times. In his heart of hearts he wasn't sorry about the first failure. He hadn't wanted to leave the knapsack full of explosives and fléchettes near a schoolyard. *I cannot kill children!* he'd almost protested when he'd been given the assignment…but he hadn't. He'd saluted his superior, taken the knapsack—one of ten he himself had so carefully assembled—and had said, *Yes, sir!*

And he'd tried to carry it out. He really had. But except for the danger to himself from the woman who'd seen him at the schoolyard and might be able to identify him, he hadn't been sorry his mission had failed. The other attacks—the Zakharian National Forces training facility, the refugee processing center, the train from the eastern border and the other six bombings scattered across Zakhar—had mostly targeted adults, and Sergeant Vasska was philosophical about it. War was war, after all. The Zakharian Liberation Front was waging war, and there would be casualties.

But not children.

It bothered him children had been targeted to begin with, even though the school chosen did contain many refugee children. It was almost as if the intent was maximum fright, though. Not to make a point about refugees. Which would mean the refugees were merely an excuse. A means to an end unknown to most of the members of the Zakharian Liberation Front. Was that possible? Could Colonel Borka have another agenda? And if so, what did that have to do with why his life had been spared?

Sergeant Vasska didn't know, and that ate at him. He truly believed in the cause the Zakharian Liberation Front espoused, and he would gladly sacrifice his life, if necessary. He'd been honest with Colonel Borka—in his mind he deserved the death penalty, because he could no longer be trusted to successfully carry out a mission. Plus, he could be identified…making him a danger to the cause. So why was he still alive? What purpose was served?

Tahra leaned back against the white wicker chair in the secluded gazebo in the Royal Garden, to which Marek had led her an hour ago, picnic basket in hand. Replete, she gazed at the man sitting across from her, thinking she'd never seen someone so self-assured, so completely confident in who he was and his purpose in life, as Marek. Except maybe her new boss, Alec. *Alec's not your* new *boss*, she reminded herself with a touch of impatience. *He* has *been for more than a year and a half. You just don't remember, that's all.*

That made her ask, "Will you tell me about Alec… and Angelina?"

He wiped his hands on a napkin. "What about them?"

She wasn't sure what she was really asking, only, "You said this morning we are…friends with them."

"Yes." He cut an apple in two and cored it, then handed her one half. He hadn't even asked her if she wanted it peeled—which she didn't. Another tiny sign he knew her well, she realized.

He bit into his half with relish, and Tahra stared at the apple in her hand but didn't eat it just yet. "You remind me of Alec," she confessed. "At least…what I remember about him, which isn't all that much. All I remember is when he first took over as RSO, I was very impressed with him. But then, I never cared for the previous RSO. He really didn't do his job—not the way I thought he should, anyway."

Marek swallowed and smiled. "You were very perceptive. Alec's predecessor at the embassy was convicted eight months ago in a bribery and human trafficking conspiracy case."

Tahra gawked at him. "He was?"

He nodded. "Your sister covered the trial."

She took a bite of her apple and chewed thoughtfully. After a moment she said with forced lightness, "There's so much missing from my memory. Carly got engaged… and I don't remember it. You and I got engaged…and I don't remember it. And now you tell me my former boss at the embassy is a convicted felon…and I don't remember *any* of it."

He seemed to divine her need for reassurance, because he reached out a hand to lightly caress her cheek. "Do not struggle so hard, *mariskya.* I will tell you anything you need to know. But I do not want to tell you everything, for then we will never know if you truly remember…or if you are only 'remembering' what I tell you."

She finished her apple, then said shyly, "You're very wise. Did I always think so?"

He laughed and stood, drawing her out of her chair.

"Let us walk, shall we? It is a beautiful evening and the sun has not yet set. The Royal Garden is just beginning to bloom. You will enjoy it, I think."

"Okay."

After they'd been walking for a couple of minutes, Tahra remembered her earlier question. "You never answered. Did I always think you were wise?"

"Now, how am I to answer that? If I say 'yes,' you will think me conceited. If I say 'no,' you will think me a liar. Or worse."

"I don't think you're conceited. Supremely self-confident." She smiled as she remembered how she'd described him to the queen. "And über-alpha. But not conceited."

He stopped in front of a rosebush that was just coming into flower and plucked one bloom, carefully stripping off the thorns before he held it out to her. "What is über-alpha?"

She ignored the rose and cleared her throat. "Well… you see…it's a way of describing a man who is…well…" She wasn't about to discuss the sexual connotations, so she focused on the other aspects. "Well, somewhat domineering. And controlling."

The smile faded from his face, and he was rather white about the mouth. "Is that how you see me, Tahra? Domineering? Controlling?"

She couldn't lie to him. "In some ways."

"I see." The words were spoken very quietly, with absolutely no emotion. But from the way he deliberately focused on the rose in his hand, she knew she'd wounded him with that assessment. "Because I would keep you safe? That is why?"

Her heart ached for him, and she rushed to say, "It's

not that. Truly. And it's not the criticism you might think it is. It's just..." How to explain? "Some people are just the take-charge kind. And there's nothing wrong with that, especially when the chips are down. Carly's that way." She laughed suddenly, remembering what her sister had told her in the hospital. "She even proposed to her fiancé."

Confusion played over Marek's face. "This is what you wish? To be the one proposing?"

"No, I—"

"You wish me to be a...a lapdog? That *is* the English expression, yes? A little dog that runs when you call?"

She covered her face in her hands, despite the cast on her right wrist, exasperation and laughter fighting for dominance. She looked at him again when she finally had herself under control. "You're totally missing the point."

"Then what is the point? Explain it to me." The set expression on his face told her it wasn't much use explaining, because he couldn't possibly understand, but she tried anyway.

"I'm not very assertive. I know that. Ever since I was a little girl, I was a... I guess you could say I was a follower. Not a leader. Carly always looked out for me, especially after our parents died, and I...I never learned to look out for myself."

He didn't say anything, so she went on. "I love my sister. I do. But it wasn't easy being myself when she was around."

"I do not understand."

She sighed. "I'm not sure I understand it all myself. All I know is, it was always easier to let Carly tell me what I should do, rather than figure it out on my own.

But that meant when I was finally out on my own, I wasn't..." She faltered. "I wasn't really prepared." She shivered suddenly, remembering. "Some people will take advantage of you...if you let them."

His brows drew together in a ferocious frown. "If you are talking about the man who—"

"You know?" Had she confided in Marek about that horrifying experience?

He confirmed it, saying, "You told me...oh, more than a year ago...about the man who viciously attacked you. About your arrest after you defended yourself. About how your sister came to your rescue, and how you ended up here at the embassy in Zakhar."

"I told you," she whispered to herself. Knowing she'd confided in him, that she'd trusted him with the details, conveyed a wealth of information about him...about *them*...she hadn't realized before. He'd told her they were engaged, and she'd believed him because she had no reason *not* to believe him. But now she believed they were engaged, because she knew herself well enough to know she could *never* have told him...if she hadn't loved him.

It also explained...a little more...his fierce protectiveness toward her. Because he knew she'd almost failed to protect herself. So maybe what she saw as his controlling behavior *was* nothing more than a desire to keep her safe...in the only way he knew how, especially given his upbringing. As the queen had said, Zakharian men liked to see themselves as masters of their fate.

Thinking of the queen reminded Tahra of something else. "So when were you going to tell me...about Viscount Saint-Yves?"

Chapter 7

Marek went very still. “Someone has been talking.”

Tahra nodded. “I had lunch with Queen Juliana today. She told me.”

“What else did she tell you?”

She lifted his right hand, which was clasping her left one, and tilted it until she saw the slight genetic defect she’d missed before. “That you’re also the king’s second cousin.”

“She was just a fount of information, was she not?”

“Not completely. She wouldn’t tell me what *mariskya* meant. She said I should ask you.”

“That is something, anyway,” he said drily.

Tahra peeked at him. “She *did* say Marianescus love once, then never again. And that if I was your *mariskya*, I was a very fortunate woman.”

He laughed softly. “And she would know. The king—”

"Your second cousin."

"My king," he reiterated firmly. "Always. If you would know me, Tahra, you must know that. He is my king first and foremost. I would die to keep him safe. The same goes for the queen and the crown prince—because they are *his*. Can you understand that?"

She nodded solemnly. "I think so. Because duty is honor to you, isn't it?" When he silently assented, she said, "Yes, I understand." She glanced down and realized he still held the flower he'd picked for her. "May I have my rose?"

He seemed as surprised as she'd been that he still had it, but all he said was "Of course." Then he brushed his lips against the petals in a romantic gesture that made Tahra sigh soundlessly, and offered her the rose, which she took in her right hand. She couldn't lift anything *heavy* with that hand, but her surgeon had encouraged her to use her muscles in that arm whenever she could do so without putting a strain on her wrist.

They resumed walking, and after a few minutes Marek said out of the blue, "I failed him once. I will never fail him again."

She stopped abruptly, and when he turned, a question on his face, she asked, "How did you fail him?" Because she couldn't imagine it. Not a man like him.

His lips tightened. "It was several years ago. I had orders to arrest Prince Nikolai. Instead, he almost killed the king and his then-fiancée…the woman who is now queen."

"But…"

"The king forgave me. He even took the blame on himself. Then he made me the head of the queen's security detail. He *trusted* me to keep her safe for him. I have not forgotten."

Puzzled, she said, "But that's not your job now."

Marek shook his head. "After the assassination attempt on the crown prince—"

"What?"

"I forgot you did not know. It happened right after I met you."

"Someone tried to murder a baby?" She couldn't fathom it.

"Why are you surprised? If people would kill dozens of children in a schoolyard—which you prevented—why should one child be any different?"

"But…the prince is okay, right? I mean, the assassination attempt failed." She tapped the flat of her left hand against her head in frustration over her stupidity. "Of course he's okay. Otherwise—"

"Yes, otherwise I would not be the head of his security detail."

"So how did you… What happened with… Please explain."

"After the assassination attempt on the crown prince on his christening day—which was foiled by Angelina, with some assistance from Alec, by the way—the man who was the head of the crown prince's security detail offered his resignation…which the king eventually accepted. The king asked me to step into that role, and he promoted Angelina in my place. That is all."

Tahra took Marek's arm and started walking again but sniffed at the rose in her right hand at the same time, breathing in the delicate scent and loving it. "No wonder the queen seemed to understand what the parents of the children in that preschool would have felt," she said, almost to herself.

"Yes, she nearly lost her son. It was a clever plot and a close call. Angelina—like you did days ago—figured out what was happening and prevented it." He squeezed her hand. "That is why I say I am not the same man I was before. You and Angelina have opened my eyes."

Tahra glanced up and read the truth on his face. "You are nothing like Angelina," he continued. "You are not tall and lean—no, this is not an insult," he added quickly when he saw her reaction. "You are perfect as you are. Soft and rounded and…and delectable."

"Nice save," she told him, choosing not to be offended. She knew she wasn't tall and lean. She wasn't short, but she had definite curves, just like her older sister.

"Nice save?" The puzzlement on his face matched his tone.

"Sports reference. American sports reference? It just means you prevented the other team from scoring or making a play that would have hurt your team."

"Ahhh." From puzzled his face turned amused. "So perhaps I should not mention you could never take me down—as Angelina did once."

Tahra looked him over. So tall. So über-masculine—although she wasn't about to use the word *über* to him again, she thought with an inner smile. *Impressively masculine*, she substituted in her mind. *That's a better description anyway.* "I can't imagine why I'd want to take you down," she said aloud, letting her eyes twinkle at him, "but you're right. You probably shouldn't mention it."

That made him laugh. He stopped short and drew her into his embrace, dropping a kiss onto her upturned face. "You are a constant delight." He stared down at her, and Tahra caught her breath. Everything he was feeling was there in his eyes, his face. Love and desire, and something else. Something she suddenly realized was even more important to her. Admiration.

"No," he said, shaking his head. "You are nothing like Angelina. And yet you are just like her in one crucial way."

Her pulse wasn't steady and neither was her breathing when she asked, "What way?"

"You have a warrior's heart."

The sun had long since set before Marek, carrying the picnic basket they'd retrieved from the gazebo, led Tahra back inside the palace through the side door they'd used earlier. The guard posted there wasn't the same man who'd been on the door before, but he snapped a salute at Marek and addressed them both by name…in English.

"Good evening, Captain Zale, Miss Edwards." He held the door for them.

Marek returned the salute, answering in Zakharan. A quick exchange followed, and though Tahra thought she was ignoring a conversation she wasn't part of in a language she didn't know, she was startled when she recognized a half-dozen words. She waited until they were out of earshot of the guard before she asked Marek about it.

"Yes," he replied as he led her down a short corridor lined with doors. "You have been taking lessons in Zakharan for as long as I have known you."

"I have?"

"Yes. Zakharan is not an easy language to learn as

Major Stesha wasn't a major in the Zakharian National Forces any longer, but Marek gave him the traditional salute anyway. He'd been Marek's superior officer years ago, before the king had personally asked a then-Lieutenant Zale to go to Hollywood on his behalf and had asked the major to reform the secret intelligence service as soon as the king had ascended the throne. *No sinecure, that*, Marek thought to himself. But Major Stesha had quickly brought order out of chaos. Even more, he'd returned *esprit de corps* to a service that had sunk in nearly everyone's estimation, especially in the eyes of the men in the Zakharian National Forces. The secret intelligence service was necessary to national security, though, and under Major Stesha it had established itself as second to none.

But that was before the Zakharian Liberation Front had emerged onto the national scene.

Major Stesha returned Marek's salute, then offered him a chair and reseated himself behind his desk. "What can I do for you, Captain?"

"Thank you for seeing me on such short notice, sir. I have been trying to ascertain some information on the nurse's aide who attempted to kill my fiancée last week." The lie came easily to Marek's lips because in his heart it wasn't a lie—Tahra *was* his fiancée...until she renounced their engagement.

"Ah yes, Miss Edwards. The woman who saved the children."

"Yes, sir. I have just come from the police station, where they would tell me nothing about the supposed suicide. Understandable, in a way, since I am not officially involved in the investigation. But—"

"But it was your fiancée whose life was almost taken."

Major Stesha smiled, not unkindly. "Your motivation in seeking this information is also understandable."

Marek drew a deep breath. "If anyone knows anything, it is you, sir. I am not asking for classified information. Nor am I asking to be part of the official investigation into the woman's death or its connection to the Zakharian Liberation Front. But you know me, sir. I cannot—*cannot*—simply do nothing."

The major considered this for a moment, then asked abruptly, "What do you intend to do with this information…assuming I give it to you?"

"Nothing that would interfere with you or your men," Marek assured him. "You have my word on that."

Again the major considered Marek's statement in silence. Then he reached into a side drawer and pulled out a thick file folder, which he slid across the desk to Marek.

Marek swung the folder around and opened it, reading the first few sentences. Then he glanced up sharply. "You had it ready for me, sir? Before I asked for it?"

A tiny smile touched the major's lips. "As you say, I know you, Captain Zale. I knew you would want this information. I was expecting you yesterday."

There was a slight question in his voice, and Marek rushed to explain. "I was on duty, sir. Today was my first opportunity…"

"Ah, yes. Duty. Your *sine qua non*." The major's smile took on a hint of understanding. "Just remember, there is duty to king and country…and there is duty to one's family. And then there is loyalty, to the men under your command and to one's superior officers. You are no longer my officer, Captain Zale, but you spoke up to defend me in a meeting where all looked upon me as a pariah—especially myself. That kind of loyalty earned you the file in your hands. I am breaking the rules giving it to you—do not let me down."

"No, sir. You have my word."

Marek intended to take the file home to read, then changed his mind and headed for his office in the palace. Any information relevant to the case needed to go on his whiteboard, so he might as well start from there. He never turned off his cell phone or pager—the head of the crown prince's security detail was always on call for emergencies—but he could let any phone calls to his office phone go to voice mail, allowing him to work uninterrupted.

He took a quick detour to the second floor to assure himself all was well with the crown prince, then passed Tahra's suite without stopping...although he was tempted. He jogged down the Grand Staircase, the file still clutched in one hand, and passed the Privy Council Chamber just as a meeting was letting out.

He paused politely to let the king's senior advisers precede him down the corridor and was surprised when Colonel Lermontov turned to address him. "Captain Zale. A moment, please."

Like Major Stesha, Colonel Lermontov was no longer an officer in the Zakharian National Forces, having retired after twenty years of stellar service. His impressive record as an officer had stood him in good stead when the king had ascended the throne and turned a once-appointed Privy Council into an elected one. The colonel had easily won his seat, and when the king had slowly but surely started placing more power and responsibility in the hands of the Privy Council, the ambitious and politically astute colonel had soon risen to the position of chief councillor.

All of this flashed through Marek's mind in a couple of seconds, so he saluted and gave the older man the honorific. "Yes, Colonel?"

"What is the word on your fiancée? Has she recovered her memory yet?"

The question was innocuous enough, but he was puzzled. Colonel Lermontov had never exhibited any interest in Marek's personal life before, and it made him wonder. Before he could respond, though, the colonel added, "We were just discussing Miss Edwards's bravery in council. The king announced he will hold a reception in her honor when she has fully recuperated, but he was unable to set a date because he does not know when that will be."

The tiny frown was erased from Marek's forehead. "She is making great strides physically, sir. The worst of it is a broken wrist, but the doctor assured us it should heal with no lasting damage."

"And her memory? The king mentioned Miss Edwards has no recollection of the actual incident, which is perfectly understandable under the circumstances. But apparently she has lost more than just that day. Yes?"

Chief councillor or not, Marek wasn't about to discuss Tahra's progress…or lack of it…with Colonel Lermontov. "We are hopeful her memory will return completely, sir…in God's time."

The colonel nodded thoughtfully, then clapped Marek on the shoulder. "In God's time. Yes, that is the approach to take. Please tell your fiancée the entire Privy Council is grateful to her and wishes her a speedy recovery."

"Will do, sir. And thank you for your concern."

* * *

Once Marek reached his office, he spared a moment to think of Tahra. Of how desperately he yearned for her complete recovery, mentally as well as physically. Then he sternly reminded himself, "It will happen in God's time, not mine," and dragged his focus back to the file Major Stesha had given him.

He read each document thoroughly in the order they were arranged in the file. He knew the major well enough to know that—since he'd anticipated Marek's request—the file would be impeccably assembled.

There was a small furrow between Marek's brows when he finished, and he started reading again from the beginning, thinking he must have overlooked something. But when he reached the end the second time, he realized he hadn't missed anything—but something was missing from the file. An explanation that should be there...but wasn't.

He thought about it for a minute, then picked up the phone and dialed a number he knew by heart. When a male voice answered, he said, "Alec? It is Marek."

"Hey, I was just thinking about calling you. How's Tahra doing?"

It took him a second to pull his mind off what was worrying him and say, "She is fine physically." Marek had seen her that morning, and she was doing remarkably well for a woman who just a week ago had been in a coma. "But she still does not remember anything from the past eighteen months."

"Damn. I was hoping something would have clicked by now. We... *I* really miss her at work. The admin I've got on loan tries, I'll give her that. But she's not Tahra, not by a long shot."

Marek smiled. "Tahra would love to hear that…from you. I realize she is a security risk at the moment, since her memory is impaired, but you could call her, try to jog her memory in some way. I have tried, but…" He sighed.

"That's not a bad idea," Alec said slowly. "I'll give it some thought." Then he changed gears. "So what's up? Why are you calling?"

"I need to discuss something with Angelina. Is she there?"

"She's feeding the baby right now, and before you ask," Alec said drily, "no, this isn't something I can do for her, no matter how much we try to share parenting duties."

Marek knew from Alec's tone of voice he was making a joke, but this wasn't the kind of thing he felt comfortable discussing with his friend, joke or not. Of course he knew Angelina was a woman. And like every woman, she had…female parts. And of course he knew she'd just had a baby a few months ago. But for years he'd thought of Angelina as nothing but a fellow officer and a fighting man, and it disconcerted him to envision her doing something so…so *womanly* as nursing a baby.

"Could you ask her to call me when she is free?" Marek asked now. "I am in my office and will be here for—" he checked his watch "—at least another half an hour."

"Sure thing."

The two men hung up, and Marek moved to the whiteboard. He picked up one of the colored markers and jotted down a few notes that were fresh in his mind. Then he picked up a different-colored marker for emphasis and added a few more notations. He was staring at the board, lost in thought, when the phone jangled behind him, and he answered it automatically. "Captain Zale."

A warm contralto sounded in his ear. "Marek? You asked me to call?"

"Angelina." He faced the whiteboard again, the furrow returning to between his brows. "I need to bounce an idea off you…about the Zakharian Liberation Front."

Tahra was restless and bored. She'd read all the books in her suite. She'd flicked on the TV in her sitting room, but since her Zakharan wasn't fluent enough to follow fast-paced dialogue and there were no English subtitles, she'd impatiently flicked it off again.

She'd browsed the internet on her laptop, but most of the news stories she read assumed she knew what had taken place in the world during the past eighteen months…which she didn't. The same went for all the posts on her Facebook feed. Frustrated, she'd logged off and closed her laptop with a decided *click*.

She'd even tried calling Carly through the palace switchboard—Zakhar was six hours ahead of Washington, DC, so her sister should have been at work—but all she got was Carly's work voice mail. A call to her sister's cell phone also went right to voice mail.

"Do you wish me to try again, Miss Edwards?" the switchboard operator had asked in her pretty English.

"No, that's okay. Thanks anyway."

She paced her suite, which was luxurious in the extreme—the silk-covered walls were hung with paintings that made her think of wide vistas, and the delicate porcelain knickknacks scattered throughout the rooms would have been behind glass in most

American homes—but there was only so much she could marvel at before familiarity bred...well, not *contempt*, but a kind of indifference.

Finally she couldn't stand it anymore. She grabbed a light jacket from the closet and headed out. She didn't know where she was going. All she knew was that with the walls closing in on her she couldn't stay here another minute.

Marek had just hung up with Angelina when his cell phone rang. He didn't recognize the caller, but he answered anyway. "Captain Zale."

"Sorry to bother you, Captain. Private Markovich, perimeter security. I have a Miss Edwards here who was trying to leave the palace. My orders state she is not to—"

"Yes, Private Markovich, those are your orders. Miss Edwards is not to leave the palace unless accompanied by one of five officers—Colonel Marianescu, Majors Kostya and Branko, Captain Mateja-Jones or myself. If she is not so accompanied, it is not safe for her to leave."

"That is the problem, sir. Miss Edwards is being..." Marek could hear Tahra's voice in the background—low-pitched and restrained, but nevertheless upset.

"I'm a guest, not a prisoner, and you have no right to keep me here!"

Marek sighed internally but didn't let the private hear him. He'd hoped Tahra would never have to know she *was* a prisoner...in essence. Now he would have to explain. "Keep her there, Private Markovich, by whatever means necessary. I will be with you shortly. Where exactly are you located?"

* * *

Tahra turned at the sound of a firm military tread on the marble floor behind her, relieved—still upset, but unaccountably relieved—to see Marek. She wanted to run to him but forced herself not to, because he'd ordered her held here at gunpoint, which the private guarding the door had told her…right before he'd drawn his weapon.

"How dare you," she began, her voice shaking as she tried to control her emotions.

"In private, Tahra, if you please."

"I *don't* please. You have no right to—"

He gave her a stern look, but all he said was "Please."

Tahra hadn't been this justifiably angry since the police had arrested *her* after she'd fought off her would-be rapist—a foreign diplomat who she hadn't known was married when she'd first started dating him—sending him to the hospital with severe but not fatal wounds. And then, when her boss and the people she worked with at the State Department hadn't believed her…when they'd taken the word of a lying, cheating SOB who'd concocted a fantastical tale that *she'd* lured *him* into a relationship and had stabbed him in a fit of rage when he refused to leave his wife for her, she'd been even more furious…and devastated.

The memory of the incident flashed through her mind, and she almost told Marek exactly what he could do with his "please." But then she remembered two things. First, she'd sworn she'd never trust another man again after the incident, but somehow Marek had overcome that, because she had to have trusted him if she'd agreed to marry him. And somehow he'd won her love. That meant he deserved the benefit of the doubt.

He deserved a chance to explain—in private—why she was a prisoner in the palace. Second, she'd been raised a lady. And a lady never let her emotions control her actions in public. No matter the provocation.

So she pressed her lips firmly together to keep her hot words unsaid. And when he held his right hand out to her, she took it.

"Thank you, Private Markovich," Marek told the guard, who'd already holstered his weapon. "You may return to your post."

"Yes, sir!"

When they were alone, Marek brought her left hand up to his cheek and held it there for a moment. "Thank you."

She struggled to find words she could say to him. "I'm still upset. You ordered him to hold me at gunpoint!"

He turned his face so he could press his lips into her palm. Briefly. Then he let her hand go. "I did not actually use those words. But yes, I did tell him to use whatever means necessary."

Only one word came to mind. "Why?"

He glanced around the corridor. "Not here. Let us return to your suite and I will try to explain."

It took Marek less time to take Tahra back than it had taken her to get here—partly because he didn't make a false turn and have to wend his way backward, as she'd done. Once the door to her suite closed behind them, she confronted him again. "Why?"

"Because you are a witness."

She gaped at him. "I'm a prisoner because I'm a witness?"

"A witness who is in danger. Have you never heard of protective custody?"

"Yes, but..." Her mind a whirl, she snatched at the first complete thought that came to her. "Why didn't you tell me? Why did you say I'm being *housed* in the palace for the time being? That makes it sound as if I have a choice."

"I would have spared you this, *maris*—"

"Stop it! Just stop it!" When his expression turned puzzled, she grabbed onto her temper and held tight, forcing her voice lower. "Stop *protecting* me. I'm not a half-wit and I'm not five years old. I don't want you to 'spare' me, I want you to treat me as an equal."

"You ask the impossible. This is who I am. You must take me as I am, or..."

"Or what?" she asked softly, her heart aching for him...and for herself. "Or what?"

"Set me free."

"Set you free?" Tahra shook her head slowly. "I'm not the one holding you prisoner. You're doing it to yourself. But not the way you're doing it to me."

"I am not...you do not understand. It is not my decree that holds you here, it is the king's."

"But you agree with it, don't you?" When he didn't answer, she insisted, "Don't you?"

"Yes." The word was forced through clenched teeth.

"I can't live that way. I can't. I'm not talking about protective custody. I get that I'm a witness. I'm talking about someone making decisions about what's best for me. Someone trying to shield me from life. I've lived that way before, and it's no good. Can't you see that? It's not good for me. Carly..."

She gulped, because she loved her sister more than anything, and what she was about to say seemed a betrayal of that love, but... "I told you before, Carly always protected me. Smoothed my path in life. Shielded me from whatever she could. *She* made the decisions—what I should focus on in high school, what college I should attend, what I should major in, even what career was best for me. And I let her. I just…let her. She wasn't doing it to hurt me—Carly would *never* deliberately hurt me. But she *was* hurting me by never letting me fall. Never letting me pick myself up. Never letting me make bad decisions so I could learn from them. She shielded me my entire life…until the one time she wasn't there. And I almost crashed and burned."

Tahra laughed a little hysterically at the bewildered look Marek gave her when she uttered the last sentence. "It's an American expression," she explained. "Plane crash? Fireball? I know it sounds insensitive, but it's not meant to be."

She drew a deep breath. "It's not that I don't want to be loved. I do. I want that more than anything. But I also need to know I'm strong enough to get back up after I've been knocked down. I'm not a little girl, I'm a woman. If you love me, love *me*. Not someone who always needs to be sheltered from life. Love someone who can stand at your side and carry her share of the load. Someone who will protect *you*, if necessary. Love me, but let me be that woman. Please."

Chapter 9

Marek tried to follow what Tahra was saying, but every word seemed an indictment of him. Of his love. All he could hear was her saying his love was hurting her somehow. And that sliced right to the bone, because hurting her was the *last* thing he ever wanted to do. Couldn't she see that? Couldn't she understand that all he wanted to do was protect her? Shelter her? Shield her? Spare her?

Cripple her.

The realization stunned him, but as soon as the thought coalesced in his brain he couldn't deny it. *She is right. Tahra is right and I am wrong. I have not loved her the way she needed me to love her. Selfish love, not selfless. Oh, God, what have I done?*

He tried to speak, but self-condemnation closed his throat, and when he didn't answer, she added quietly,

"You said I had a warrior's heart. If you truly believe that, then help me believe it, too. I need to know I can stand on my own before I can stand at your side."

Could he do it? Could he sit back and let Tahra stumble and fall and *not* reach out a hand to help her? Even if it was what she wanted, what she needed? Could he do it?

"I cannot promise," he said in a low voice, needing to be honest with her. He took her left hand in his, staring at his engagement ring there. Thinking of what it symbolized. "But I will try. Because I *do* love you, Tahra. More than I can ever express. So I will try to love you the way you need me to love you...and not the way I want to love you."

She gazed up at him, suddenly misty-eyed. "That's all I'm asking," she whispered. She moved until she was standing so close he could feel her trembling. "I'll be honest—I'm terrified I'll fail. That's why I need you to believe in me. So I can believe in myself."

He slid his arms around her waist and drew her into his embrace, but he didn't kiss her. He pressed her head against his shoulder and stroked her dark head, a new kind of love welling up in him. Love mixed with renewed admiration for her courage. Not just the physical courage she'd displayed a week ago, but the emotional courage to demand the best of herself...now and always.

"You *do* have a warrior's heart, *mariskya*. Never doubt it...and never doubt yourself."

The apartment building had been built at the dawn of the previous century and had been upgraded numerous times to bring it up to code—electrical wiring, natural gas lines, plumbing, fire alarms and reinforced steel fire doors in the stairwells. It stood on a rise overlooking the river winding its way through Drago, with an excellent view of the royal palace in the distance. The perspective had in some ways made up for its inconveniences, including the less-than-reliable boilers that sometimes but not always provided hot water for the tenants and the elevator that broke down with frustrating regularity, turning the building into an eight-story walk-up.

Until a year ago the residents had all been native-born Zakharians. But over the past twelve months almost half of the tenants had sacrificed the views for more reliable conveniences, opening up an increasing number of apartments to the latest wave of immigrants…many of whose rents were fully or partially subsidized by the king and the Zakharian government on a temporary basis until they were fully assimilated.

The building was mostly empty in the daytime. Many of the immigrant tenants worked at least one job and sometimes two to get ahead. And their children attended school and after-school study halls to catch up with their age groups and to learn their adopted language as quickly as possible. Even the stay-at-home mothers were usually out and about during the day—shopping or taking their children to the parks and museums that abounded in Drago. But the sun had set hours ago, and all the residents were fast asleep.

Three men dressed all in black, carrying knapsacks and duffel bags, slipped from the shadows through the unlocked front door into the lobby. Draconian laws on the books that Zakharian judges and juries never hesitated to apply in criminal trials made electronic security unnecessary in Drago for the most part.

No one saw the three men descend the staircase into

the bowels of the building or push open the unlocked boiler room door. No one saw them swiftly unpack their duffel bags and knapsacks.

No one saw one man lay charges around the room, run detonating cords to a central device or glance at his watch to set the timer, as the other two propped open the fire doors at the basement level, then climbed the stairways and did the same with the fire doors on each subsequent landing.

No one saw them make their escape, either, sliding into the passenger seats of a late-model sedan.

"All set?" the driver asked in Zakharan as he put the car in gear and glided away into the darkness without turning on his headlights.

The man in the front seat smiled and answered for the three of them. "All set." He glanced at the glowing digital clock on the car's dashboard. "Colonel Borka will be pleased. Twenty minutes from now there will be fewer refugees in Zakhar."

Tahra was soundly sleeping when a series of loud explosions rent the night, shocking her awake. She tossed the covers to one side and leaped from the bed, rushing in her nightclothes to the French doors leading to the balcony outside her suite. She threw them open and stumbled outside, still not really awake yet.

Flames engulfed a building a few miles from the palace, but clearly visible. "Oh, my God!" she whispered, only seconds before sirens split the night air, and the lights of emergency vehicles converged on the fiery building from all directions. "Oh, my God."

Tahra turned and hurried back inside, scrambling into the first clothes she could find. Then she made her way into the corridor outside her suite, which was already teeming with people. A man passed her wearing camouflage clothing and desert-style boots, carrying a lethal-looking rifle—the same uniform as the man who'd stopped her from leaving the palace earlier that evening—and she figured he probably knew what was going on. He certainly couldn't know less than she did. She grabbed his arm. "Please," she begged. "Can you tell me what's happening? How can I help?"

The doors to the ancient chapel on the first floor in the older part of the palace were already wide-open when Tahra made her way there. The seriously injured victims of the explosions and subsequent fire had been taken by ambulance to one of Drago's hospitals, but those who had escaped with only minor injuries or were miraculously unhurt had been transported here for first aid and temporary housing.

Almost all the victims were wearing nightclothes, and many were barefoot—they had obviously barely escaped with their lives. Tahra saw Queen Juliana, looking especially petite next to a tall blonde woman watching over her with vigilant eyes, going from one cluster of survivors to another, handing out blankets from a stack carried by one footman and socks from a box in the arms of another. A third, who hovered at her side with a notebook and a pen, appeared to be taking down names and other vital information.

Tahra turned, and her gaze was immediately drawn to a boy who couldn't have been more than twelve or thirteen, awkwardly holding a crying baby while a toddler and a young girl clung to his side, their eyes wide with terror.

"Let me help you," Tahra said, taking the wailing infant from him and cuddling it in her arms. "Shh," she soothed, jiggling the baby against her right shoulder so her left hand could do most of the work and not put a strain on her right wrist as she attempted to calm the little girl. She smiled down at the tearful face. "Shh. You're okay, honey," she said in English, hoping that even though her words might not be understood, her calming tone would get through. "You're okay."

When the crying finally ceased, Tahra wiped away the tearstains with the tips of her fingers and popped a kiss on the button nose. "There you go," she murmured. "You're a sweetheart, aren't you?" Then she returned her attention to the boy. He was kneeling between the young girl and the toddler, who were obviously his sister and brother, and he was hugging them fiercely, whispering to them in a language Tahra didn't understand.

He glanced up after a moment. In broken Zakharan she had only a little difficulty following, he said, "My father…" He gulped and a lone tear slid down his cheek. "He went back…for my mother. He got us all out safely, then went back inside to…to find my mother. I do not know if…" Another tear slid down, following the path of the first one as he struggled to hold emotions in check he should never have had to experience in the first place.

Tahra swallowed hard, blinking rapidly to keep her own tears at bay. "I'm so sorry," she whispered, thankful her Zakharan was good enough for these simple words of comfort. Her arms tightened instinctively around the baby she cradled against her shoulder… whose parents most likely weren't ever coming back. An orphan, like her.

* * *

Marek found Tahra just before dawn, precariously dozing in one of the pews…and his heart turned over. Her head was pillowed on a folded blanket, and her body was curved protectively around an infant in a pink sleeper and a very young boy in footed pj's, both peacefully unconscious in the shelter of her embrace. At the other end of the pew, a boy and a young girl slept with worn-out abandon beneath a blanket.

He touched her shoulder. He hated to wake her, but… "Tahra," he whispered. "Wake up, *mariskya*. You must wake up."

She came groggily awake and almost fell off the pew, but Marek caught her and helped her into a sitting position. She covered the sleeping children with the blanket she'd been using as a pillow, then scooted a little away and rubbed her eyes tiredly. "What are you doing here, Marek?" she said, her voice pitched low in an obvious attempt not to waken anyone else. She yawned and glanced around, seeming surprised to find the chapel almost empty. Then she abruptly focused on him and the two soldiers behind him, her eyes widening. "What…?"

Marek squatted so his eyes were on a level with hers. "The Red Cross has found shelter for everyone, including these children," he told her in an undertone. "They are the last. These men…" He indicated the two soldiers with a tilt of his head. "They will take the children now."

"Where? Where are they going?"

"A husband and wife who know the family slightly and speak the children's native tongue have volunteered to take them in…until we can be sure what happened to their parents."

Tahra darted a glance at the two older children, but they were still fast asleep. "Rafiq—he's the oldest," she said, her soft blue eyes full of shadows. "He told me his father got all four children out, then went back into the fire for their mother." Her voice broke and her eyes filled with tears. "I think they're orphans."

Pain speared through him at the sight of Tahra's tears and the desolate way she uttered those last four words. He remembered her confiding in him months ago about how she'd been orphaned herself at the tender age of ten. *"Carly was wonderful,"* she'd confessed in a voice that wasn't quite steady. *"I don't know what I would have done without her. But I missed my mom so much I cried myself to sleep for a month."*

It killed him that he couldn't turn back time—not for these newest orphans and not for Tahra. But he vowed whoever had set the bombs tonight would be brought to justice…one way or another.

Tahra gently shook Rafiq's shoulder, then his younger sister's. They sat up, rubbing their eyes just as she'd done, and while they were doing that she picked up the baby, nuzzling her awake.

"Here, miss, I will take her," the older of the two soldiers said, relieving Tahra of her precious burden before she could stop him. "I have one almost the same age."

The other soldier lifted the small boy from the pew where he still slept, and cuddled him. "Go back to sleep, little one," he murmured, gently pressing the boy's head against his shoulder.

Tahra quickly introduced the children to the soldiers. "This is Rafiq Ibrahim, who is twelve," she said, lightly squeezing the oldest boy's arm. "His sister Aaliyah is seven." She indicated the sleeping toddler in the soldier's arms. "Tamir—he's two and a half. And Safirah—" she brushed her fingers over the baby's head "—just turned one." She drew a trembling breath. "And you are…?"

"Sergeant Troian," the older of the two soldiers said. "And this is Corporal Zelimir. We will take good care of the children—you have my word."

She nodded, then turned to Rafiq and Aaliyah, sitting and drawing them to her side. "Go with Sergeant Troian and Corporal Zelimir," she managed in Zakharan. "They'll take you to someone who knows you. Someone who will look after you until…" She glanced up at Marek, an appeal in her eyes.

"Until we know what happened to your parents," he explained gently. "If we can locate them at the hospital, we will let them know where you are. And if they are now with God—" A whimper from Aaliyah made him pause for a moment, until Rafiq put his arm around her. *So young*, Marek thought with a flash of admiration, *and yet his first thought is to comfort his sister. To protect her. Rafiq is not Zakharian-born, but he is assuredly Zakharian-bred. He will grow into a man Zakhar will be proud to call a citizen.*

"If they are now with God," he continued, even more gently, "the king himself will make the arrangements your parents would have wished for you. You are not to worry about that," he assured them. "Just go with these men now."

Tahra managed not to break down and cry until the children were out of sight. Then she sank back in the wooden pew, buried her face in her hands and wept. She was vaguely aware of Marek, solid and warm at her side. Wrapping his arms around her and holding her so close she could hear the beat of his heart when he pressed her face against his chest and let her cry the tears she'd been wanting to cry since she'd first seen Rafiq with his sisters and brother.

"It's not right," she sobbed. "Why do bad things happen to good people? My parents…their parents…"

"I know." His voice rumbled beneath her ear. "It is inconceivable that any man could deliberately do something like this."

"What?" she gasped as she raised her head to stare at him, struggling for breath as shocked comprehension dawned.

"The explosions and fire were no accident," Marek confirmed grimly. "Of this we are sure. And it is worse than you know. Almost exactly the same thing happened in five other cities tonight across Zakhar. Reports are still coming in, but the overall death toll could exceed a thousand. We do not know who—no one has yet claimed responsibility—but I can hazard a guess."

"The Zakharian Liberation Front?" Tahra barely breathed the name.

Marek nodded, his eyes hard and cold. "*Someone* targeted those six apartment buildings—many of whose residents are refugees—the same way the Zakharian Liberation Front targeted refugees last week."

"Oh, my God." Suddenly cognizant of where they were, she closed her eyes and her lips moved soundlessly in a silent prayer for the innocent victims who'd been in that apartment building when it had exploded. Then she whispered "Amen" at the end.

"Amen," Marek repeated after her, but in Zakharan.

Then in English he promised, "We will catch them, Tahra. I give you my word."

Frustration rose out of nowhere. "If only I could *remember*." She hit the heel of her hand against her skull three times in rapid succession, as if she could force her memory to return. When Marek caught her hand in his, she buried her face against his shoulder, and a touch of despair crept into her voice. "It makes me so angry at myself. If I could remember, we might be able to catch him—the man who left the bomb. The man the witnesses say I saw. And if we can catch *him*, then..."

"You did your part when you saved the children at the preschool," he reminded her. "When you berate yourself, remember *how* you came to lose your memory." His arms tightened around her. "I can never forget."

She grasped his shirt in one tightly clenched fist. "I know. I *know*. It's just..."

"It is just that your tender heart will always overrule your practical brain. Yes, *mariskya*, this I have known about you almost from the beginning." He brushed a kiss against her forehead.

"And I suppose you never let your heart overrule your head," she said without thinking.

His whole body tightened against hers. "My heart has overruled my head since the moment I met you." And something in those simple words...the quiet way they were spoken...made Tahra's heart ache. And she realized she didn't just want to remember so they could catch the man who'd left the bomb near the schoolyard. She wanted to remember this man as well, wanted to remember the love they'd shared.

"We were happy," she said, looking up into his face for confirmation. "Weren't we?"

She almost missed the nearly imperceptible hesitation before he nodded slowly. "Yes. We were happy. We did not fall in love the way you fall into a hole and just as easily clamber out. Although I think I knew you were The One the moment we first spoke, I just did not admit it to myself. Instead of falling, we *grew* into love. We grew into…" There was that tiny hesitation again before he finished his sentence with "Trust. We grew into trust."

Tahra sighed deeply. She wanted to ask Marek why he'd hesitated. Twice. But…she didn't want another confrontation with him that in any way resembled their clash earlier tonight. *Last night, actually*, she acknowledged as the first rays of dawn crept into the chapel through the stained glass windows, casting jeweled light over the two of them. She didn't regret their heated discussion last night—she'd said things that *had* to be said—but there was such solace sitting here in Marek's arms, she wasn't willing to risk saying anything that might remotely come across as confrontational.

So instead she pulled the blanket she'd used to cover the children onto her lap and refolded it, saying, "The queen was here before I arrived, handing out blankets and socks and…and words of comfort to everyone. She was so gracious. She seemed to know exactly what to say, just like Carly. I wish I could be like that." She sighed again, then added, "The king joined her, but not until much later." She tried not to let that sound like a criticism of the king Marek practically worshipped, but…

He answered her unspoken question as if he could read her mind. "The king called an emergency meeting of the Privy Council," he explained. "Followed by a meeting with Colonel Marianescu and Major Stesha—the heads of internal security and the secret intelligence service—among others."

"Is that where you were?"

He shook his head. "I was with the crown prince." His face took on a faraway expression. "I wonder if you can understand how important Crown Prince Raoul is to all of us in Zakhar—not just to his parents."

She thought a moment. "I think so. Because he's the future king, right?"

"It is not just that. He represents the future of our country, and as such is doubly precious to us. The line of direct descent from father to son has *never* been broken."

"Never?"

"No, never. The first Andre Alexei was succeeded by his son, Raoul, in the sixteenth century, and from that day to this, every reigning monarch has been succeeded by his son. I was not yet born when the current king was born, but my father told me the national jubilation at his birth was nearly as epic as at the crown prince's. It is the continuation of a dynasty more than five hundred years old, you understand."

He laughed a little under his breath, surprising her. "We are not superstitious, of course." He smiled and his blue eyes twinkled at her. "But Zakhar has prospered wondrously in all that time, under good kings. Some were even great kings. Are those things connected? *Probably* not, but no Zakharian wishes to risk testing it by breaking the line of direct descent. So my duty was to ensure Crown Prince Raoul's safety, just as Angelina's duty—Captain Mateja-Jones, that is, your boss's wife—her duty was to ensure the safety of the queen and the baby she carries."

"A lovely blonde woman, quite tall, with sharply watchful eyes? That's Angelina?"

"Yes." His smile faded and his face took on a serious mien. "I should not have told you…about the baby. Please keep that to yourself for now—it is not public knowledge."

"I already knew," she confessed. "The queen told me herself, and I was thrilled for her. For *them*. But I didn't know you knew about it."

He let out his breath, as if he'd been worried he'd revealed something he shouldn't have. "The king confided in me because I will have to expand the security detail when Crown Prince Raoul has a brother or sister in the not-too-distant future." A faint smile touched his lips. "A brother would be best for Zakhar, of course, because—"

"'An heir and a spare,'" Tahra quoted drily.

"Well…yes. Although the king would welcome a daughter."

Tahra wasn't so sure about that, but she wasn't going to say so. She knew from what Queen Juliana had told her that women weren't in the line of succession in Zakhar, and her State Department briefing had indicated Zakhar was fifty years behind the times where women were concerned. But all she said was "Let's get back to what we were discussing."

"Of course." Marek thought for a moment, then said, "With the queen and the crown prince out of danger, the king could focus on other things. When the explosions occurred, there was concern the palace itself might be under attack. The king's first thought was for the safety of his wife and his son…as it should be. His second thought was for his subjects. Not just the ones attacked tonight, and not just those who live in Drago, but *all* his subjects. That is why he was not with the queen from the beginning."

"I…I didn't mean to criticize him."

"You did, but that is not to the point. The king was forced to make an extremely difficult decision, but he had no choice where the safety of his subjects is concerned."

"What do you mean?"

"At the urging of the Privy Council, the king has called out the Zakharian National Forces. The country is now under martial law."

Chapter 10

Tahra gasped, and Marek was sorry he'd had to spring this on her with little warning. Then he remembered her adamantly insisting, *"Stop* protecting *me,"* and his own response, *"I cannot promise... But I will try."*

So instead of downplaying the seriousness of the king's action, he admitted, "Armed soldiers will be posted at all the main points of congress within the country—airports, train stations, bus stations, churches, schools, border crossings. You name it, an armed presence will make itself felt."

"He's closing the borders?"

"No. That would play into the hands of the Zakharian Liberation Front, giving them exactly what they are asking for—cutting off the flow of refugees. But the border guards will be complemented by soldiers, making sure the émigrés who make it inside our borders are safe. No impact for the US embassy here, but it *will* cause your State Department to issue a travel warning to US citizens."

"Oh. I hadn't thought about that. Does Alec know?"

"The king officially notified all the ambassadors—" he glanced at his watch "—more than an hour ago. I would assume this was important enough for their staffs to wake them. So yes, I would also assume the regional security officer of your embassy would know by now… through official channels."

She turned questioning eyes on him. "Angelina wouldn't tell him? Her own husband?"

He shook his head, regret creeping into his voice. "You know the answer to that question…it is buried somewhere in the currently inaccessible recesses of your brain. We are friends with them—I told you this, yes?" When she nodded, he said, "Angelina and Alec are… Let us just say that honor and duty are everything to both of them. Angelina would not tell Alec anything concerning Zakharian national security…*and he would not expect her to.* Just as he would tell her nothing he learned through his job as the US embassy's RSO, and she would not want him to, either."

"But…you told me."

"It is not a secret, you understand. Not now that the ambassadors have been officially notified and the king made an announcement on national television and radio at the same time the letters went to the ambassadors."

He took her left hand in his, rubbing a finger over the engagement ring. "I explained when we became affianced that I could not tell you everything. And you said you understood—you have secret clearance for your job at the embassy, and you take that seriously, *mariskya.*"

"Yes, I do."

"So you understand I cannot—this is completely separate from my love for you—but I cannot betray the oath I took. Not just my oath as an officer in the Zakharian National Forces, but also the one I swore to the king when I took over security for his wife and then his son."

Tahra entwined her fingers with Marek's. "I understand. Honest." She yawned suddenly, covering her mouth with her free hand, the one with a cast around her wrist. "Sorry," she said quickly. "I didn't get a lot of sleep last night, and—"

He interrupted her. "And I have kept you talking when you should have been in bed." He took the blanket from her and laid it on the pew next to him. "Leave this—someone will collect it later today with all the rest." Then he rose and helped her to her feet, drawing her into the circle of his arms. "Yes, and you are still recovering," he said, the remorse he felt over keeping her from her bed reflected in his voice. He kissed her lightly on the lips. "Come, I will walk you to your suite."

"You should be in bed, too," Tahra told him as they made their way out of the chapel. "You probably got less sleep than I did, since I napped earlier."

He almost told her he'd gotten *no* sleep last night, and not just because of the explosions. He'd been awake when the phone call had come urgently requesting his presence at the palace. Awake, because he hadn't been able to sleep for thinking about everything that had happened last night. Everything she'd said to him.

Not to mention the lie begun with the best intentions that had grown to huge proportions weighing heavily on his conscience, the lie that they were engaged. How long could he keep up that pretense? And would Tahra ever forgive him if—*when*—she regained her memory?

Then there was the other lie robbing him of sleep, the one he'd told her last night—*"...take me as I am or set me free."* A lie, because it was not possible. Tahra could not set him free, because he could not *be* set free—Marianescus loved once, then never again. And Tahra had seemed to know it when she replied, *"I'm not the one holding you prisoner. You're doing it to yourself..."*

Not *quite* true...because he hadn't chosen his fate. *It has to be something in our blood,* he reasoned, because he was only a Marianescu on the distaff side. And yet his father had warned him when he'd barely entered his teens. *"Some call it the Marianescu curse,"* his father had explained. *"But it is no curse—not to the men who truly love."* The Count of Mortagne had smiled as he said this, a smile conveying he was one of the lucky ones for whom the curse was not a curse.

Marek had thought he understood...as much as a teenaged boy could understand such things, but he hadn't been unduly concerned how it might affect him. And he'd gone for years without giving it much thought. Until King Andre Alexei IV had ascended the throne and had assigned a then-Lieutenant Zale to head up the team surreptitiously guarding Juliana Richardson in Hollywood. And Marek had seen for himself just how powerful the hold was.

It is her...or no one.

The first Andre Alexei had said that about his Eleonora when she'd been kidnapped and held to ransom for five seemingly endless years. King Andre hadn't had to say those words to Marek about the women he eventually made his queen...but Marek had known. He'd placed his hands between the king's and had sworn an oath to keep Juliana safe or die trying. And he'd moved heaven and earth to keep that vow, both in Hollywood and Zakhar, even saving Juliana's life once.

And again Marek had thought he understood. But it was like a seeing man trying to describe sight to a man who had always been blind. One could understand the concept *in theory*, without having any idea what it was really like.

Then Tahra had entered his life, and Marek had known. The scales had fallen from his eyes and he'd finally, *finally* understood. He'd known, too, that he must win her heart—failure was not an option.

It still wasn't.

He opened the door to Tahra's suite and ushered her inside but didn't dare follow her in. Not now. Not when heart, mind and body were all clamoring for him to take advantage of the shy invitation on the face Tahra turned to him—an invitation he wasn't even sure she was consciously aware of.

He barely had the strength of will to resist her invitation *and* his own desires, but somehow he managed it. He gazed down into her face, cataloging her features, and trying—not for the first time—to figure out what it was about her that had irrevocably ensnared his heart. Tahra was beautiful, but he'd known more beautiful women… Zorina among them. But he hadn't loved Zorina any more than he'd loved the other women he'd known. Tahra had curves in all the right places, but he'd been with more voluptuous women… Again, Zorina among them. Tahra was not the first woman he'd desired…but she was the only woman for whom he'd forsworn his desire. The only woman he wanted from now until eternity, and he'd craved the sanctity of marriage before…

Was that why—like his noble ancestor, like his royal cousin—he knew with unshakable faith that it was Tahra…or no one?

It is her eyes, he realized, wondering how he'd missed it before. *Her eyes are windows into her soul. She will age as my mother has aged, but she will always be the caring, loving woman she is now. And I will love her thirty years from now…forty…fifty…as my father still loves my mother. That will never change.*

But would Tahra still love him? She'd loved him before the explosion had wiped out the past eighteen months… *And will again,* he vowed fiercely, *whether or not she ever regains her memory.* Somehow he would untangle the web of lies he'd spun and find his way back to her heart.

He kissed her cheek. Then, because his heart swelled with love and he couldn't help himself, he brushed his lips against hers.

Failure is not an option.

"Failure is not an option," Colonel Marianescu adamantly asserted to the men—and one woman—assembled around the conference table in the War Room later that morning. "The king has declared a state of martial law, but that cannot endure indefinitely, and no one knows that better than the king himself. So he has tasked me—and now I am tasking *you*—with putting an end to the unconscionable attacks the Zakharian Liberation Front has inflicted upon Zakhar, including its most innocent victims—its children."

Everyone in the room knew the Zakharian Liberation

Front had publicly taken credit for the early-morning bombings at apartment buildings across the country. And everyone in the room knew that of the nine hundred fifty-seven fatalities, six hundred eighty-nine of them were children…four hundred seventy-two of whom were children under the age of ten.

"*Unconscionable* is the word," Marek whispered to Angelina, the lone woman in the room. "How any man could plan and carry out something like this is unconscionable."

Angelina nodded, and her eyes met Marek's. "That could have been me," she whispered back. "Before I married Alec, I used to live in the apartment building that was firebombed here in Drago…on the top floor."

Marek understood exactly what she meant. Flames and smoke had shot up the elevator shaft and the stairwells, because—as the fire investigators had already determined—someone had propped open the fire doors on every floor. Almost no one on the seventh or eighth floors had escaped. Not all the victims had died from the fire. Many had succumbed to asphyxiation, especially those on the higher floors, overcome by smoke that in a normal fire would not have blocked the escape routes.

"So, gentlemen. What do we know about this organization so far?" Colonel Marianescu demanded. "Major Stesha?"

Marek's former superior opened a thick folder he'd brought with him to this meeting. It looked to be a duplicate of the one he'd given Marek the day before. Marek had forgotten about it with everything that had happened since then, but now the idea the file had raised came roaring back to mind.

"Excuse me, Major Stesha," Marek said, rising to his feet. "I have something to offer, if I may." The major waved a hand, ceding him the floor. "All the targets, including the ones early this morning, appear to be related to the refugee issue. And yes, 'Zakhar for Zakharians' sounds as if their goal is…" He fumbled for the right word. "Ahhh…ethnically related." He drew a deep breath. "But not all the victims have been immigrants. A fair amount have been native-born Zakharians. And if the bomb had been allowed to explode at the preschool, even more native-born Zakharians would have died. Yes, nearly half the children in that schoolyard were relatively new immigrants—*but more than half were not.*"

"What are you trying to say, Captain?" Major Stesha barked.

"What if the asylum seekers are not truly the issue?" he asked softly. "If they were, would this organization have taken the lives of so many native-born Zakharians?" He didn't wait for an answer before continuing. "What if the refugees are a…a blind, a way of dividing the country? A way of diverting national security attention from their true goal?"

Angelina rose to stand at his side, nodding slowly. "Captain Zale is correct. Last week we all sat in this room and assumed the refugees were the target. Even the king believed this to be the case. But what if he was wrong?"

A smothered gasp went around the room, and Marek had to bite his lip not to smile. Angelina had uttered what amounted to heresy to the men gathered here. The king could not be wrong because God would not *let* him be wrong. He'd believed that, too…until he'd read

Major Stesha's file. Until the idea the refugees were not the real target had grabbed hold of him and refused to let go. He wouldn't have worded his statement quite that bluntly, however…even though he was thinking it.

"Captain Mateja-Jones is right," Marek said now. "What if the king is wrong? What if this is nothing more than an attempt to seize power from our rightful monarch? To assassinate the entire royal family and take over Zakhar?" He let that suggestion sink in for a moment, then added, "Even their name supports the idea. Zakharian *Liberation* Front. Nothing about that name indicates keeping Zakhar 'pure' or keeping the ethnic makeup of our citizens as it has been for centuries. Yes, their publicly stated credo would lead you to believe this, but again, that could be a diversion tactic."

The arrested expression on Major Stesha's face was followed by a flash of admiration, then agreement. "There is much in what you say, Captain Zale." He turned to Colonel Marianescu. "The secret intelligence service has focused exclusively on learning as much as it can about the Zakharian Liberation Front as it relates to the influx of émigrés. And yes, we have made some progress in that area. But if Captain Zale is correct, the threat is even greater than we have so far imagined."

Tahra woke when her body told her she'd had enough sleep…and when she heard a slight noise from the other room. "Who's there?" she called sharply, sudden fear ratcheting up her heartbeat. She'd never been fearful like this…until she'd nearly been raped. But ever since then, she'd experienced instances of panic attacks, which the psychologist she'd consulted had assured her would become less and less frequent over time. The woman had been right…at least as far as Tahra could remember. They had nearly ceased by the time she'd been transferred to Zakhar. In fact, one of the reasons she'd welcomed the transfer was Drago's reputation as one of the safest capitals in the world.

Tahra couldn't swear she hadn't had a panic attack in the past year and a half—she couldn't swear to *anything* that might or might not have happened during that time. But that wasn't really relevant. She was having one now.

Another sound from the other room, then the door to the bedroom was pushed ajar, and a smiling face peered in. "You are awake, Miss Edwards. Did you sleep well?"

Tahra let out the breath she'd been holding and leaned back against the pillows, ordering her heart to relax. The door opened further, and Ani entered the room, carrying a bed tray. "I have brought your lunch, miss."

Lunch in bed seemed so…decadent. So…un-American. But Ani didn't seem to see it that way, and besides, Tahra still found meals awkward with the cast on her right wrist. So when the little maid set the tray on a side table, opened the curtains to let the noonday sun in and moved to fluff up Tahra's pillows, she leaned forward and let her.

"Oh, miss!"

The empathetic dismay in Ani's voice reminded Tahra she was wearing one of her sleeveless nightgowns… and those pinkish scars the fléchettes had inflicted were clearly visible in the sunlight. She sat back hurriedly, hiding the scars from view. She'd almost forgotten about them, especially since they didn't hurt and she couldn't see them herself unless she posed naked in front of a mirror and craned her neck—something she wasn't about to do.

"Oh, miss," Ani said again, and this time there were tears in her eyes. "We knew you were a heroine, saving those children as you did—all the household staff vied to look after you, and I was proud when I was chosen—but we… I never knew what you suffered."

Tahra couldn't help it; bright color flooded her cheeks. "It doesn't hurt. Truly it doesn't. And I don't remember, but Marek—Captain Zale—told me what I did. You would probably have done the same thing."

Ani shook her head. "Not me, miss. I would have been frozen with fear." She settled the bed tray across Tahra's lap, then removed the cover to reveal a tempting meal…one that wouldn't require her to use her right wrist at all.

"Thank you." She wasn't sure if the chef had known or if Ani had reminded him, but she was grateful one way or the other.

"There is a note, too, miss," the maid said. "Let me fetch it." She was gone and back in less than a minute. "It is from your fiancé. Captain Zale."

Tahra put down her fork and took the envelope, laying it on the tray momentarily. "How do you know?"

Ani smiled in a way that made her seem older than Tahra, who was probably ten years her senior. "How do I know it came from Captain Zale? Or how do I know he is your fiancé?"

"Both."

"A footman brought the note and told me who had sent it." Ani's smile deepened. "And everyone who works in the palace knows Captain Zale. Many women have tried to catch his eye—oh, many, many. He is so handsome and such a gentleman!" She sighed a little. "But ever since he came to work here in the palace he seemed to have eyes only for his duty. So of course when we learned his fiancée was the heroine who was all over the news and was coming to recuperate in the palace, well! Word spread like wildfire."

Tahra knew she shouldn't ask, but she couldn't help it. "Many, many?"

Ani was straightening the room as she gossiped, picking up the clothes Tahra had worn in the early hours of the morning—an event that seemed so far away from her now, after six hours of sleep—and placing them in the laundry hamper. "You would not believe how silly some women are when a man ignores them," Ani said. "And when a man looks like Captain Zale, like a prince in a fairy tale..." Her dark eyes twinkled at Tahra.

The color deepened in Tahra's cheeks, and she tried to focus on the delicacies on her plate. Then she saw the envelope on the tray next to her plate, with her name written across it in a bold hand. And though the room was warm and the sun was shining brightly through the window, a chill ran through her at the sight of her name in Marek's handwriting.

Her hand was trembling so much she almost couldn't pick the envelope up. *Why?* Her frantic brain scrambled for an answer, but none was forthcoming. All she knew was that she dreaded reading what was enclosed. Which was crazy. *Crazy!*

Why would she react this way? It made no sense. None.

Then she remembered that moment in his office when she'd known without a doubt he'd done something to break her heart. She didn't know what. And she didn't know why. She just knew she'd wept bitter tears over him. And if she wasn't careful, he just might break her heart again.

Chapter 11

Tahra finally snatched at the envelope, despite her sense of foreboding, and ripped it open, then drew out the crisp notepaper and forced herself to read what was written there.

Dear Tahra, the note said. *We have been invited to dinner with the Joneses on Friday evening. They keep early hours because of their baby. I did mention Alec and Angelina have a new baby, did I not? So Angelina asked me if 6:00 p.m. would be good for us. If you agree, I will let Angelina know. Sincerely, Marek.*

Completely innocuous. Nothing to be afraid of. Then she turned the note over and saw something written on the other side.

I regret to inform you I could find no trace of the Ibrahim children's parents at any of the hospitals. Recovery of the bodies from the apartment building is still ongoing, but it could be days or weeks before all are identified and we know for sure. In the meantime, please take comfort in knowing the children are being cared for. Sincerely, M.

"Oh, God," she whispered. She suddenly had no more appetite, although she'd been hungry before she'd read Marek's note.

"What is it, miss?"

"Some children I met in the chapel early this morning," she managed to answer. She didn't think she had to explain to Ani—everyone who worked in the palace must know the use to which the chapel had been put after the bombing and fire at the apartment building. "Marek—Captain Zale—checked the hospitals. There's no sign of the children's parents."

The maid crossed herself and whispered something in Zakharan that Tahra was able to translate in her mind: *God have them in his keeping.*

Yes, she thought as waves of sadness swept through her. *God have them all in his keeping—Rafiq, Aaliyah, Tamir and Safirah. And their parents.*

She stared at the note, suddenly realizing she hadn't even had to ask. Marek had found out for her. He'd anticipated her question and had quietly made it his job to find the answer. Another in a growing list of reasons to love him.

Which was why she couldn't understand—could barely accept—that he'd broken her heart somehow. But just as she knew he loved her, she knew the other was true, too.

Keeping a wrist cast clean and dry wasn't easy…not if you preferred showers to baths, as Tahra did. But her suite had an amazing marble tub big enough for two, which made up for the necessity. She let Ani draw her a bath but dispensed with further assistance. "I think I can manage from here," she said firmly.

"Should I wait in the other room, miss? Just in case?"

Ummm, no, definitely not! Tahra thought, uncomfortable with being waited on hand and foot. Okay, so doing some things for herself with her right hand in a cast took two or three times longer than they normally did. Eating with her left hand, for instance, was a challenge. Dressing, especially anything with buttons or zippers, was also more difficult than she would have thought. But she wasn't an invalid, and she wasn't about to act like one. She didn't want to hurt Ani's feelings, however, so all she said was "I'll be fine. You don't have to wait."

Ani was already making the bed, something Tahra would have done herself if she'd had two good hands. "Let me at least lay out your clothes, miss. What will you wear today?"

"You don't have to do that."

Ani fluffed the pillows and tucked them inside their decorative covers. Satisfied with the pristine condition of the bed, she turned to Tahra, a hurt expression on her face. "That is my job, miss. A job I take great pride in. If you are not satisfied with my work, the master of the household will reassign me and find some—"

"Oh, no!" Tahra rushed to reassure her. "You do a splendid job. It's just that I'm not used to…" She waved a helpless hand around the bedroom.

"Ahhh," the maid said. "I understand, miss. You are American, like Queen Juliana. Daphne—the queen's personal maid—explained it to me. The queen herself had difficulty accepting her new status at first, but eventually she came around. This is Zakhar," she said proudly. "Our ways suit us, and you will adapt in time. Especially after you marry Captain Zale. You will be Zakharian then." She switched gears. "Now, what would you like to wear today?"

"Oh...anything. You pick for me."

"That is good," Ani said with a determined nod and a self-satisfied smile. "A woman's maid knows best. You will see." She bustled toward the closet and emerged with slacks and a long-sleeved cotton sweater in an appealing shade of blue. The sweater happened to be one of Tahra's favorites because it almost exactly matched the color of her eyes. "Captain Zale will love you in this color, miss."

Tahra shook her head. "He's very busy. I probably won't even see him today."

Ani's smile morphed into a knowing one. "You will see him. No matter how busy he is, you will see him. This I know." Then her voice turned brisk. "Your bathwater is cooling, miss."

Satisfied with the results of his snap inspection, Marek left the crown prince's suite, exhaustion tugging at him. No sleep last night before he'd been called out, and no sleep since had him drawing upon all his energy reserves to finish out the day. Some men might have gone home to sleep after this morning's meeting, feeling justified in doing so—but those men were not Marek Zale.

He started down the Grand Staircase, intending to do some work in his office on the first floor, but changed his mind and headed for Princess Mara's suite instead, which was where the master of the household had placed

Tahra. *She probably does not know the honor being accorded her*, he thought with a private smile. The suite was usually kept vacant except for the few times a year Princess Mara and her family were able to visit from Colorado. Even the master of the household would not have dared to assign that suite to Tahra…if the king's orders hadn't made it perfectly clear he wanted nothing but the best for the woman who'd been injured saving so many children.

He rapped on the oak door, which was almost immediately opened by Tahra's diminutive maid. The young woman smiled what could only be called an "I knew it!" smile and let him in. "Miss Edwards is…unavailable at the moment," she explained as she led Marek into the sitting room. "Please have a seat. I will let her know you are here."

He stayed standing. He was afraid if he sat down on the sofa he'd fall asleep, so he leaned against the marble side of the large, meticulously maintained fireplace that hadn't needed a fire to heat the room for many years. But it was beautiful and complemented the decor in the suite.

A sound made him look up, and there was Tahra framed in the doorway, so lovely in a royal blue sweater with her dark hair curling on her shoulders, she took his breath away. *That is nothing new—Tahra always takes your breath away*, he thought as he moved toward her. He barely noticed the maid gently pushing Tahra into the room and then closing the double doors behind her, giving them privacy. "You are awake" was all he could think of to say. "When your maid said you were unavailable, I thought you might still be—"

Warm color tinged her cheeks. "I was taking a bath."

She held her right arm up, displaying the cast on her wrist. "It's not easy when you have to wrap a plastic bag around most of your arm so you don't get the darn thing wet. Makes me wish I were left-handed, too, because everything takes longer—even pulling on a sweater or zipping up."

"If we were married, I could help you with those things," he said in a low, teasing voice as he dipped his head for a quick kiss. "You are even lovelier than I remembered," he murmured when his lips left hers.

She laughed a little self-consciously and protested, "You just saw me this morning."

"Yes." He let his eyes speak for him for a few seconds, and the color in her cheeks deepened. "But the reality of you is always a shock to my senses."

How did Marek manage to say such things—to pay her such flowery compliments—and not come across as anything other than the über-alpha male he was? Tahra had no idea. She knew most American men wouldn't be caught dead saying something like that. Not to mention most American men these days wouldn't think marriage was a necessary precursor to physical intimacy. And in theory she agreed with her countrymen. Marriage wasn't the be-all and end-all for a woman these days. Her own sister hadn't "saved herself for marriage," and there was absolutely nothing wrong with it. But there wasn't anything wrong with marriage, either, or a man who respected you enough to wait until you were truly ready for that next step in a relationship heading for marriage. A man who didn't push for sex from the very first date.

She liked that about Marek. A lot. And the woman

she'd been for the past eighteen months must have liked that about him, too. Because if they'd never been lovers, it *had* to be his doing. The desire for more that pulsed through her body whenever he kissed her? She *must* have felt it before. Which meant he'd set the boundaries in their physical relationship. Which meant…

Tahra sighed softly and leaned into Marek, loving how warm and tingly she felt when his arms tightened around her and he pulled her close for another mind-blowing kiss…before letting her go.

Only when she was free to gaze up into his face did she realize there were tiny lines of exhaustion around his eyes. "You've been up all night." Concern for him lent an accusing edge to her tone. "Oh, Marek, why? Why didn't you go home to bed?"

His lips twitched. "I could not. There was a national security meeting earlier this morning, a meeting I could not miss, not with the country under martial law—and besides, I am on duty."

"And duty is everything to you," she said softly, understanding. "But you're entitled to time off for lunch, aren't you? Wait right here." She rushed out of the sitting room and into her bedroom, relieved to see Ani hadn't yet removed her lunch tray. The food was cold by now, but still edible. She grabbed the plate with her left hand, the fork with her right, and hurried back into the sitting room.

"Sit down," she ordered, channeling her older sister. And when Marek had done so, she handed him the largely untouched plate. "I…I wasn't hungry earlier," she explained. She sat next to him on the sofa, enjoying the sight of him wolfing down the food. When he was done, she took the plate and fork from him and placed them on an end table. Then she tugged on his sleeve.

"What are you—" he began, but Tahra cut him off.

"Half an hour," she insisted, pulling his head onto her lap. He resisted at first, but she was adamant. "Sleep for half an hour. I promise I won't let it be longer than that."

He was asleep almost as soon as his head rested on her thighs, and Tahra's heart turned over. Falling in love with Marek was the easy part—she was far beyond halfway there after only a week of knowing him, despite the overprotectiveness and patronizing attitude toward women that were relics of his Zakharian upbringing. Every moment spent in his company only drew her deeper under his spell.

The question was, what wasn't he telling her? Why was she so sure he'd broken her heart before? And could she go forward with a relationship with him if she never remembered? If he never told her the truth?

She couldn't answer those questions. All she knew was that in this moment he was hers to protect. And if anyone tried to wake him in the next thirty minutes? They'd have to deal with her first.

Sergeant Thimo Vasska lowered his binoculars and said quietly to his two companions, "That is the third troop carrier in the past hour. That makes eleven since the announcement early this morning." He didn't have to be more specific—his companions knew he was referring to the declaration that the country was now under martial law. Zakharian National Forces troops were being dispatched to all the borders to beef up security. All the borders, not just the eastern one, although Sergeant Vasska theorized more were being sent there because that was where the refugees were first entering Zakhar.

But the increased security had nothing to do with stemming the tide; the soldiers were there to provide extra security *for* the refugees, not against them. So Sergeant Vasska didn't understand why the captain and the major who'd accompanied him on this expedition into the mountains were looking on this as a good thing. Not that they came right out and admitted as much. But the sergeant could read more than they realized he was seeing in the tiny smiles they shared when they thought his face was turned elsewhere.

The sound of a truck laboring up a hill in the distance made the sergeant raise his binoculars again. "Here comes another one," he announced. "That makes twelve all told."

"Twelve here," said the major. "At least half that many on the other three borders, which makes at least thirty."

"Fifty men to a carrier," intoned the captain, "times thirty carriers means at least fifteen hundred men here, not there."

Out of the corner of his eye Sergeant Vasska saw the major and the captain share another secret smile. *Fifteen hundred new soldiers on the borders*, he thought to himself. *What the hell is worth smiling at about that?*

Three people stood at attention in front of Colonel Marianescu's desk. "At ease, gentlemen," he said, even though one of the soldiers was a woman. "Please be seated."

Marek sat, glancing to his right at Major Damon Kostya, before looking left and catching Angelina's eyes. She just shook her head slightly, indicating she had no more idea than he did what this was all about.

Colonel Marianescu got right to the point. "Three men were arrested early this morning in the city of Timon, near the eastern border. They were attempting to set explosive devices in an apartment building there, similar to what was done here. That they were caught at all was a fluke. Two officers at the air force base outside Timon who live in that apartment building had been out...ahhh...celebrating their recent promotions—"

Celebrating at a bar, Marek translated.

"—and returned home very late. They noticed the fire doors had been propped open on the ground floor, and upon investigation managed to apprehend the two men in the stairwells, just as they were returning."

Not too *drunk, then*, Marek thought approvingly. He partook of spirits on occasion, but never to excess. He never forgot that a man who imbibed too much was not in control of himself or the situation around him. Drunkenness was an action unbecoming to an officer in the Zakharian National Forces.

"Neither suspect would say a word when the officers made a citizen's arrest," Colonel Marianescu continued, "but then a third man emerged from the basement and was also apprehended. The officers held all three men until the police could be summoned. We suspect a fourth man was involved—a driver who must have fled when he heard the police sirens. The similarity to the bombings here and elsewhere across the country was too obvious to miss, and the Timon police notified the secret intelligence service—Major Stesha's men—who took the three suspects into custody. They are being held under tight security at the air force base outside the city.

"Normal interrogation tactics have been useless. None of the men have spoken a word. Major Stesha is wishing to utilize…ahhh…extraordinary interrogation tactics."

Marek had no difficulty grasping that Colonel Marianescu was referring to torture, a form of interrogation he both deplored and held little faith in. A man would say anything to stop the torture, so information gleaned from that source was rarely reliable. Nor was it evidence that could be used at trial.

The colonel focused his attention on Angelina. "I immediately thought of you, Captain Mateja-Jones. Your success interrogating the cameraman involved in the conspiracy to assassinate the crown prince stands as a classic example of what might work in this case. All we need is one man to talk, to tell us what he knows of the Zakharian Liberation Front. Are you willing to give it a shot, Captain?"

Angelina didn't hesitate, Marek noted with approval. "Of course, sir." Then she glanced Marek's way and added, "But Captain Zale was also instrumental in that previous interrogation, sir. He helped me assess the best way to approach the cameraman. If you send me, send him, too. That will improve our chances for success."

Colonel Marianescu nodded. "Good idea. I was going to ask Captain Zale and Major Kostya to cover for you with regard to the queen's security detail in your absence." He turned his gaze on the major. "Now I must ask you to cover for both Captain Mateja-Jones and Captain Zale. Be honest. Is this too much to ask of one man?"

Major Kostya shook his head. "Not if the queen is willing to cooperate."

"Which she will," Angelina assured them all. "The queen will make any personal sacrifice necessary to ensure the safety of all Zakharians…especially children."

"Then we have a plan, gentlemen." Colonel Marianescu stood, and everyone else did, too. "I have a military jet standing by, Captain Mateja-Jones, Captain Zale. I need not tell you time is of the essence here, just as I need not tell you this is top secret." His voice softened, but his face hardened. "If you are correct, Captain Zale, the Zakharian Liberation Front is a threat to the royal family. A threat that *cannot* be tolerated. Not for an instant."

Chapter 12

Tahra was taken to St. Anne's Hospital on Wednesday morning for a follow-up examination by her surgeon. She'd hoped Marek would be free to accompany her, but she was sadly disappointed to find someone else waiting beside the limousine to which she was guided.

"Miss Edwards?" the man asked courteously. He was dressed in regular business clothes, but something about him made her instantly think, *military*. When Tahra nodded, he offered her his hand and said, "Major Lukas Branko, at your service," confirming her supposition. "The king has ordered me to see you safely to and from the hospital."

He held the limo door open for Tahra. She glanced back at the door through which she'd just come, praying Marek would miraculously appear…but he didn't. So she allowed Major Branko to hand her into the limo, then go around and get in the other side.

They rode in silence almost the entire way. The major reminded Tahra a lot of Marek—a little older perhaps, but that same military air, that same old-fashioned courtesy. *Handsome, too*, she acknowledged, *even more handsome than Marek, if that's possible*. But somehow the major left her cold, and it wasn't just because he didn't talk to her except for some banal comment on the weather.

Tahra's checkup went smoothly. She was taken for X-rays first—and no waiting in line. She was whisked in and out with smiling promptitude, which made her wonder if that was just the way it was in Zakhar, or if she was being accorded special treatment because of what she'd done and the interest the king had taken in her case. *Probably a mix of both*, she thought with a little smile.

Her surgeon examined her nicely healing scars, including the laparoscopic one from her surgery, and reviewed her X-rays with her, explaining in detail what he was looking for and that there was absolutely no cause for concern. He questioned her at great length about her lost memory, which still hadn't returned. Tahra found herself confiding in him the flashes of certainty she'd had about some aspects of those missing months, even though she still didn't remember.

"I was *afraid* when I saw his note," she confessed. "Not physically afraid, more like I…I *dreaded* reading it."

The surgeon nodded. "I understand. The mind is a very complex organ, Miss Edwards. And yet very simple in some ways. It tries to protect us from being hurt. For instance, we learn early not to touch something on the stove that could burn us. Most of us do not consciously *remember* the moment our fingers were burned…but our subconscious brain retains the lesson and stops us from doing it again."

Her thoughts were churning, but all she said was "I…see."

"Perhaps you received a note in the past from your fiancé containing bad news. Your brain might subconsciously equate a note from him with bad news, and the unthinking dread is generated." He smiled. "Do not be alarmed. This is actually a good sign. Those memories are still there in your brain—otherwise your subconscious would not react as it does. Be patient. Give yourself time."

He mentioned again how lucky she was her broken wrist was really a simple fracture that would heal quickly, but cautioned her not to try to use her right hand too much too soon.

"I won't," she promised, hiding the dart of guilt over the things she'd already done.

Major Branko was waiting for her when she exited the doctor's office, guiding her back through the bewildering series of corridors and doors they'd used to get here in the first place—he was taking no chances with her safety, so they hadn't just walked in the hospital's front door.

As the limousine pulled away from the curb, Tahra suddenly remembered something she'd intended to do while she was out. "Could we stop at my apartment? I want to pick up some books and a few more clothes." Then she realized, "Oh, but I don't know the address." She began fumbling in her purse, which had been recovered from the park and restored to her intact, hoping any identification she might have would have the address.

"Marek—Captain Zale—took me there when I was discharged from the hospital, but I—"

Major Branko interrupted her. "Just a moment." He leaned forward and slid open the privacy glass to speak to the driver in Zakharan, but too quickly for her ears to catch. The driver nodded and immediately signaled a lane change. The major closed the window and sat back. "He is the same driver who drove you the other day, and he remembers." The major unbent enough to smile at her. "Your wish is my command, Miss Edwards."

Tahra was smart enough to interpret this statement to mean, *the king's wish is my command.* And since Zakhar's ruler had placed Major Branko at her disposal for this trip, her wish—by extension—was almost the same as if the king had uttered it. She hadn't yet met King Andre Alexei IV—not that she remembered, anyway, although the queen had said they'd previously been introduced at a reception. But the unswerving devotion he evoked in the men who served him—including Marek and Major Branko—as well as the wife who obviously adored him, made Tahra hope she would have the chance soon. He loomed large, and encountering him could possibly be daunting. Nevertheless, she wanted to meet Marek's king in person.

Major Branko followed Tahra into the elevator like a tall, determined shadow, and his protective air—so like Marek's—made her ask, "You're a bodyguard, too, aren't you? Like Captain Zale?"

"I have the honor to be one of the *king's* bodyguards, yes."

"Ahhh." Tahra almost giggled at the way he said this, as if the major thought being the king's man put him in a different class than Marek, who was "only" responsible for the crown prince. But she managed to maintain an expression of bland interest when his gaze swept her face.

Tahra's purse still contained her apartment key, and she used it to let herself and Major Branko into her apartment, the same way she'd done last week with Marek. And just as Marek had done, the major made her stay by the door while he inspected the apartment.

"All clear," he said as he returned to the living room. "Let me know if you need assistance. Otherwise I will wait here for you."

Last week Tahra had packed what she'd thought she would need for her stay in the palace, but she only had the one dress. She wanted a second for Friday night's dinner date with Marek and the Joneses.

Dresses were her weakness. She didn't mind suits or slacks and a blazer for work, but she loved dressing up and always did so for a date. Now she went through her closet, searching for another one that wouldn't reveal the scars on her back and the backs of her arms. Dark nylons would cover the backs of her legs nicely, so she wasn't worried about that.

She found another dress she thought would do, although she didn't recognize it—a lightweight voile in swirling shades of blue, one of which matched her eyes—with a floating skirt. *Must have bought this here in Zakhar*, she reasoned. *For Marek.* She smiled to herself. The dress was delightfully feminine, designed to hint but not reveal. Which made it perfect for covering up what she didn't want to display in public.

Then she searched for dark nylons to go with it, first pulling open one drawer, then another. And that was where she found the notes from Marek. They were hidden beneath two unopened packages of nylons—but how had she missed them when she was packing last week? *Because you just grabbed the first pair in the right shade*, she reminded herself, *and closed the drawer.*

The dread she'd experienced before returned in waves. The dread her surgeon had said was a good sign because her subconscious was remembering and making a connection. But it didn't *feel* like a good sign. It felt...well...almost as if her heart had been squeezed. As if unbearable pain was about to descend.

The envelopes weren't sealed—the flaps must have been tucked inside and the notes hand delivered. But the flaps were pulled out, as if she'd read the contents, then returned the notes to their envelopes and hid them away. Out of sight. *But not out of mind?*

Her fingers trembled ever so slightly as she picked up the first one, drew the thick paper out, unfolded it and began reading.

Dearest Tahra, the note began. *It is not unknown to you that I have found uncommon delight in your company since the moment we met. And you cannot deny you have indicated the same to me. You must know I would be a good provider, would never hurt you in word or deed. I would be a good father should God bless us with children. And I would honor and cherish you all the days of my life.*

The dread faded, and Tahra smiled with tenderness as she read Marek's words. "I knew Zakhar was fifty years behind the times," she murmured to herself. "But Marek sounds practically Victorian." There was something appealing about it, though—the old-fashioned courtesy, the formal way he put things. Enumerating his qualifications as a husband and father, without once mentioning the passionate love they shared, passion that flared between them every time they kissed. Every time they touched. As if—in the long run—these other things were equally as important as passion.

Which…when you got right down to it, they were. Not that passionate love couldn't survive over a lifetime. But that alone couldn't sustain a relationship. Not for the long term. She knew it, and apparently Marek did, too.

But Tahra's smile faded as she continued reading. *You are upset because I kept a secret from you. You returned my ring—*

She stopped right there. "I *knew* it," she whispered. "I just knew it." She'd suspected he wasn't being completely honest with her since she'd come out of the coma, and now she knew what he'd been concealing. They *weren't* really engaged. He'd broken her heart and she'd given him back his ring.

Tahra glanced down at the ring on her left hand. Despite everything, though, the ring seemed…right somehow. And the man who'd placed it on her finger… it seemed right when she was with him. So what had happened?

She picked up reading where she'd left off. *You returned my ring—the ring you first accepted with joy and then returned because you said you could not marry a man who did not trust you. That is not true—I would trust you with my life. I cannot believe you will let this insignificant truth irrevocably separate us.*

I am still the same man. I am still Captain Marek Zale, still a professional soldier. Still the head of the crown prince's security detail. This is work I do because I am the best there is—I will not pretend otherwise.

But I have not confessed to something that besmirches my moral character. I am still the same man you profess to love. How can this secret make a difference in how you feel?

Which begged the question. What secret?

And why hadn't he told her…whatever it was? It had to be important, or why would she have returned his ring after accepting it? Why would she have accused him of not trusting her?

The note was signed merely *Marek*. Not *Love, Marek*. Just *Marek*. As if he would not presume on their love…or as if it was a given. Either way it was a telling thing. She put the first note down on top of its envelope and picked up the second one.

Dearest Tahra, this note began, just like the first. *Your silence tells me you are still upset, and I apologize. It was never that I did not trust you. But you must understand I had a good reason not to tell you before now, a reason I cannot put on paper.*

"What reason? And what secret?" she asked herself. She kept reading, and the second question was quickly answered. But not the first one.

I am ambitious, yes. But ambition does not rule me. Like Colonel Marianescu—Prince Xavier, I should say—I have never cared to use my inherited title. I earned my rank in the Zakharian National Forces, and I am proud to be a captain. Proud of the job I do protecting the royal heir.

"His inherited title. So *that* was it." Tahra's thoughts flew back to her lunch with Queen Juliana, to the moment when the queen had first mentioned the name Viscount Saint-Yves…and her own reaction. The sudden chill at hearing a name she felt she should recognize, but didn't. The feeling had disappeared when the queen had revealed that not only was Marek Viscount Saint-Yves, he was also a Marianescu.

Then Tahra remembered Marek's startled and guarded reaction when she'd greeted him at the door to her suite that evening with the accusation, *"Why didn't you tell me who you really are?"*

She'd been distracted, though, by wanting to know what *mariskya* meant, and they hadn't gotten around to discussing his title until after their picnic dinner. But it hadn't upset her unduly *because she'd thought he'd told her a long time ago.* That the knowledge of his true identity was in those missing memories. Which it *was*, but…she hadn't realized he'd kept it a secret until after he proposed.

She forced herself to put those thoughts aside and keep reading.

Everything important about me you have known for months. Yes, I am a viscount and will someday be a count, and yes, I am related to the king. But how can this impact our love? Do not let this meaningless secret assume importance beyond forgiveness, mariskya. *Life is too short, and we can never know what the future holds. You trusted me once—your trust was not misplaced. Please let me explain. Marek.*

Trust. Marek said she'd trusted him. But she'd trusted a man once before—and had almost paid too high a price. She didn't want to believe Marek was like *him…* but how could she know for sure? If he could deceive her about one thing, what else would he deceive her about? Besides, trust was a two-way street. Marek hadn't trusted her. How could she do the same?

She put the second note down on top of the first and picked up the third and final one.

Dearest Tahra, I will not write to you again. Nor will I try to see you again. I will wait with the patience I have shown for all these months for you to realize we belong together. That what we share is precious and granted to very few. When you are ready to hear my explanation with an open mind and the loving heart I know you possess, I will give it. Until then, may God hold you in the palm of his hand and keep you safe. Marek.

Tahra slowly returned each note to its envelope. Then tucked all three envelopes in her purse to take back with her. Her heart was aching—not just for herself, but for Marek, too. Because the last note reminded her that Marek *had* shown unbelievable patience in their relationship. That he'd never pushed her for sex. Had never even taken advantage of her desire for him. She didn't *remember*, but he couldn't have. Which meant he wasn't *anything* like the foreign diplomat she'd trusted, the one who'd deceived her and eventually ended up trying to rape her.

Why hadn't she given Marek the chance to explain? That was what she couldn't understand. Or had she? Had Marek explained…and his explanation wasn't worthy of forgiveness?

One thing's for sure, she thought as she gathered a few more things to take with her back to the palace, gathering up her courage at the same time. *I'm going to ask Marek about it the first chance I get.*

But Tahra was doomed to wait for an explanation. No sooner was she back in the limousine and they were heading to the palace when Major Branko volunteered, "It is too bad Colonel Marianescu sent your fiancé to the eastern border. Otherwise the king would most likely have assigned him to guard you today instead of me." He smiled, the second smile she'd seen from him, but somehow this smile, like the first one, didn't soften the hard lines of his face the way Marek's did. "The king is thoughtful in that manner."

"Marek's not here?" She hadn't known, and she couldn't help the touch of dismay in her voice. "We're supposed to have dinner on Friday with—"

"Captain Zale will return tomorrow or the next day," the major assured her.

"What about…you know…the crown prince's security detail?" Tahra couldn't imagine what Marek could possibly have to do at the eastern border. Not when the crown prince was here in Drago.

"Major Kostya is covering for him. And the king is aware, of course. Colonel Marianescu would not send Captain Zale and— That is, Colonel Marianescu would not undertake this action without the king's blessing."

What action? she wondered. But she didn't ask the question out loud. *And why didn't Marek tell me he was leaving?* She sighed softly. She totally got that there were things Marek couldn't share with her about his job. But telling her he was leaving town wasn't one of them. So now she'd have to confront him about this, too. And unlike her sister, she didn't do confrontation well. At all.

Marek buckled into his seat on the military plane that had flown Angelina and him to Timon Tuesday afternoon, which was now taking them back to Drago early on this Friday morning. Mission accomplished… thanks to Angelina.

He smiled over at the woman who had once worked for him, who had earned her promotion to captain by outstanding work—saving the crown prince's life as well as interrogating their prisoner and tricking him into revealing information he had no intention of revealing… just as she'd done here. "You could write a textbook."

Angelina buckled her seat belt and shook her head. "My interrogation techniques would only work in Zakhar," she said drily. "And only on men."

Marek laughed. "Perhaps." He stretched his tired muscles, but it was a good ache. They hadn't had much sleep over the past two and a half days, but success made it worthwhile.

"And do not downplay your own contributions," Angelina added. "I could not have succeeded without your astute observations."

"We make a good team," he agreed. "We always did."

"How did you know which one of the three was most vulnerable to my…brand of interrogation? It is amazing and saved us many hours."

He grinned at her. "I picked the one most like Alec… and me." Angelina shot him a narrow-eyed look; she didn't take criticism of her beloved husband well, even if said in jest. "I honestly do not know," he confessed. "I just had a feeling, and it turned out to be correct, thank God." His smile faded. "That is the good news. That, and the fact he does not know he revealed we have played into their hands by diluting our military force here in Drago. As far as he and the Zakharian Liberation Front are concerned, we know no more now than an adult, but you told me when we met that you felt, since you worked at the embassy here in Drago, it was important to at least try." He turned a corner, then unlocked a door, opened it, turned on the light and ushered Tahra inside. "Here we are. I have been wanting to show you my office, but the occasion never arose."

Marek's office was small but immaculate. No clutter anywhere. Everything had a place, everything was tidied away. Not even a piece of notepaper by the phone or a pen lying haphazardly on the expanse of his desk. And Tahra wondered, *If that's the way he is at work, how is he at home?* Would he be driven to distraction by how she left things here and there? Would he try to control her that way, too? She was neat and tidy at work, but that was at work. At home she liked to be...well... not *messy*, but not quite so organized, either.

A whiteboard covered the wall behind his desk, with a grid of days, dates and what appeared to be blocks of time across the top, and names neatly lettered down the left side. *X*s were scattered across the grid in various boxes. When he saw the direction of Tahra's gaze, he explained, "That is a chart of who is on duty when."

"Guarding the crown prince."

"Precisely."

"I hadn't realized there were so many," she murmured.

"Unlike the king, who chafes under the necessity and will accept only one bodyguard at a time, there are always two men on duty guarding the crown prince twenty-four hours a day. Eight-hour shifts times two men per shift means a minimum of six men per day. But of course, they must be relieved for meals and such, which means an additional man per shift, who acts as supervisor in my absence. And then I must also allow for the fact that a man cannot work seven days a week, fifty-two weeks in a year, so additional men are necessary. The queen, too, requires two bodyguards at all times, but that is Angelina's responsibility now. We share men, so there is always full coverage of the queen and the crown prince and yet no man's time is wasted."

"Only men?"

Marek had the grace to look abashed. "On the crown prince's detail, yes. The queen insisted from the beginning that a certain number of her bodyguards be women, which is how Angelina came to be assigned in the first place. But every bodyguard is a member of the Zakharian National Forces on detached duty. That is, while they are on special assignment as bodyguards and the normal chain of command does not apply, they are still in the military. Which means they are referred to as 'men,' even those who are women."

"Oh." She tried not to judge, but it seemed somewhat archaic.

"You must be patient with us. Zakhar is still adapting to the change."

"The change?"

"It has only been since the king ascended the throne that women were allowed in the Zakharian National Forces. And it has not even been three years since they were allowed to serve in combat."

"I see." And now that he'd brought it up, Tahra remembered her State Department briefing on the history of Zakhar, its political structure and its attitudes on a variety of issues, including women's rights. "The king instituted a lot of changes, didn't he?"

"He is the king." Implicit in his words and tone was a firm conviction that Zakhar's ruler was always right.

Tahra smiled to herself. She would never tell Marek, because it was obvious he believed God Himself would not *allow* the king to be wrong, but she was too American to accept that those in positions of power were perfect beings. Everyone was human. And everyone made mistakes. She was just glad, for Marek's sake, that the king he admired and served with such dedication seemed to live up to his ideals.

"So what's this?" she asked as she glanced at the whiteboard on the wall across from Marek's desk, where a series of squares had been blocked out—four in the first row, then three and three. She moved closer when she saw her name written in a box in the top right corner, circled in red.

"I think best when I can visualize what is happening. Ten nearly simultaneous attacks in one day..."

"This is everything that happened that day?" She turned to look at him and he nodded. She faced the board again, touching the numbers written in each of the squares, a chill running down her spine as she recognized what those numbers signified. "Oh, God," she whispered, tears springing to her eyes. "So many dead."

Scarcely two seconds later, strong arms enfolded her from behind. "None from the preschool," he reminded her in a deep voice. "Thanks to you."

"Yes, but why? I mean why all these attacks?" She turned and burrowed into Marek's comforting embrace. "Who would do something like this?"

He hesitated, as if there were things he knew he couldn't share with her. Finally he said, "An organization called the Zakharian Liberation Front has taken public responsibility. Have you heard of it?"

She didn't even raise her head from where it resided. "No."

"Their credo is 'Zakhar for Zakharians.'"

This time she was forced to look up. "Immigrants?" she asked, appalled. "Those pitiful refugees? *That's* their reason for mass murder?"

"That is what they say, yes."

Something in his voice made her ask, "You don't believe it?"

He didn't answer right away, just stared over her head at everything written on the whiteboard. "I do not know," he said slowly. Deliberately. "All the targets so far have some connection with those who have made their way to Zakhar and are settling here with the king's blessing and encouragement."

He pointed to the top left. "A train from the eastern border, packed with asylum seekers." His finger moved across the top to the next square. "The refugee processing center in the middle of Drago." He pointed to the next block. "The Zakharian National Forces training facility, where seventy percent of the new recruits were male émigrés." He hesitated, then indicated top right. "A preschool, where almost half the children enrolled are émigrés. And the other six targets across Zakhar have similar makeups."

"Seems pretty obvious to me the refugees *are* the focus."

"It would seem that way, yes. And yet… It is nothing I can name, just a feeling there is something we are overlooking."

"What's being done about it?"

"The king has stated the Zakharian Liberation Front's actions are unacceptable to him, and has expressed his desire for three things." Tahra correctly interpreted "expressed his desire" to mean "issued a royal command," at least where Marek and the men who served the king were concerned.

"What are those three things?"

"Protect the refugees at all costs. Bring to justice all who are involved in the attacks. Root out and destroy the Zakharian Liberation Front so something like this never occurs again."

"Is that what you're doing?"

"Not me personally, but yes, the secret intelligence service, assisted by the Drago police and the Zakharian National Forces, is doing everything in its power to make his wishes a reality."

"What else?"

"The head of the king's protection detail asked Angelina and me to form a task force with him, so any potential threat to the royal family is immediately nullified. We have already met twice. I cannot disclose the specifics, but rest assured the royals are as safe as we can make them."

"Yes, but what exactly are *you* doing?" She didn't know how she knew, just that she did—Marek wouldn't sit back and wait for someone else to solve the mystery and bring the perpetrators to justice. Even if she wasn't involved, even if she wasn't still a potential target, Marek was too über-alpha—*there's that word again*, she chastised herself silently—too much of a take-charge man to sit quietly on the sidelines while someone else ran the ball.

"What makes you think I am doing anything?" he parried. "My job is to ensure the safety of the crown prince, and tangentially the safety of the royal family as a whole. That I am doing. Always." But she knew he was keeping something from her…again.

Again?

Tahra stiffened. Where had that thought come from? What would make her think Marek had deceived her about something in the past? The past she couldn't remember. *That has to be it,* she reasoned. Because she couldn't think of anything he'd said or not said since she'd woken up in the hospital that could qualify for "again" in that context.

She started to ask him but changed her mind at the last minute because Marek had been right earlier—if he told her too much about her past, how would she know if she ever really regained her memory, or just thought she had?

There's another reason, too, a little voice in the back of her mind taunted her. *You're afraid to know.*

Shocked, Tahra acknowledged the little voice was right. She *was* afraid. Because despite the strikes Marek had against him—that control thing he had going, not to mention his less-than-ideal attitude toward women—he was drawing her under his spell, like a fragile moth to a far-too-tempting flame. She was falling in love with him all over again…in the space of four days.

Four days? She mentally counted back to what she referred to as Day One, when she'd woken from a coma in the hospital in the wee hours of the morning, Marek at her bedside. And yes, today was only Day Four.

Okay, it wasn't really four days. She'd grown to love him at some point in the past year and a half. But she didn't *remember* that. Didn't remember him. So in some ways it was as if she'd opened her eyes, taken one look at his handsome features and incredible body, and decided he was the man she'd been waiting for all these years. *Not* like her at all.

Unless...subconsciously...she remembered him, her body as well as her heart. Which was where the fear came in. Because he'd done something—*what*, she hadn't a clue—but *something* to break her heart. She was sure of it.

Chapter 8

Marek walked out of the police station on his day off with more questions than answers. The nurse's aide who'd attempted to kill Tahra—who'd been *bribed* to try to kill her—was dead. Ostensibly by her own hand, but he wasn't buying it. The aide had been talking to investigators, telling them what little she knew in exchange for a plea deal, and it made no sense she would have committed suicide. Which meant she'd been murdered…while in custody.

No one at the police station seemed to know how it could have happened. At least…no one who was talking to him. But if they wouldn't talk to him, he knew who the police *would* talk to…and probably already had.

"Major Stesha will see you now," the major's administrative assistant told Marek, who'd been cooling his heels in the outer office for the past twenty minutes.

we did before. The bad news is I was right. I did not wish to be."

Her expression was suddenly serious, too. "I know."

He broke the long silence that followed, saying, "Are we still on for dinner tonight? You have not seen Alec and your baby for more than two days. Tahra and I will understand if you prefer to postpone."

"Alec would be disappointed," she said firmly. "So no, let us not postpone. Besides, I have already ordered the meal from Mischa's." She laughed softly. "I would not afflict you with my own cooking."

Angelina excused herself after takeoff, and Marek correctly interpreted the slight strain on her face as she picked up the overnight case she'd brought on board and carried it with her to the restroom in the rear. He reclined his seat back and shifted to a more comfortable position, realizing as he did so that it still bothered him to think of Angelina doing what breast-feeding mothers who worked outside the home had to do as a matter of course.

He didn't want that for Tahra. And he believed she felt the same way. Except for one brief time in his life, he had never touched his inherited wealth, preferring to live modestly on his soldier's salary. But he could afford for Tahra to be a full-time mother if she wished it. And when they'd talked before—in a roundabout way—of children, she'd given him the impression that was her desire, too. To be a full-time mother as her own had been before she died when Tahra was ten.

Tahra...and children. Little girls with their mother's soft eyes and tender, loving heart. Little boys with his muscle and devotion to king and country.

And all he had to do to make that happen was undo

the damage that had been done. All he had to do was win Tahra's heart again, no matter how long it took.

Failure is not an option, he reminded himself as he fell asleep. *Failure is not an option.*

Chapter 13

"That is all we know," Angelina concluded, then sat down. This top secret convocation had been assembled as soon as they returned, and both Angelina and Marek had been summoned to report on what they'd uncovered in Timon.

Good job! Marek mouthed at her, and she rewarded him with a tiny smile.

"So what are your conclusions, Captain Zale?" Major Stesha asked.

Marek almost responded that the question should have been addressed to Angelina first—she was the one who'd tricked answers out of the suspect, after all, not him—but she shook her head at him. *Do not*, her eyes warned. *This is not the moment to fight that battle.*

Instead, Marek rose and addressed the assemblage. "We know now we have been lured into reducing the overall strength of our fighting force here in Drago to dangerous levels by the erroneous belief that the target was the refugees. Cold-blooded murder on such a vast scale *must* have a reason. The oldest motive in the world comes to mind—a grab for power. And *that* means the Zakharian Liberation Front's true target is the royal family, as I previously suggested."

Having gone this far, he cared not that he was a mere captain in a room of higher-ranking officers. "I strongly recommend we send no more soldiers to the borders and the cities and towns where they have been deployed. I also strongly recommend surreptitiously recalling as many fighting men as possible. I say surreptitiously because we do not wish to show our hand—we must let the Zakharian Liberation Front *think* we have been duped."

"And how do you propose we do this, Captain?" General Miroslav was the head of the Zakharian National Forces, and at sixty-two was the oldest man in the room. He'd seen action in Iraq during the first Gulf War as a coalition fighter pilot and had commanded the Zakharian peacekeeping contingent in Afghanistan. The king himself—when he'd been the crown prince—had served under the general's command. General Miroslav had ordered the troop deployment as soon as the king had declared martial law. And now Marek was telling him both he and the king had been wrong.

"The troop carriers must stay where they are. The country has seen them rolling out—they are unmistakable. Which means the Zakharian Liberation Front has also seen them deployed. But the men those troop carriers drove to the borders and elsewhere? Leave a token force in place, sir, but recall two of every three. Quietly. By plane, if possible, but not via military transports—

that would be too noticeable. So commercial flights. *Not* in uniform. Tell the men to leave their gear and their weapons behind—they can be recovered later."

"Commercial flights will be expensive," the general said.

"But fast, sir. And right now I think speed is more important than cost. We do not know *when* the Zakharian Liberation Front intends to strike, but I am not willing to risk my king's life that it will not be tomorrow."

"How do we know the Zakharian Liberation Front has not infiltrated the Zakharian National Forces? If the order goes out—quietly or not—to recall two-thirds of the troops, how do we know the enemy will not instantly know what we have done?"

Marek took a deep breath. "We do not *know*, sir. But that is the beauty of this solution. If they do not know of the recall and attempt to take over the government, we will have the manpower necessary to defeat them. If they *do* know of the recall, they will know their deception has failed, and they will attempt no coup. Not now. Which gives *us* time to infiltrate *their* organization and bring them down. The immediate threat is *now*. Our solution must meet the current threat. Future threats can be dealt with in the future."

"Thank you, Captain," Colonel Marianescu said from the head of the table. "We will take your suggestions under advisement."

"Yes, sir." Marek started to sit, then changed his mind. "One more thing, sir," he said, looking straight at Colonel Marianescu. "With regard to the Privy Council."

When the colonel smiled, which he didn't do often, he looked remarkably like the king. "So you see that, too, Captain. Quite astute of you. Fear not—no matter what is decided here, the Privy Council will know nothing of what was discussed and the conclusions reached. The king—yes, of course. But not the Privy Council."

"Yes, sir." Marek sat down, surprised to find his legs were glad they no longer had to support him, and breathed deeply to let some of the tension out—tension he hadn't even been aware of until this moment.

He glanced at Angelina, who mouthed, *Good job!* The same thing he'd told her earlier, after her speech before these high-ranking officers.

Discussion went on around the table, fast and furious. But Marek was glad to hear no one was refuting his assumptions. And no one was refuting his suggestions. He spoke only once in the next twenty-five minutes, and only when he was specifically addressed. Angelina didn't speak at all. But then, both of them had already said all they needed to say.

Finally the discussion came to an end. "Thank you, gentlemen," Colonel Marianescu said. While technically General Miroslav outranked him, as head of internal security answering directly to the king, Colonel Marianescu chaired the national security meeting. "A show of hands, please. All in favor of Captain Zale's suggestion?" Every hand was raised, including General Miroslav's and Colonel Marianescu's. "I think we have our path forward, gentlemen. Thank you, Captain Mateja-Jones and Captain Zale. You are dismissed."

Marek glanced at his watch as he and Angelina walked out of the national security meeting. "It is already after four," he informed her. "Are you going to check in with Major Kostya? Or head home?"

"Home. But I will stop by to tell the queen I am back and will see her tomorrow."

Marek laughed softly. “That is why we make such a great team. We think alike. I was planning to drop in on the crown prince for just a moment. But no more than that. I must go home and change, then swing back here and pick up Tahra and make it to your house by six.”

“Do not worry if you are a few minutes late,” Angelina told him as they both mounted the Grand Staircase to the second floor, where their respective destinations were. They parted at the door to the queen’s suite, where Angelina knocked and gained admittance. “See you shortly.”

As he’d told Angelina, Marek’s visit to the crown prince’s suite—next door to his mother’s—was brief. His duty done, Marek headed out. He almost stopped at Tahra’s suite, but after another check of his watch he decided against it. He barely had enough time as it was, and if he stopped to see her—as he was strongly tempted to do—they would be late. Very late. He couldn’t risk it.

Tahra had been dressed and waiting for Marek since five o’clock. He’d told her dinner with Alec and Angelina was at six, but he hadn’t said how long it would take to get there, or when he’d pick her up, or anything. And she didn’t know if he’d even made it back from the eastern border. Major Branko had *said* he would, but since Marek hadn’t even bothered to inform her he was leaving Drago, she hadn’t expected he’d call to let her know he was back. And sure enough, he hadn’t.

But Tahra had been raised to believe a commitment was a commitment. And though part of her wanted to be anywhere but here when—*if*—Marek showed up, another part of her had dressed so she was ready and waiting for him.

She'd tried to sit as she waited, but too many emotions were roiling through her, and she nervously paced instead. She loved this room usually, but neither the paintings nor the priceless objets d'art scattered about could hold her interest for long. The clock on the fireplace mantel ticked away the minutes until Tahra was as wound up as the clock was, and she greeted the rapping on the door with a gasp of relief.

Her first thought when she opened the door was how exhausted Marek looked. As if he hadn't gotten nearly enough sleep for days. As if no one—least of all him—cared enough for *him* to insist he wasn't made of iron. And she wanted to throw her arms around him, pull him into the room, then put him to bed and let him sleep the clock around. Her second thought was that she was angry with him. She went with the second thought.

"Thank you for letting me know when you'd arrive," she said, her tone dripping ice. "Shall we go? I don't want to be late." She ducked away from his kiss and slid out the door, pulling it shut behind her.

A flicker of disappointment crossed his face, then disappeared, replaced by a bland mask that revealed nothing of what he was thinking. And yet…she knew her coldness hurt him. She *knew* it and felt a kindred ache…because fool that she was, she'd fallen in love with him. Again.

Her heart clutched at the thought, and she almost stopped then and there to tell him, but she managed to hold on and not blurt it out. Because she was still angry at the way he seemed to take her for granted, despite loving her.

They didn't speak at all on the way to the Joneses' house—a drive that reminded Tahra poignantly of her ride with Major Branko to the hospital on Wednesday. She racked her brain to think of something to say, something that wouldn't be accusing because she had no intention of having it out with Marek...not in the limousine. Even though there was a glass partition for privacy, she'd been raised a lady. She would say nothing to him about how upset she was...how *hurt* she was...until *after* they'd left Alec and Angelina's. She would be polite to him throughout the evening...even if it killed her.

Tahra was furious with him—it didn't take any special training to see that. Icily polite in a way that reminded him of his grandmother, the one who'd once been a royal princess. His grandmother who could flay a man alive with a few well-chosen words without raising her voice.

He knew one reason why Tahra was upset—he'd forgotten to tell her when he would pick her up, a social solecism he didn't usually make. His excuse was that he'd been sent to Timon to conduct interrogations with Angelina on absolutely no notice and had only just returned. In fact, dinner with the Joneses tonight had completely slipped his mind until he and Angelina were flying home this morning. But it didn't seem as if this alone would be enough to affect her this strongly.

Then it hit him. He hadn't told Tahra he was leaving. He hadn't called her, texted her or given her any reason to know she was constantly in the back of his mind, no matter how focused he was on the task at hand.

Not the way to convince a woman of your steadfast devotion.

He cudgeled his brain to think of something to say to her, some way of apologizing that wouldn't come across as caddish or self-serving, but nothing came to mind. It wasn't until they were standing on the Joneses' doorstep ringing the bell that he said, "Angelina just returned home today, when I did. I asked her if we should postpone dinner tonight, but she refused. Then we both went immediately into a national security meeting that did not end until after four, so she has barely had time to see her husband and her baby. I intend to leave early this evening. I hope you do not mind."

She turned startled eyes on him. "Angelina was with you at the eastern border?"

The front door swung open. "Hey there," Alec said. "You're right on time. Come on in." He pushed the door wider and stepped back, saying, "You look a thousand times better than the last time I saw you, Tahra. Of course, you were just barely out of a coma, so I probably shouldn't have mentioned it." He grinned. "Women can be touchy about their appearance...even in the hospital."

Tahra tilted her head to one side, obviously puzzled. "You came to see me in the hospital?"

"Three times. Okay, so the first time you were in surgery, and it hardly counts. The second time you were still in a coma. And the third time you were sleeping. I spent a half hour talking with your sister—soon to be my sister-in-law—waiting for you to wake up, but you never did."

Alec was leading them into the living room as he spoke. "Have a seat. Angelina will be here in a minute." Just as he said this, the tall blonde woman Tahra recognized from her attendance on the queen in the chapel the other night came into the room carrying a baby dressed in a Denver Broncos orange-and-blue football jersey and baby jeans. And Tahra was drawn forward as if the baby was a magnet and she was a little pile of metal shavings.

"Oh, what's his name? May I hold him? Please?"

The woman relinquished the baby into Tahra's arms with a little smile. "Of course. You do not remember, I know, but I am Angelina. Our son's full name is Andrew Drago Jones, but we call him Drew."

Tahra was already cooing over little Drew in a way that made Marek's heart ache with sudden yearning to see her with *their* baby, but she looked up abruptly at Angelina's last sentence. "That's an unusual middle name," she said. "I know Drago is the capital of Zakhar, but—"

Alec broke in. "Don't blame me. Angelina picked both names. Andrew after the king—although I insisted on the American Andrew instead of Andre. And Drago because that's where he was..." He cleared his throat self-consciously.

Angelina's lips twitched into a tiny smile. "Alec's mother gave all her children middle names of the cities where they were conceived. I wanted to honor her in some way when Drew was born, so I continued the tradition."

Tahra turned her gaze on Alec and raised her eyebrows. "Oh?" she asked delicately.

"It's on my birth certificate and my passport," Alec growled, "but I'm not volunteering anything."

Tahra gurgled with laughter, then returned her attention to the baby, tickling him until he laughed with her. "Your daddy's funny, isn't he?" she cooed. "And you're a sweetheart. You are. Yes, you *are*." Her voice was soft, warm and oh-so-sweet to the man who loved her, very different from her icy tone earlier.

She glanced up, her blue eyes bright. "Oh, Angelina, he's wearing the little outfit I gave you at his baby shower. It's so darling on him." Marek froze, and so did everyone else in the room, something that was obviously not lost on Tahra. "What?" she asked, the smile fading from her face. "What did I say?"

Marek struggled for words, but Angelina forestalled him. "You remembered," she said softly, and there was a note of gladness in her voice.

Tahra caught her breath and looked down at the laughing baby in her arms, and the outfit that had triggered a memory. "Oh, God. You're right. I remember. I remember ordering it off the internet and thinking Alec would get a kick out of it. And I remember you opening the box and laughing." Her eyes sought Marek's, and they were suddenly swimming in tears. "I remembered something." And in her face he saw joy far beyond what the simple memory would evoke. He also saw a dawning belief that if she remembered *this*, then the rest of her memories might be restored. Including her memories of him. Of them.

It wasn't quite nine when Marek called for the limousine to pick them up, politely declining Alec and Angelina's urgings to stay. "Another time," he said, shaking his head. But his eyes were on Tahra as he spoke, and she knew it wasn't just that he wanted to give Angelina more private time with Alec and Drew. He wanted private time with her, too.

Her earlier anger with Marek was gone, wiped out by the excitement of knowing maybe—just *maybe*—those eighteen months weren't permanently lost. But that didn't mean they didn't need to talk. They did. She was still wearing his engagement ring, for one thing, and before they went any further, she needed to hear the explanation he'd begged her to allow him to give in those notes she'd found.

So once they were seated in the privacy of the limousine, she said quietly, "Before we return to the palace, can we go somewhere to talk? Somewhere where we won't be interrupted or overheard, or…"

"Can we not talk in your suite at the palace?"

"I'd rather not."

"What do you wish to talk about that requires such privacy?"

She drew a deep breath. "I *know*, Marek." She held up her left hand, wiggling her fingers a little so he could see the ring in the darkness. "I know this is… make-believe."

Chapter 14

"You…remember?" The note of intense happiness in his voice was overlaid with something she couldn't place at first, until she realized it was…resignation. As if Marek had prayed devoutly for her memory to return, even if it meant the death of his hopes for them.

She shook her head. "No. I don't remember. But Major Kostya took me to my apartment on Wednesday, after my checkup at the hospital, and—"

"You saw your surgeon? What did he say?"

"I'm fine. The X-rays all look good, and he's still hopeful my memory will return. But don't change the subject. I started to say I went to my apartment on Wednesday, and I…I found the notes you sent me."

There was a long silence. Then, "I see." He didn't actually move away from her, but she sensed his inner withdrawal. "That is what you wish to discuss in private, of course."

"Yes." She searched for something to add to that one word but came up blank.

He leaned forward suddenly and opened the glass panel to the driver's section of the limousine. She only understood one word in three he spoke to the driver, but then he closed the glass, sat back and told her, "My apartment is not far from here. So is yours, but I would not subject you to another confrontation with a man in the sanctuary of your own home, *mariskya*, even though I would never do what he did."

Once again Tahra was touched by Marek's thoughtfulness, his consideration for her feelings. *No, there's no comparison between them*, she acknowledged. Marek was a true gentleman. *Nothing* like the man who'd attacked her. She was as safe with Marek as she wanted to be. Which made her ask herself—how safe did she want to be?

Marek's apartment was exactly as she'd envisioned it would be after seeing his meticulously neat office. Everything in its place. Spotlessly clean. And almost spartan in appearance. There were no feminine touches anywhere, and though Tahra told herself she shouldn't be glad, she was. Fiercely glad. No woman had ever lived here.

"Please be seated," Marek invited, indicating the sofa, before going to stand as far away from her as he could. Leaning against the wall, one hand in his pocket. All expression wiped from his face.

Stoic, Tahra thought. *That word perfectly describes him.* She had no idea how she knew, but somehow she did—Marek was steeling himself against the pain he believed she was about to inflict.

"I don't want to hurt you," she blurted out. "But I have to know. Why did you lie to me?"

She could have sworn he flinched. "To which lie are you referring?"

"How many are there?"

He didn't answer at first. Then, "Only one lie—from which other…deceptions were…inevitable."

"You mean the lie that we're engaged."

He nodded slowly. "And yet…when I uttered it, I did not think it a lie. Only afterward, when I begged your sister not to reveal the truth—"

"Carly knew?" Tahra couldn't believe it. "Carly knew we weren't really engaged and didn't tell me?"

"She knew my intentions. And she knew I loved you." A faint smile touched his lips. "She threatened me should anything happen to you because of me—but she agreed to keep the secret."

Tahra suddenly remembered Carly kissing her goodbye in the hospital, saying, *"You're in good hands,"* and those words that were no longer enigmatic, *"Be kind to him."*

"Who else knew it was a lie?"

"No one, *mariskya*, you have my word. Alec and Angelina may have suspected, but they did not *know.* Only your sister, and only because you had confided to her everything that had taken place the night I proposed. The night you accepted my proposal…then rejected it. And me."

Tahra drew a trembling breath at the unutterable pain in his voice when he said, "And me." As if she'd taken a knife to his heart when she'd rejected his proposal.

"But you deceived me," she pleaded, as if she had to justify her actions to him. "You didn't tell me who you really were. And no, I don't remember, but the notes make it clear that's why I…turned you down."

She waited for him to say something, and when he didn't, she added, "I don't *know* what I was feeling that night. All I can tell you is what I felt when I read your notes and realized what must have been going through my mind." She swallowed hard. "I trusted another man once…to my eternal regret. I know you're nothing like him. I know that. But it would have been a shock to learn you had deceived me, too. You broke my heart, Marek. I've known that for days now. Not that I *remember*, but I *know*."

Her words hung in the air between them, and Marek drew a rasping breath. He'd never spoken of what he was going to tell Tahra—not even to those closest to him—because it was a shameful episode in his past he never wanted even to remember. He'd locked it away in the secret recesses of his heart. But it had shaped the man he was, and he owed it to Tahra to explain as best he could why he'd kept his identity secret from her.

"I was not quite twenty-one, and but a lowly second lieutenant," he began in a husky voice. "With dreams of rising through the ranks in service to my country. Then I met Zorina. She was beautiful. Entrancing. Captivating in a way I had never known before."

"I don't think I want to hear—"

"You *must* hear, to understand why I kept my secret."

Tahra breathed deeply, as if preparing herself to listen to what he'd once felt for another woman. It couldn't be easy for her—no woman wanted to hear the details of how the man she loved had once been infatuated with another. But just as he needed to get this off his chest, she needed to hear it.

"I did not love Zorina, but I…desired her." He paused for a moment. "More than that—I was bewitched by her." Suddenly restless, he strode around the room, self-directed anger rolling off him in waves. "These things are not easy for me to say to you, you understand. A man can desire a woman…be enthralled by her…without loving her. *Knowing* he does not love her."

He forced himself to look at Tahra and was surprised when her lips twitched with sudden amusement. "It's the same for a woman, you know. She can desire a man without loving him."

After a moment he acknowledged the truth of her words. "Yes. That is true." He drew a deep breath, then continued. "In Zorina's case, she neither loved me nor desired me. She merely…tolerated me at first. I did not know this at the time, but she desired only the things money can buy…and the men who would give them to her. When she learned I had money and a title, however, she set her sights on me. But I was not her ultimate goal. I was merely a stepping stone to bigger and better things. She planned her every move with a cold calculation to which I was blind…until she dragged my pride through the mud."

"What did she do?"

A cynical smile touched his lips. "We had been lovers for less than a month when she made a play for the king, who was the crown prince at the time."

"What?"

"When I first met Zorina, she was…uninterested in me until—fool that I was—I tried to impress her with my title. My wealth. I wanted her to know I was more than just a lowly second lieutenant. Then and only then did she seem to look upon me with favor. She deliberately set out to entice me, and I believed her lies. But she was just using me as an entrée to Prince Andre's world. He was three years my senior, and—of course—would have been a splendid conquest for her. She did not know the crown prince was indifferent by then to all lures thrown out to him—the woman who is now queen already owned his heart by the time he was the age I was then." His cynical smile grew. "When Zorina's plans came to naught with Prince Andre, she turned her eyes on Zax—Prince Xavier. Who, in addition to being a royal prince, had inherited a fortune from his father that put my fortune to shame."

"Oh, Marek." Her tone conveyed her tender heart ached for the blow to his pride. Her yearning expression told him she longed to comfort that not-quite-twenty-one-year-old man he'd once been.

"Prince Xavier would have none of her, either. Not because he was not attracted to her—Zorina's beauty of face and figure was considerable—but because he knew of my relationship with her. He is an extremely honorable man, and he would not poach on another man's preserves."

Tahra looked as if she were about to say that Marek hadn't *owned* Zorina, and the attitudes of the two men left much to be desired. But before she could, he said, "But Zorina was nothing if not ambitious. When Prince Xavier turned her down, she switched her attention… and her charms…onto Niko—Prince Nikolai. Who was *not* the man his brother, Prince Xavier, was. As a royal prince Niko was exempt from the military service required of every other Zakharian male—something he had accepted as his due when he turned eighteen, unlike his brother. Unlike the king. They both served in the Zakharian National Forces. But not Niko."

This last was said with a touch of contempt. Then he mentally girded his loins to finish his confession. "Prince Nikolai and Zorina became lovers barely a week after they met—while Zorina was still pretending to care for me. And he...taunted me with his conquest. I had known nothing...seen nothing...until that moment."

All Tahra could say was "Oh, Marek" again. That wouldn't have been just a blow to his pride—it would have cut to the bone.

"Only then did Prince Andre and Prince Xavier tell me how she had tried to entice them before she settled for Niko," he continued, in that same determinedly detached voice. "They are— You are not a man, so perhaps you cannot understand just how much they tried to spare my pride by not speaking up earlier. A man does not tell another man things like that...especially one to whom you are related by blood and have known since childhood. It was only later—after Zorina chose Prince Nikolai over me—they tried to cushion the blow by informing me of her true character."

His face hardened. "But I did not need their explanations to understand what Zorina had done. Choosing a man like Prince Nikolai—a man with no honor—over me... Not that I thought myself perfect. Please do not think that. And one should never speak ill of the dead. But if you had ever known Niko, you would understand that—"

"Knowing he taunted you over Zorina tells me all I need to know about him."

A flash of something that looked like gratitude came and went in his eyes so quickly she wasn't sure it had even been there before he continued, "I swore then no woman would ever have an opportunity to use me in that fashion ever again. No woman would ever know I was anything except an officer in the Zakharian National Forces."

His blue eyes darkened. "That is why, Tahra. That is why I did not tell you who I was. I wanted you to love me for *me*...not for my title or my connections."

She was silent for a moment, digesting everything. "I understand...probably more than you realize. And if you had told me later, after you got to know me, after you realized I— But you didn't. You didn't trust me. You wanted me to love you for yourself, but you didn't trust I wouldn't somehow be swayed by your title. Like Cinderella falling for Prince Charming just because he's a prince."

"I am not a prince, and I do not see—"

"Oh, Marek, must you take everything so literally?" She wanted to laugh and cry at the same time. "All I'm saying is you didn't trust me with the truth of who you really are." Her voice faltered as the realization overwhelmed her for a moment, as the memory of the other deception and betrayal she'd suffered at the hands of a man she'd trusted came into sharp focus. But then she found the strength to add, "The notes I found make it very clear you didn't tell me until I'd already agreed to marry you, thinking you were nothing more than Captain Marek Zale. Don't you see what that says about how you see me?"

"Everything important about me you knew," he said in an implacable tone. "You knew the man I am—my character. You knew that honor and duty go hand in hand for me. You knew I would die to protect you. What else was there to know? My childhood? I never lied to you about that. I had a happy, uneventful childhood. How I came to be in the Zakharian National Forces, how I came to head up first the queen's security detail and then the crown prince's? You knew that, too. The things I did not tell you are extraneous. They are not the man I am."

In one sense he was right. But in another he was wrong. At least from her perspective back then. How to explain so he'd understand? In an intense undertone, she said, "My first reaction when I read the notes was, if you can deceive me about something like this, what else would you deceive me about? If you know what led to my almost being...raped, you know I believed every lie he told me. I was a naive fool, but I believed him. Only to find it was all lies—*all* of it."

She'd dated the foreign diplomat for two months, believing him when he professed to be single. She'd gently refused to sleep with him, shyly explaining why, then had again believed him implicitly when he said he was looking for an "old-fashioned girl" like her.

None of it had been true. When she'd learned he was married, she'd confronted him. And fool that she was, she'd done it in the privacy of her apartment, wanting to spare him public humiliation.

But instead of apologizing, he'd turned ugly. She would have been brutally raped—she'd seen it in his eyes when he'd ripped her dress and tried to pin her to the floor. But she'd fought him off, then scrambled to her feet and run for the door. And when he'd blocked her escape that way, she'd made a dash for the kitchen and the knives in the butcher block her frantic mind remembered.

She'd almost lost her career over the incident, until Carly had come to her rescue…again. And Tahra had sworn then she'd learn to stand up for herself. That never again would she rely on someone else to rescue her, not even her sister. She'd saved herself from being raped—fighting for her pride and dignity should be child's play after that.

She'd also sworn she'd never trust another man again. So learning that her trust had once again been betrayed would explain why she'd returned his ring. It would have been the death knell to her dreams of a life with Marek…but not her love. Nothing could kill that.

"There is no comparison between him and me. I would not lie to—" Marek broke off, as if he suddenly realized he *had* lied to her…ever since she'd woken up in the hospital. "I would not lie to you for *my* benefit." His voice was very low. Very deep. "Keep a shameful secret to myself, yes. I admit that. But I would *never* take advantage of you as *he* tried to do."

"I know." She touched her hand to her heart. "I know it now. Maybe I needed to lose my memories of you to realize how different you are from him. To understand the kind of man you are. Maybe I needed to understand myself better, too."

He looked puzzled. "In what way, *mariskya*?"

"If you'd told me eighteen months ago that I would risk my life to save someone else…I wouldn't have believed you." She struggled to find the right words. "I never saw myself as…as *brave*, I guess is the right word."

"But you are. You are the bravest woman I know."

Tahra's heart turned over at the simple way those words were spoken. Not as if Marek was trying to convince her, but as if they were merely a statement of fact recognized by everyone.

"As brave as Angelina?" At his startled expression, she rushed to explain. "You told me how she saved the crown prince. And she— You admire her. I can tell."

"Are you honestly asking me to compare you to Angelina?" he queried, incredulous.

Tahra wasn't prepared for how swiftly Marek moved. And she wasn't prepared for the way he snatched her up, or the way his arms tightened around her. "There is no comparison," he insisted, once he had her in his embrace. "Angelina is a trained soldier and a bodyguard. I would expect no less of her than exactly what she did. But you—you are not a soldier or a bodyguard. Yet you placed your body between danger and those children in the playground *without hesitation*. That is the definition of bravery, *mariskya*. Overcoming fear in an instant to do what *must* be done to save others, even at the risk of your own life."

He kissed her eyes, her cheeks, the curve of her chin. Everywhere except her lips. "You are the bravest woman I know, bar none," he breathed. "And I have nothing but pride in you for what you did. If you had died… I have said this before, but I will say it again. If you had died, I would also have died. And while I would have taken that risk for you if I could, I would not wish for you to do other than you did, because you were the only one who could do it. Can you understand that?"

Tahra was lost in a world of emotion and swirling desire, things she always felt when Marek kissed her. But she heard his words in a distant recess of her brain and they gladdened her heart, because she wanted Marek to be proud of her. Because she wanted to be the kind of woman he admired as well as loved.

Her gaze met his, and she knew what she wanted. She loved Marek. Would always love him. And despite the lies and deceptions, he was an honorable man at heart. A man who deserved to be loved. She just had to convince him she loved him for the man he was. "Please," she whispered, twining her arms around his neck. "Please."

He couldn't let her go.

Marek had tried so hard to chain the wolf inside him, but he could almost hear the chain snap when Tahra touched him that way. When she placed her lips on his lips and pressed her body all along the length of his. When she whispered, "Please."

He swung her into his arms and carried her into the bedroom, setting her down on her feet and taking a step back. "Are you sure, *mariskya*? If you are not *sure*, please tell me now. I have waited so long, and I…"

She smiled up at him. "I'm sure."

He had them both naked in minutes. His clothes, he merely ripped off. Tahra's were drawn from her body with reverence, and with each piece he removed, he paused to give her time to change her mind. *Please do not*, he begged her in his mind, but knowing he had to offer her that opportunity.

Want and need clawed through him when he saw Tahra's softly rounded body completely naked, and he wanted to claim her in the most primitive way. But he managed to restrain his desires. Barely. *Slow*, his mind chanted, forcing his body to obey his command. *Take it slow.*

So his hands caressed…instead of seizing. His lips coaxed…instead of devouring. And he whispered words of love in her ear…instead of growling his possession. But underneath it all was the wolf who feared this might be his only chance to convince her she belonged to him the way he belonged to her. Forever.

Then they were on the bed. Tahra moaned his name and arched like a bow when he tested her readiness…and found her damp. He almost fitted himself into place in that instant but gritted his teeth and remembered to don a condom at the last minute, praying there was no expiration date on them. He hadn't used one in more than eighteen months…because he hadn't been with a woman since he'd met Tahra.

Then he was *there*. Finally. His mind still chanting, *Take it slow*, as he pressed inexorably inward. Until something blocked his way.

He snatched at a ragged breath as comprehension dawned. "You lied to me, *mariskya*."

But when he would have withdrawn, she clutched at his hips, anchoring him where he was. "Please," she begged. "If you love me…please. *Please.*"

He wasn't proof against the combination of her desire and his. "It will hurt," he warned her, steeling himself against her pain that would also be his. "Just this once."

And it *did* hurt—he knew by the way her breath caught in her throat and her eyes squeezed shut. But by then he was deep inside her. Waiting. By sheer force of will he held himself immobile, waiting for her body to accept his. He kissed the little hollow beneath her ear, and her nipples tightened against the wall of his chest.

Then he felt something else. A softening. A lessening of the tension in her inner muscles. An *acceptance* that this was as it should be. That not only his heart belonged to her, but his body did, too.

He began to move. Slowly. Kissing her eyes, her lips, whispering words of love in the language of his heart. She was moving, too, her hips rising to meet his, her left hand clinging to his back, her fingernails digging in a little as she held on. The cast on her right wrist rough against his bare skin as she clung with that hand, too, as best she could.

Her breathing was ragged—but in a good way now. He could tell by the tiny sounds issuing from her throat that the pain was gone and all she felt now was pleasure. Intense pleasure.

"Yes," he encouraged her when her movements became frantic.

"Please." She gasped the word. And then, as if she couldn't help it, gasped again. *"Please."*

He clung to control by a thread, picking up the pace until she arched beneath him. Until her orgasm crashed through her body and she cried out, a wordless sound of entreaty urging him on, and he let go. Just let go and took what he needed from her, loving how her body embraced his in the ultimate act of giving.

Chapter 15

Marek insisted on a shower for both of them. "Do not argue with me on this, Tahra," he said grimly as he picked her up, cradled her against his chest and carried her into the bathroom. He waited for the water to be warm enough before wrapping a towel around the cast on her right wrist and drawing her into the shower with him. Washing her body with a touching gentleness. Refusing to let her hide the scars.

"Shh," he soothed her when she made a sound of distress and tried to keep her back to the wall. "I know the scars are there. Do you think they affect my desire for you? Can you not see they do not?"

She choked on laughter, because she had to admit, no, they didn't. He was already aroused again—apparently ready, willing and able to prove his point. But he didn't do anything about it, just dried them both and carried her back to the bed, ignoring her faint protest that she could walk. He settled against the pillows he bunched up behind him and drew her back into his embrace. Then said again, "You lied to me, *mariskya*."

Tahra didn't pretend she didn't know what he meant. "No, I didn't."

"Yes, you did. You said, and I quote, '…if you knew I wasn't a virgin, we would have been lovers long ago… but you wouldn't have asked me to be your wife.'" He paused for a moment, then added in a low voice, "Those words I can never forget. Your accusation was untrue, but I will admit it hurt me…as you intended it to do."

"I *did* want to hurt you," she admitted. "But I didn't say I wasn't a virgin. I merely postulated a what-if scenario by prefacing my statement with 'if.' *If* you knew…"

"Play no word games with me," he said, a stern expression on his face. "You deliberately led me to believe you were…experienced."

"No." She raised her head and gazed at him, dead serious. "But you can't be naive enough to think virginity and experience are two sides of the same coin. A virgin who is raped—as I nearly was—is technically no longer a virgin. But that doesn't mean she made a *choice*. I wasn't 'saving myself for marriage.' That went out of style decades ago. But I *was* waiting for a man I could love, because I wanted him to be the first. The only." She shivered as she remembered how nearly that choice had been taken from her a few years ago.

Marek gently tugged her back into place against his shoulder, tightening his arms around her, as if he knew what she was thinking. A supposition confirmed when he said, "I understand. When you told me what happened, I was… Let us just say I was furious. Not for me, but for you and any other woman so treated."

Tahra was watching Marek's face and saw the steel enter his eyes as he continued. "I will not lie to you—even here in Zakhar these things happen. But the king has instituted new laws with severe penalties, and I pray this will be a deterrent." He clenched his jaw. "But that is for the future. I had to make sure the man who attacked you paid for his crime once he returned to his own country."

Startled, she sat up straight, pulling the bedclothes around her, staring at him. "What did you do?"

A faint smile touched his lips, but a smile with no humor, and she suddenly saw a family resemblance to the king. "He will live. But he will never again touch another woman against her will." And despite her pleas for the details, he would disclose nothing more than that.

They cuddled for a bit, then Marek sighed deeply and said with regret, "I must take you back to the palace."

"Why can't I stay here?"

"Because…" He kissed her, a kiss she figured he'd intended to be quick, but which soon turned into more. When he finally lifted his head, he said, "Because you have a reputation to maintain, *mariskya*. As do I. The limousine driver…if I send him back to the palace alone, he will know you are with me. If I do not send him back, he will know you are with me…*and* he will be unhappy he will not sleep in his own bed. The driver knows better than to say anything outside the palace, but I would spare you backstairs gossip if I can. And no," he said firmly, "this is not in any way related to making decisions for you or trying to control your life."

"But we're engaged," she protested. "In the US—"

"Yes, but this is Zakhar. I can change myself for you, but I cannot change the entire country. Besides..." His hands cradled her face so she couldn't look away. "A woman's first time...your body must be..." He cleared his throat. "That is, it would be selfish of me to..."

"I'm fine," she hastened to reassure him. But now that he mentioned it, she *was* sore. The initial pain had soon been replaced with the kind of emotional and physical ecstasy she'd only read about and dreamed of, but now her body was confirming Marek's assumptions. And his consideration, his tender care for her, was just another in a long list of reasons why she loved him. "You didn't hurt me," she whispered, suddenly a little shy talking about this. "You made it beautiful for me."

"I am glad." His smile was suddenly very male. "It was beyond beautiful for me...as you no doubt could tell."

They dressed silently, Marek helping her by fastening her bra in the back and zipping up her dress because of the cast on her right wrist. Tahra decided to forego donning her nylons again. It was just too difficult with the cast—it had taken almost ten minutes to wiggle into them and not create a run back at the palace—and since Marek didn't care about the scars on the backs of her legs, she wouldn't, either. She stuffed the nylons in her purse, hoping the limo driver wouldn't notice.

Marek caught her arm as she started to walk out the door, tugging her gently into his embrace. "Wait," he said. "I have one more thing to say."

"Yes?"

He didn't immediately respond, just drew her left hand up and kissed it, then stared down at his ring there, varied expressions flitting across his face. Finally, his voice very deep, he admitted, "You should already know this, but I will say it anyway. I would have loved you even if…even if you had not waited." And she knew what he was trying to say.

She smiled tenderly. "I know."

He raised his eyes to meet hers. "But I must confess I am…honored…" Then he frowned. "I wish now I could have given you the same gift, but I cannot. All I can offer is my word that since the moment I met you there has been no other. Nor will there ever be."

Honesty shone from his face, and Tahra's heart skipped a beat. She'd never heard a more romantic declaration in a movie or read one in a book than the one Marek had just made to her. She wished she could tell him what those words meant to her…as well as the love that inspired them. But all she could think of to say was "I'm so glad I waited for you."

The first commercial plane carrying recalled soldiers from the northern border landed at the Drago airport shortly before 5:00 a.m. The second plane, from the western border, landed shortly thereafter. In keeping with the clandestine nature of the recall, none of the soldiers were in uniform. None of the soldiers carried their belongings in a military duffel bag, either. And none of the soldiers were picked up by a military transport—they made their way in twos and threes via taxis to a huge warehouse that had been rented the day before and furnished overnight with the dispatch and efficiency for which the Zakharian National Forces was justifiably famous.

Cots, complete with blankets and pillows, were already set up in neat rows, and a footlocker stood at the foot of each. One wall was lined with racks of weapons to replace the ones the soldiers had been forced to leave behind. Along another wall was a makeshift mess area—officers and enlisted men would eat side by side. A third was roped off and screened. Behind the screen were makeshift showers and portable latrines.

Four privates with clipboards stood at the entrance, each one responsible for one-fourth of the expected influx, and each one checking soldiers off their list and assigning them to cots. The sixty in the first wave were processed and eating breakfast by seven.

Tahra was already awake when the phone by her bed jangled. She'd woken before dawn feeling wondrously refreshed and deliriously happy. So she'd just lain there, her left hand tucked under her cheek, thinking of Marek. Thinking no woman could have had a more tender lover—especially for her first time. Wishing she could have woken beside him this morning. Wishing for a repeat performance of last night.

She replayed every moment in her mind, loving them all. But three instances stood out above the rest. Marek taking a step back in the bedroom, saying, *"Are you sure,* mariskya*? If you are not* sure, *please tell me now. I have waited so long, and I..."* As if he was afraid he wouldn't be able to stop if she changed her mind later. "But he would have," she whispered to herself, knowing it for the truth. He'd hesitated as he undressed her, giving her time to change her mind. And as soon as her body betrayed he was her first lover, he'd tried to draw back. And he would have, if she'd let him.

Then there was the memory of Marek washing her so gently in the shower, saying, *"I know the scars are there. Do you think they affect my desire for you?"* as his body proved beyond a shadow of a doubt they were meaningless.

And Marek confessing, *"I wish now I could have given you the same gift, but I cannot. All I can offer is my word that since the moment I met you there has been no other. Nor will there ever be."*

What woman could resist a man like that? "Not me," she acknowledged just as the phone rang. She picked it up. "Hello?"

Marek's deep voice sounded in her ear. "Good morning, *mariskya*."

A wave of heat washed through her. "Good morning."

"I am sorry to call so early, but I… That is… How are you feeling this morning?"

She smiled, even though he couldn't see her. "I'm fine. More than fine. I was just lying here, thinking of you. Thinking of last night." Then she remembered how exhausted he'd appeared when he'd picked her up for dinner, and said, "How did you sleep last night after you brought me back to the palace? You looked so tired yesterday."

"I slept like a man without a care in the world. Thank you very much."

She laughed softly. "I slept dreamlessly for the first time in…oh…forever. Thank *you* very much." She turned onto her back and stretched deliciously. Remembering. Emboldened, she asked, "Will I see you today?"

"I would like nothing more, but duty calls."

"It's Saturday."

"Yes, and I have been absent for most of three days."

She didn't want to be one of those women where it was all about her, so she said quickly, "I understand."

But she couldn't help adding, "Call me before you go to bed tonight? Please? Just so I know you're okay?"

She could hear the smile in his voice. "A man would have to be made of ice to turn you down when you say 'please,' *mariskya.* And I am not made of ice." Something in his voice told her he was remembering last night…and the many times she'd said "please." Especially right at the very end. And Tahra blushed.

She grasped at the first thing she could think of to change the subject. "You know, you never did explain where you were, or why you didn't tell me you were leaving."

There was dead silence at the other end. Then he said, "I should have told you I was leaving, yes. But where I was and why I had to leave on short notice—these things I cannot tell you. Not because they are secret from *you*, but because they are *secret.* Top secret."

She thought about this for a minute. Much as she wanted to know, she was also—in an odd sort of way—proud that he *wouldn't* tell her. He took his oath on Zakharian national security as seriously as she took hers regarding her clearance with the US government. A life with Marek wouldn't be easy because there was so much he couldn't share with her. She would have to take him on faith. To trust that when he wasn't there, he wasn't out somewhere doing what he shouldn't do.

But that wasn't all. She also had to accept that he could die in the line of duty. Like wives and husbands of police officers, firefighters and soldiers, she would have to kiss him goodbye in the morning, never knowing if he would return at the end of the day. *But you already accepted that…didn't you?* a little voice in the back of her head demanded. *You had to know what you were getting into with an officer in the Zakharian National Forces who is also a royal bodyguard when you started dating him.*

"I understand," she said finally. "But if you want me to trust you, you have to trust me. No more secrets except those related to your work. And no more 'sheltering' me from the harsh realities of life. Promise?"

"Promise."

The word was uttered without the slightest hesitation, and inside Tahra was thrilled. But all she said was "I should let you go. You probably have a million things to do today. Just...please remember to call me tonight."

He said something under his breath in Zakharan that she didn't catch, and when she asked him to repeat it he did, but then he translated it into English for her. "You are a woman in a thousand. And I will never again leave without telling you—you have my word."

Marek hung up the phone and threw back the bedclothes, then stood and stretched, naked. He ordered himself to ignore the way his early-morning arousal had been inflamed into an urgent ache by merely hearing Tahra's voice on the phone...and remembering last night. He could have dealt with his problem in five minutes—the same way he'd dealt with similar occurrences over the past year and a half—but now that he'd finally...*finally*...made love to Tahra, seeking release without her was anathema to him.

He dressed swiftly in jogging clothes and running shoes, and headed out for his daily five-mile run. The sun was just rising over the mountains to the east as he settled into a steady pace. The daily regimen helped him stay in the peak physical condition he needed to maintain as head of the crown prince's security detail. He was the best at what he did, better than any man who served under him, and he had no intention of ever letting that change; no man would ever be able to claim Captain Zale wasn't up to the challenge.

But running for Marek wasn't just about exercise. He also used the time to puzzle out the answers to knotty questions, and this morning was no exception. He had two equally important yet totally separate issues weighing on his mind. One was the Zakharian Liberation Front. The other was Tahra. And of the two, what to do about Tahra occupied more of his thoughts as he took the turn that would take him past the river that flowed through the center of Drago.

Last night had changed his world. The reality of making love to Tahra was far, far better than his imagination had painted it when he'd dreamed of having her in his bed—her passion had nearly matched his. And if it hadn't been her first time, if he hadn't been absolutely sure she wasn't physically ready for anything more, he might not have been able to take her back to the palace, reputation be damned. But… *Someday soon*, he promised himself. Someday soon he would make love to her all night long. Someday soon he would take her to new heights, and in doing so he would take himself there, as well.

But not until we are married, he vowed, knowing it would take even more strength of will than it had previously…because now he *knew*. Now he knew how soft Tahra's skin was…everywhere. Now he knew the little sounds she made when she reached the peak and tumbled over the other side. Now he knew just how easily his self-control was shattered by one word from Tahra—*please.*

And for the first time since she'd returned his engagement ring a few weeks ago, he knew—*really knew*—Tahra loved him. Last night would never have happened if that weren't the case. Which meant they would be married. Not as soon as he'd like—which would have been today if he'd had a choice—but soon. As soon as her memory returned.

Which could be any day now. The spontaneously resurfaced recollection of the baby shower gift had to be a sign Tahra's memory would return completely. Or at least most of it, except for the actual explosion. And if her memory returned, if she could identify the man who'd left the bomb at the preschool…

That brought Marek's thoughts right back to the Zakharian Liberation Front, and the confirmation he and Angelina had received in Timon about the real goal behind the terrorist attacks all over Zakhar: *assassination.*

Assassinate King Andre, who would be succeeded by Crown Prince Raoul. Assassinate Queen Juliana and Prince Xavier—Colonel Marianescu—whom the king had named as regents. That would leave the crown prince, who wasn't even two years old yet and far too young to rule, with no one to act as regent.

The Zakharian Liberation Front, through the traitor who—*as he'd already intimated to Colonel Marianescu*—sat on the Privy Council, would move swiftly into that power vacuum, seizing the young king and seizing power at the same time. Setting the little boy up as a puppet and ruling in his name…for the time being. Until they'd consolidated power and no longer needed the legal myth of the crown, and they took sole control as a totalitarian dictatorship.

But they couldn't just assassinate the crown prince after his father and immediately seize power; the citizenry wouldn't stand for it. Zakharians were fiercely devoted to the much-loved monarchy and were proud the House of Marianescu had reigned in an unbroken line for centuries. So the Zakharian Liberation Front needed the legal fiction of maintaining the monarchy. And to do that, they needed Crown Prince Raoul alive. For now.

Marek didn't know *who* the traitor on the Privy Council was—just that one of its members *had* to be the one heading up the Zakharian Liberation Front. Nothing else made sense. And by the time the king was dead and the traitor stepped forward to act as regent, it would be too late.

Once upon a time the Privy Council had been appointed by the king, acting as his advisers but having no real authority. But when King Andre Alexei IV ascended the throne several years earlier, he'd slowly placed more power—and responsibility—in the hands of the Privy Council, an *elected* Privy Council, a change he had instituted over the objections of nearly everyone. As the king had explained to his intimates, absolute monarchs were passé in the twenty-first century, and Zakhar needed to modify its political structure.

Marek agreed with the king…in theory. But now he saw the fallacy in his reasoning, because a taste for power by someone on the Privy Council had led them all into this…quagmire. For just the second time in his life Marek realized the king was only human, with human failings. And instead of weakening his devotion, it increased it. Because if the king wasn't a godlike being who was never wrong, that meant he *needed* men like Marek, now more than ever. And not just as a bodyguard for his son.

Chapter 16

The phone rang just as Tahra was finishing dinner, and she picked it up eagerly, hoping it was Marek. Instead, it was one of the palace switchboard operators, who said, "I have an overseas call for you, Miss Edwards. She says she is your sister. Would you like to take the call?"

"Of course." Tahra had tried calling Carly several times but had never gotten through. She'd left messages, though, and finally her sister was calling her back.

"Tahra?" Carly's voice sounded in her sister's ear, with the hint of the Virginia roots she'd tried so hard to eradicate from her speech for her on-camera TV job, an accent that always crept in when she was excited about something.

"Carly? I've been trying to reach you for days. I've left messages, and—"

"I know, I know, and I'm so sorry. I just got back from Antarctica and called you as soon as I could."

"What were you doing there?"

"Covering a story, of course—and freezing my ass off. Global warming is *not* a myth, as anyone who sees my exposé in two weeks will clearly understand. But that's not why I called you." That excitement was back in her tone. "Can you fly back from Zakhar a month from now?"

Tahra thought quickly. "Well, I'm on medical disability leave from my job right now. And if my memory returns, I'll have to return to the embassy. But I *do* have two weeks of vacation left. What's up?"

"How would you like to be my maid of honor?"

Tahra gasped. "Oh, Carly, really? Really? You and Shane?"

"I know it sounds crazy because we haven't known each other all that long. But I'm thirty-five. Shane's forty-one. And he's The One, Tahra. I want to grow old with him."

The rock-solid assurance in Carly's voice was good to hear. She'd prayed Carly would find a man who deserved her—Tiger Shark might be her nickname in the TV industry, but Carly had a loving heart, which Tahra knew all too well—and after everything her sister had gone through, she deserved to be deliriously happy.

The two sisters chatted excitedly over the details of Carly and Shane's upcoming nuptials for several minutes, then Carly said, "I forgot. You called me and left messages for me to call you back. Is something wrong?"

"Oh." Tahra came down from the wedding high she'd been floating on. "I wanted to ask you why you didn't tell me the truth…about my own engagement."

She knew she'd taken her sister by surprise from the

sudden silence at the other end. Then Carly said, "Your memory returned?"

"No." Tahra shook her head, even though she knew her sister couldn't see it. "But I figured out our engagement was a fake and confronted Marek. He admitted it, and told me you knew." She took a deep breath. "Why? Why didn't you tell me?"

"Because…" Carly sighed. "Okay, because ever since I fell in love with Shane, I've been… I can't really explain it except to say I'm a sucker for a man in love. And Marek loves you so much, Tahra. He made his case for why he'd lied, and I…I bought it." When Tahra didn't say anything, Carly continued, her voice taking on a fierce note. "Did he do something? Did he try to take advantage of you? Because if he did, I'll kill him. He swore to me that—"

Tahra's "No!" was sharp, cutting off the flow of words from the other end of the line. "No, he didn't," she said, forcing herself to a calmness she was far from feeling. "And you don't have to fight my battles for me anymore," she told her sister. "I can take care of myself."

"Are you sure?" Tahra was surprised by the hint of uncertainty in Carly's tone—Carly, who always seemed so self-assured. "I don't mean, are you sure you can take care of yourself. I mean, are you sure he didn't try to take advantage of the situation."

Tahra laughed a little. "The shoe's on the other foot, actually. If one of us took advantage of the other, blame me, not him."

"Does that mean what I think it means?"

A tapping at the door to her suite gave Tahra a welcome opportunity not to answer the question. "Hang on, someone's here. I'll be right back." She put the receiver down, and when she opened the door, there stood Ani.

"Finished with your dinner, miss? You didn't ring, but I thought perhaps..."

Tahra pushed the door open. "I was on the phone, but I was just about done. So yes, you may take the tray."

"Sorry," she told Carly after Ani left. "My maid was here to take the dinner tray."

"Must be nice living in the lap of luxury," her sister teased.

Tahra suddenly remembered how Marek had convinced her to accept Ani's services, and couldn't help but smile. "When in Rome," she began. "Or in this case, in the royal palace in Drago..."

Her sister let out a huge sigh of relief. "Oh, Tahra, you have no idea how happy it makes me to hear you talk this way. Just like your old self. I was so worried when you were in the hospital..."

"I'm fine. More than fine, actually. And last night I remembered something from those missing months." She filled Carly in on the details. "So I'm really hopeful everything will come back soon," she finished.

"And...Marek? How are things between you? I mean, if you know the engagement was fake, do you know *why* it was fake? Why you gave him back his ring?"

"I know. And we're working on that trust thing." She breathed deeply. "But I'm still wearing the ring." She held the phone between her ear and her shoulder so she could look at her left hand and Marek's ring, which seemed so *right* on her finger. "And...I love him, Carly. I know it's hard to believe, because it's as if we just met when I came out of the coma last week. But..."

"You're preaching to the choir," Carly said, a dry

note in her voice. "I think I fell in love with Shane almost from the moment I met him, but I was sure he was The One in less than a week."

"Maybe it's an Edwards thing," Tahra joked.

"Maybe it is." But there was no laughter in Carly's voice. "Dad said something to me once. I've never forgotten. I must have been…oh…fifteen? He said he took one look at Mom and he knew. Convincing her took longer, but he never had a doubt. And they'd been married for almost twenty years when they…well…you know."

The little ache in her heart that never quite went away made Tahra confess, "I've never envied you anything, Carly…except that. You had Mom and Dad for so many more years than I did."

"I kinda sorta knew that. You went through a phase, remember?"

Actually, Tahra had forgotten. But now that Carly reminded her… "How you managed to put up with me, I'll never know."

"You were my sister," Carly said simply. "You were all I had."

Tahra choked back tears. "Oh, Carly…"

"And anyway," Carly said with what sounded suspiciously like tears in her own voice, tears she was trying to hold back, "that phase didn't last long, thank God."

"If I never said it, thank you for sharing those memories of Mom and Dad with me." She sighed with regret. "Sometimes I wonder if I really remember them…or if I'm just remembering things you told me about them over the years."

"Does it really matter one way or the other?"

In her mind she heard Marek say, *"Do not struggle so hard,* mariskya. *I will tell you anything you need to know. But I do not want to tell you everything, for then we will never know if you truly remember...or if you are only 'remembering' what I tell you."*

And suddenly she missed Marek so much it was a physical ache. She closed her eyes for a few seconds as longing speared through her. Not sexual desire. Just a yearning to see his face, hear his voice, touch his hand. Watch him smile. And because all her life she'd shared what she was feeling with her older sister, she blurted out, "Does it hurt when Shane isn't there?" Then she rushed to apologize. "Sorry, that was totally out of left field, wasn't it?"

But Carly seemed to understand. "I thought I was losing my mind when I was in Antarctica because it hurt so much." Her voice softened. "What makes it bearable is knowing he feels the same way."

And again a memory came to her. Marek saying, *"You almost died, Tahra. If that had happened, I would also have died. I would have gone on breathing, but..."*

She and Marek shared the kind of love granted to very few. A very lucky few. Like Carly and Shane. Like Queen Juliana and King Andre. And the realization struck her like a lightning bolt. She wasn't just Marek's *mariskya*—he was hers, too. Something she couldn't live without.

Soldiers from the Zakharian National Forces who had been deployed elsewhere had continued to arrive in Drago throughout the day and into the evening in a seemingly random stream, which was actually highly organized. Two of every three who had shipped out were to return in secret—so the orders had read, and so the senior commanders had complied. The orders had not specified the best and the brightest, but the senior commanders had read between the lines. The Zakharian National Forces were preparing for war. Only the best would do.

By the time the last commercial plane carrying recalled soldiers in civilian garb landed, two more warehouses had been prepared to receive and house the returning men. The sixty soldiers in the last wave were processed and eating a late dinner by nine that night.

The lights in all three warehouses went out at ten. And the soldiers—being soldiers, men who could sleep anytime, anywhere, almost as if on command—were soon fast asleep. The only sounds were the creak of cots as men turned over…and the occasional snore.

Tahra had tried to stay awake for Marek's call, but after a long, relaxing bath—not quite as long as the one she'd taken last night after Marek returned her to the palace, but long enough—she curled up on top of the covers on her bed. Still in her robe, and with one of the books she'd brought back from her apartment, a murder mystery that she told herself would keep her awake. Then she put the book facedown after a few pages, intending merely to "rest her eyes" for a moment. And promptly fell asleep.

The phone rang at half past ten, jolting her awake, and she scrambled to answer it. "Hello? Marek?"

"I woke you," he said with obvious regret. "It is late and I should have realized…but you had asked me to call you before I went to bed tonight. And you had said 'please.'" His voice dropped. "I cannot resist you when you say 'please,' *mariskya*."

The longing that swept through her this time *was*

sexual. Desire for Marek's hands, his lips, his rock-hard body on hers. *In* hers. Moving with controlled male power. Taking his time, making sure she was with him every step of the way. Carrying her into that place where all she could feel was him. Where all she could hear was the frantic sound of their breathing and her voice almost begging for release. Where all she could see was Marek's face transformed. His blue eyes alight with passion…and love.

Tahra's breath caught in her throat, and she couldn't have spoken even if her brain could function enough to form words.

"That is why you must promise me not to say 'please.'"

She swallowed, and her words came out in a croak. "What do you mean?"

"I have sworn to myself I will not… That is, *we* will not… Not until we are married. But since I cannot resist that word on your lips, you must refrain from using it…in that context."

Tahra would have laughed…if Marek didn't sound so dead serious. Okay, yes, things had changed in the United States in the past fifty years…and Zakhar hadn't moved with the times. But it used to be the *woman* who wanted to wait for marriage…not the man. Yet here was Marek telling her "no more sex" until the knot was tied.

"How is that fair? You're putting all the responsibility on me."

"No, no, you misunderstand. I will undertake to be responsible for controlling my own desires…but I cannot withstand yours *and* mine. So you must refrain from asking me."

She could almost see him nodding decisively. As if

that settled that. And she strangled the laughter that threatened to bubble out of her. "I'll…" Cough, cough. Gurgle. Snort. "I'll think about it."

Oh, how she loved this man. Would always love him. And as Carly had said about her fiancé, she wanted to grow old with him. But first she wanted to make babies with him. Beautiful babies, like Alec and Angelina's son, Drew. And just as marriage was a prerequisite for sex to Marek—where she was concerned, anyway—marriage was a prerequisite to babies for her. Because even though the world had changed…she hadn't.

And speaking of marriages…

"Carly called me tonight," Tahra told him. "She and Shane are getting married next month. She wants me to be her maid of honor. Will you come with me?"

"Next month?" He seemed to be weighing her statement, as if trying to fit that date into some timeline of his own. "That should be…possible. What is the exact date?" When she told him, he said, "May I give you a definite answer next week? There are some…arrangements…I will have to make."

"Of course. And if you can't make it, I'll understand. But…" She let her voice soften into almost a coaxing tone. "I would love to have you with me."

"I will do my best."

She almost said, "You always do," but thought better of it. If for some reason Marek couldn't go—maybe he had too many men on the crown prince's security detail already scheduled for vacation next month—she didn't want him to feel bad about not being able to accompany her.

She yawned suddenly, and though she tried to smother

the sound, Marek heard her. "It is late and you are tired, *mariskya*. I am keeping you from your bed."

"Well, actually," she admitted, "I'm already in bed." On top of the covers, but technically she *was* in bed.

A groan sounded in her ear. "Why did you say that? Now I will never sleep, imagining you as you were last night in my bed. So perfect."

"Not exactly perf—"

"Perfect," he insisted. "There are no words in English beautiful enough to describe you, so I can only say…" He whispered to her in Zakharan. Soft, seductive words that rolled off his tongue and made her blush, even though she had absolutely no idea what he was saying—apparently her Zakharan lessons hadn't encompassed these words. But she blushed because just the tenor of his voice, the pitch, the melodious words sounded…sexy. Enticing. "Someday I will translate for you, *mariskya*," he concluded. "And then you will know just how perfect you are."

Something is not right, Sergeant Vasska told himself as he packed his binoculars away and headed back into town under the cover of darkness. The air force base outside of Timon looked curiously…he struggled for the right word…*vacant*. Yes, that was it. The base looked somehow *vacant* compared to yesterday, although the troop carriers were still lined up in plain sight. Soldiers had come and gone all day, which made sense, since they were supplementing the border guards five miles away in addition to everything else they normally did. And planes had taken off and landed in the training exercises the pilots here conducted most days. But he couldn't shake the feeling something wasn't quite as it should be.

A feeling wasn't something he would put into his report, though. He'd made that mistake once…and had been reamed for it. He wouldn't make that mistake again. Facts and figures. He'd been ordered to observe the comings and goings at the base, and that's what would go into his report. Period.

Anything else was irrelevant.

Marek tried to turn off his brain and go to sleep, but he couldn't, even though he was exhausted and the hands of the clock on his nightstand stood at a quarter to midnight. He consoled himself with the reminder that he was off tomorrow, and though he rarely slept in even on his days off, perhaps this one time he would. Too much work and too little sleep this past week was putting a strain on even his iron constitution.

At first he knew exactly why he couldn't sleep—Tahra. Because his memories of last night had been brought vividly to life by his phone conversation with her. Because his imagination was working overtime, fantasizing about everything he planned to do with her…once they were married.

But eventually he forced himself to think of something else. Because as incredible as his fantasies were, he'd already determined this morning he wouldn't avail himself of the easy solution he could carry out in less than five minutes. To his everlasting regret, he hadn't waited for Tahra the way she'd waited for him. Shadowy memories of the women he'd made love to before Tahra—*had sex with*, his mind stubbornly substituted—would haunt him. Not just Zorina. Tahra knew about

Zorina, but she didn't know about the others. Nothing serious. But still. And he hadn't seen it until Tahra had accused him of having a double standard where women were concerned.

No, he hadn't waited for Tahra before; he damned well was going to wait for her now…even if it killed him.

So he turned his thoughts away from Tahra on to his other pressing concern—the Zakharian Liberation Front…and the Privy Council.

Who? he asked himself. *Who on the Privy Council is the traitor behind this terrorist organization? Who is ambitious enough...and ruthless enough...to kill all these civilians just as a decoy?*

He narrowed the candidates down to three. Then down to one. And he was shocked how easy it was—once you looked at it that way. Once you got past the barricades your mind automatically put up because you didn't *want* to think someone you knew could do this.

He sat up abruptly and picked up the phone. His first instinct—to call Major Stesha—was put on hold because he didn't know his home phone number. *Probably unlisted, too,* he theorized. But there *was* one number he knew by heart—had known it since the king had assigned him to head up the queen's security detail years ago—and he dialed it now.

"Colonel Marianescu." Almost midnight, but the colonel's voice was as crisp and alert as if he never slept.

"Captain Zale, sir. Sorry to call so late, but—"

"What is it, Captain?"

I think I know who the traitor on the Privy Council is."

Chapter 17

"I have no proof," Marek told King Andre, Colonel Marianescu and Major Stesha in the king's private office in the palace, to which he'd been summoned for this early-morning meeting. "Nothing that would hold up in court."

"Then what have you got?" The king leaned back in his chair, his right hand toying with a letter opener in the shape of an antique sword.

"It was merely a matter of asking myself who could do this, Sire. And who benefits. Then it was easy."

Colonel Marianescu smiled coldly. "Lay it out for him, Captain, the way you laid it out for me over the phone."

"All along it bothered me," Marek explained. "The *precision* involved in the attacks. The almost military discipline. A secret organization no one had heard of…

until they struck without warning. And once we figured out the refugees were a decoy—"

"Yes, yes," Major Stesha said testily. "This is nothing new. Get to the point."

Marek glanced at the major on the other side of Colonel Marianescu. "Yes, sir." Then he faced the king again. "Should you die, Sire, the crown prince will ascend the throne. And if the regents you named in the act of succession are also killed—the queen and you, sir," he said, his gaze flicking toward Colonel Marianescu, "there would be chaos. At least until a new regent is named. With no one related to the crown prince by blood through the male line available, who would the country turn to?"

Marek read in the king's eyes that he saw it now. "Are you saying…?"

"Yes, Sire. Who but your chief councillor on the Privy Council?"

Marek cleared his throat. "The Zakharian Liberation Front is small because he only *needs* small to achieve his goals. Flying under the radar? Done. Forcing you to declare martial law and diverting troops with his terrorist attacks? Done. Or at least he *thinks* it has been done. Assassinating the three people he needs dead in order to seize power? Easily accomplished even with a small paramilitary force, so long as it does not have to fight a large contingent of the Zakharian National Forces. Being named regent? Who else would the country insist upon in the ensuing crisis? And remember, nineteen years must pass before the new king turns twenty-one and can reign without a regent."

The king's stillness was unnerving, but Marek continued. "Once Colonel Lermontov consolidated power, once he was firmly in control…he would merely need to eliminate the young king…who would have no one to protect him. No father. No mother. No second cousin who is head of internal security," he said, referring to Colonel Marianescu, "who is as devoted to him as his own father."

Marek's gaze was drawn to the king's right hand, which now gripped the antique sword letter opener so tightly the fist was bloodless. And his face was a death mask, his eyes focused on something only he could see. "Not in this lifetime," the king vowed softly. Then he turned that deadly face on Major Stesha. "Arrest Colonel Lermontov. Immediately."

"Yes, Sire."

But Marek spoke up almost before Major Stesha's prompt reply. "On what charge, Sire? With what proof? I have none. My belief that it can be no one else is nothing more than that—my belief."

"*I* will get the proof—from Colonel Lermontov's own lips." This from Major Stesha.

Marek shook his head, but he didn't look at the major; his gaze was locked on the king's. "'Torture is not tolerated in Zakhar.' Those are your own words, Sire, and you *cannot* countenance it. Not even for this."

Seconds passed that seemed like hours, and Marek prayed, *Please God. Not my king. He has the legal authority, but do not let him do this.*

Then the deadly light in the king's eyes slowly receded. His face was still implacable, his eyes still hard and cold. But the white-hot rage that would sweep everything before it, including honor and justice, was tamped down. Barely.

"Then what do you suggest, Marek?"

The use of his first name reminded Marek of the moment years ago when—shamed to his very soul—he'd confessed his failure to the king. And the king had insisted, *"No, Marek. No blame attaches to you. If blame there is, it belongs to me and me alone..."*

The king had given him back his honor. Priceless. Now it was Marek's turn to give Zakhar's monarch something equally priceless to him—his wife and child. *"I will never fail him again,"* he remembered telling Tahra. And he never would.

"We set a trap, Sire. Risky, because no matter how carefully we plan, something could go wrong. But nothing will happen to the crown prince, and not just because Colonel Lermontov needs to keep him alive. Nothing will happen to your son…*or* your wife. Not if I have anything to say about it."

Adrenaline pumping, Marek passed Princess Mara's suite—*Tahra's* suite for now—but he didn't stop. Instead, he took the stairs two at a time down to the main floor, envisioning her in his mind's eye. Sleeping peacefully. Her long, dark hair splayed across her pillow in glorious disarray, the way she'd looked when—

He chopped that thought off. *Now is not the time*, he reminded himself sternly. He stopped off at his office and snagged the folder Major Stesha had given him, then headed for his car in the back parking lot.

He needed sleep, but he wouldn't get it. Not until he'd gone through the file one more time. Somewhere in the file was a clue to the bait that would be too tempting for Colonel Lermontov to resist. Something that would trigger an assassination attempt sooner rather than later. And since they were prepared for it now, the sooner the better.

Tahra was awake and dressed long before Ani brought her breakfast tray Monday morning. She'd made her bed, too, despite the fact that it took her twice as long as usual because of the cast on her wrist. She just *couldn't* get used to being waited on hand and foot.

She also couldn't get used to being a lady of leisure. She missed her job—what she remembered of it. She didn't have an important title…but she *was* important. Alec had told her as much at dinner on Friday. *"The temp filling in for you is pretty good...but she's not you."* Then he'd joked, *"So if I slip you a bonus under the table, would you pretend you've recovered your memory so I can remove the hold on your security clearance and you can come back to work?"*

Everyone had laughed, especially Tahra, because Alec was the straightest, most honest man she knew. He would never accept a bribe or offer one. And he would *never* compromise security at the embassy by letting her pretend to no longer be a security risk. But Alec's joke *had* made her feel needed. And proud to be his administrative assistant.

She was standing on the balcony outside her bedroom, her right hand propped on the stone railing, her left tucked into the back pocket of her jeans, smiling a little as she remembered the dinner conversation Friday evening. Then it hit her. The smile faded and a chill of recognition whispered up her spine. "How did I know?"

How did she know it was a joke? How did she know the kind of man Alec was? The explosion had wiped out most of her memories of him, along with everything else. She remembered Alec as her *new* boss…eighteen months ago. "But I *did* know," she murmured to herself. "I don't remember…but I *know*."

She darted inside and grabbed her cell phone from her purse, fumbling in her contacts until she found the name she knew had to be there, and pressed the button.

"Alec Jones."

She squeezed the phone and blurted out, "Alec, it's Tahra. Sorry to call you on your private line, but I didn't want to go through the embassy switchboard."

"Not a problem," he assured her. "But how did you know I'd be here so early?"

"I just knew."

His voice sharpened. "You remember?"

"No." She shook her head as if he could see her. "It's not a memory…not exactly. More like… I can't really explain it, but…I just *knew* you get in early so you can leave early. Because of baby Drew."

"Your memory's coming back. This proves it."

"Maybe. I have to ask you something."

"Shoot."

"Remember at dinner on Friday, when you made that joke about bribing me to pretend to remember?"

"Yeah."

"I knew it was a joke, Alec. I *knew*. Because I knew you."

"What do you mean?"

"I was just standing outside on the balcony a few minutes ago, feeling a little blue because it's Monday and I should be at work, but I'm not. Then I remembered how you said you missed me at work, and that made me feel good."

"And?"

"And I remembered your joke on Friday. Which I knew *on Friday* was a joke because you're the most honest man I know."

A tiny silence was followed by "Which you couldn't possibly have known...if you didn't somehow deep down remember working for me the past eighteen months." Alec was quick to grasp the point she was trying to make.

"Exactly. It's not like remembering the Denver Broncos outfit I gave Angelina at her baby shower. That was a specific memory. But this...this is different. Because knowledge like this is made up of *hundreds* of little moments. Maybe even thousands."

"Yeah. Like knowing your mother loves you without remembering each time she tucked you into bed, each bedtime story she read to you, each song she sang to put you to sleep."

"Yes." Tahra's throat closed at the simile, because she *did* have a few memories of her mother doing that... but precious few.

"That settles it. Your memory *is* returning. What did Marek say when you told him?"

"I...I haven't told him. I called you first because I...I just wanted you to confirm I wasn't wrong about..."

"Me being honest?" He laughed abruptly. "Well, I told Angelina Drew was beautiful when he was born, even though he was the sorriest mess I'd ever seen before they cleaned him up in the delivery room. But other than that, yeah. I try to walk the straight and narrow."

"I knew it," she whispered.

"And now you need to let Marek know about this

development, PDQ. It's a good sign, and he could use some good news."

"I will. I'll call him as soon as we're done." She let her breath out in a happy sigh. "Thanks, Alec. You have no idea how much this means to me."

"I've got a pretty fair idea." Tahra was just about to disconnect when he added drily, "Oh, and by the way, I'd just as soon you not mention what I said to Angelina."

"You mean about Drew being a sorry mess?" she teased.

"Yeah." It was little more than a growl, and Tahra laughed.

"Don't worry. My lips are sealed. Just remember what a *confidential* administrative assistant I am…when review time rolls around." Which meant they were both laughing when they disconnected.

Then another thought occurred to her. If her subconscious knowledge of Alec and the kind of man he was had returned, was it possible her subconscious was also influencing her response to Marek? Was that why she'd fallen in love with him again so quickly…because it wasn't really quickly? Because deep down she *knew* the man he was, even if she didn't remember specifics?

Tahra was just about to call Marek when she heard a knock on her door. *Breakfast*, she thought, and it was. Ani moved around and set the breakfast tray in the sitting room when she saw Tahra was already dressed and—since the bed was made—was unlikely to want breakfast there.

"You should not have done that, miss," Ani scolded her. "Not with your wrist in a cast." But she didn't dwell on it because she was practically beside herself that

Tahra had *three* letters next to her plate, two of which bore the king's royal crest.

"From the king," she explained reverently, as if Tahra couldn't figure it out for herself.

When the little maid stood there expectantly, practically holding her breath, Tahra opened the first square vellum envelope, which had her name typed neatly in the center. She read the enclosed card twice. "It's an invitation," she said blankly. "To a reception in my honor this Saturday."

"I knew *that*, miss. The master of the household announced it to the entire staff yesterday. Every Zakharian of note has been invited. It will be a huge gala event."

Tahra made a little face. "I'm not all that good with crowds," she confessed to explain her lack of enthusiasm, not wanting to go into detail about her painful shyness with strangers.

"Never you mind," Ani assured her. "The king and queen will be with you. And Captain Zale, of course." Her face grew rapt. "You will be the center of attention. What will you wear?"

Tahra laughed a little, because Ani's question had topped her list of things to worry about, too. She cast her mind over the clothes in her closet—which she'd gone through the last time she was at her apartment—and she knew she had nothing that would do credit to an event like this. "I'll have to go shopping, but I…" She made another face. "I don't even remember where I used to shop."

"The queen could advise you," Ani said with a wise air that belied the fact she wasn't even twenty. "Did you not say she was very kind to you?"

"Yes, but I don't think my budget would run to the kind of clothes she wears."

Ani's eyes twinkled. "You would be surprised, miss. The queen is quite frugal in some surprising ways, and her clothes are one of them. I know because I am friends with her personal maid, Daphne. Yes, the queen's wardrobe is extensive, because she is so very much in demand, you see, but many of her dresses are reasonably priced." Ani gave a decided nod. "You ask the queen." Then she inquired delicately, "And the other card, miss? Inscribed in the king's own handwriting?"

"Oh, is that… I didn't realize. You mean he wrote it himself?" Ani nodded, and Tahra picked up the second envelope, much in the way someone would pick up a tarantula. What could the king be writing her about?

Dear Miss Edwards, she read. *I have already officially thanked you for saving those schoolchildren by sending letters to your president, the State Department for which you work and your ambassador here in Drago, a copy of which was delivered to you by my wife, Juliana. But that is merely the beginning.*

By now you should have received an invitation to a reception in your honor this Saturday, which is Zakhar's way of expressing its gratitude and deep appreciation for your bravery. Please know that invitations have been sent to the US ambassador and the regional security officer at your embassy. I have every reason to believe they will attend.

The queen and I would also like to extend our personal invitation to you and a guest for a private dinner with us before the reception. My wife speaks very highly of you, and I am looking forward to furthering our acquaintance.

Sincerely, Andre Alexei Marianescu, by the grace of God, King of Zakhar.

"Wow." That was all Tahra could think of to say. And she knew she would cherish this personal note from the king even more than the official letter that had probably already made its way into her personnel file.

And now she had another reason to call Marek. Because just the *idea* of dining with the king and queen made her weak in the knees. The shyness that had plagued her all her life, which she'd always had to struggle to overcome, returned in full force. But she wouldn't feel shy if Marek was with her. *"You are the bravest woman I know,"* he'd told her. *"You have a warrior's heart."* She didn't need him in order to *be* those things. But she needed him to believe she *could be* those things. A fine distinction, but a clear one.

So as soon as Ani left, Tahra found Marek's name in her contacts…and hit the button. But his home phone rang and rang, until the answering machine picked up. She didn't bother leaving a message because there were two other numbers for Marek in her contacts—work and cell. She didn't want to interrupt his work, so she dashed off a text to his cell phone. Then sat down to eat her rapidly cooling breakfast.

She'd just bitten into a scone slathered with butter and strawberry jam when her cell phone rang, and she swallowed quickly. "Hello? Marek?"

"Good morning, *mariskya*. I missed you yesterday."

"I missed you, too." She wanted to ask why she hadn't seen him, but she wasn't going there. She was going to trust him. She was going to believe he had a very good reason why…as well as a very good reason why he couldn't tell her about it. So she hurried to state, "I wanted you to know I've remembered something else." Then proceeded to tell him everything she'd discussed with Alec. "Alec says it's a good sign, and I think he's right."

The sudden silence at the other end puzzled her, until Marek said, "You called Alec before you called me?"

The stiff way he spoke might have slipped right by some women, but not Tahra, and she realized it bothered him she hadn't called him first. "Only because I needed him to confirm I was right about his being the most honest man I—" *Oops*, she thought suddenly. She hadn't meant that as a jab at Marek, at the tangled web of lies and half-truths he'd told her since she'd come out of the coma. Nor had she meant it as a jab at him for the secret he'd kept from her until after he'd asked her to marry him.

She'd gotten past those things. Hadn't she?

"I understand."

Just two words, but she heard the pain underlying the stoic way they were uttered, and she rushed to say, "No, I don't think you do."

"Yes, I do. And you are right. Alec is the most honest man I know, too. He would never stoop to deception… especially not with the woman he loves."

"Stop that," she ordered, practically snapping her words off. "You did what you thought you had to do… to protect me. Right?"

She could hear his breathing accelerate. "Yes," he finally admitted in a low voice.

"So stop acting like a…" At first she couldn't think of something to liken it to, then she said, "Like an early Christian martyr."

That got an unexpected chuckle out of him. "Is that what I am acting like?"

"Yes. No. Not really. Well, sort of. But it's an exaggeration."

There was a smile in his voice when he said, "I am glad we could clear that up." Which made Tahra smile, too. "Is there anything else, *mariskya*, besides the wonderful news that your memory appears to be returning? Because much as I love hearing your voice, I have a staff meeting in twenty minutes, for which I must prepare. And Colonel Marianescu is not a man to accept excuses for being late."

"Just a couple of things."

"And they are?"

She'd never—as far as she could recall—asked a man to be her date for any reason. But if she wanted to take charge of her life… "Well…there's this reception next Saturday."

"Yes, I know. A reception in your honor, which is well deserved. Invitations have been sent to more than five hundred guests."

She faltered. "Five hundred?" Her courage failed her for a moment as she imagined facing that many strangers…all there to meet her. But then she took a mental grip on herself. *You can do this*, her new, stronger self insisted. So she forged ahead. "And the king has invited me to have dinner privately with the queen and him before the reception."

"Another honor."

"Yes, well…the invitation is for me and…a guest." *Just spit it out*, she told herself. "I was wondering if…"

"You are asking me for a date? Is this the new Tahra? The Tahra who wishes to do the proposing?"

Now she knew he was teasing her. "Just say yes."

"Yes," he said promptly.

"That was easy."

He laughed softly. "Is now the time to confess I can deny you nothing that is in my power to give you?"

And just like that her heart melted. As it tended to do whenever he was around. They still had issues to iron out—including Marek's *slight* alpha tendencies. But their love would find a way, because they saw the *world* the same way. They cared about the same issues. Prayed for the same outcomes.

Which reminded her of the other thing she'd made a mental note to discuss with Marek. "I don't mean to keep you. I know you have to get ready for your staff meeting. But I wanted to ask you about the Ibrahim children. How they're doing. And if there's any word on their parents." When he didn't answer right away, she said, "I…I didn't know who else I could ask."

"Did you not receive the card I sent you?"

Chapter 18

"Oh." Tahra looked at her tray, and sure enough, there was a third envelope by her plate. She'd been so sidetracked by the invitation to the reception in her honor and the king's handwritten note she'd completely forgotten it. She berated herself because there was her name across the front of the envelope in Marek's incisive handwriting. She ripped the envelope open, pulled out the note card and read what he'd written there.

Dearest Tahra. I could not bring myself to tell you this in person because I know your tender heart, and I cannot bear to see you cry. If that makes me a coward, then so be it—I am a coward in this way.

Ominous opening words, but Tahra forced herself to keep reading.

I regret to inform you the Ibrahim children's parents were positively identified as having perished in the fire. I have told Rafiq his parents are now with God, and he took the news like the man he will someday be. I would also have explained this to his little sister as best I could with a child so young, but Rafiq insisted it would be easier for Aaliyah to hear the news from him...in private.

Sudden tears blurred her vision, so that the words swam on the page and she could barely make out the rest.

I have spoken with the king, and as I knew he would, the king himself will make all arrangements necessary for the Ibrahim children to be cared for as their parents would have wished.

It is small comfort, I know, but rest assured the men responsible will be caught. You have my word.

Love, Marek.

Tahra was weeping silently by the time she reached the end. "Oh, Marek."

His voice was rough. "I cannot bear it when you cry."

"I'm not crying." But she caught her breath on a sob that gave the lie to her words.

He muttered something under his breath in Zakharan that sounded suspiciously like a curse. Then said in English, "I should not have told you."

"Don't you dare even *think* that." She struggled with herself, and eventually managed to get her emotions under control. "You promised, remember? No trying to shield me." She had to make him understand. "Just because I cried doesn't mean I'm not strong enough to deal with it—I am. I *hurt* for those children, okay? Because I know what they're going through right now. I've been through it myself. And crying is how I deal with that kind of emotional pain—you're going to have to learn to accept it. But I won't fall apart just because I cried. I promise."

"She should be told," Marek announced. He glanced around the conference table. Then he fixed his steady gaze on Colonel Marianescu. "She should be told our plans for the reception."

The colonel shook his head. "I think not."

"It is not fair to her, sir. She should know this reception is not just to honor her, but is also a trap for the Zakharian Liberation Front. A trap baited with the king and queen, yes, but also with her."

"Your personal involvement is coloring your perspective."

Marek stiffened. "My personal *involvement*, sir, has nothing to do with it."

"If the queen is not to be told, Miss Edwards cannot be told."

Angelina spoke up. "And I must object to that, Colonel. The queen should not be kept in the dark, either. She will be furious—and rightly so—when she finds out I did not tell her of the danger in advance. It is even possible she will never trust me again."

"Take that up with the king, both of you," Colonel Marianescu said flatly. "This is his decision."

Marek and Angelina exchanged glances, and she shook her head. He interpreted that to mean, *this is not a battle we can win.* He couldn't just leave it at that, however, even though he'd received a legal order from his superior officer. But he *could* appeal to the king directly, without disobeying a command…because the colonel himself had said, *"Take that up with the king..."*

So he merely said, "Yes, sir," and sat down. Already planning in his mind the arguments he would put forth to the king. Once upon a time Marek would never even have *thought* the king could be wrong—in anything—much less questioned his decisions. But not anymore.

Tahra sat in Queen Juliana's sitting room, watching a private fashion show, Angelina perched on the arm of the sofa beside the queen. Tahra would never have approached the queen for advice about a dress for the reception, despite Ani's recommendation. But Ani had pulled an end run around her—mentioning it to Daphne, the queen's personal maid, who had mentioned it to her mistress, who had picked up the phone and called Tahra. Insisting in a charming way that it was no imposition at all, she'd love to do this. "It'll be fun, Tahra, you'll see."

So here she sat, as formal dress after formal dress was presented for her delectation. She'd been a little nervous at first at this private showing, but the queen—who'd insisted Tahra call her Juliana—had soon put her at her ease.

"That's a lovely fabric," Juliana said when a floating chiffon number in variegated shades of misty rose made an appearance. "Don't you think so? And the color is perfect for you."

"Yes but…isn't the neckline a little…low?"

The queen's eyes twinkled. "It would be if you were

built on voluptuous lines—which you're not—or had no figure at all. Which isn't the case. And that dress will look even better on you than it does on the model. Don't you think so, Angelina?"

"What?" Angelina seemed a little distracted, but then she said, "Oh, yes, absolutely."

"But it looks a little...I don't know...more like a bridesmaid's dress than a killer evening gown," Juliana stated. "Let's see what else there is."

Several more garments passed in review, none of which caught Tahra's fancy. Then she and Juliana both spotted it at the same time. "That's the one," the queen murmured.

Tahra was speechless, but inside she was saying, *Yes, yes, yes!*

"Try it on," the queen insisted.

When she did, Tahra knew it was perfect—and she wanted to see Marek's eyes when he saw her in it. Sophisticated, but not brazen. Elegant, yet sexy. The sapphire blue color made her skin translucent, and the sequined fabric clung in all the right places, making it look as if she'd been dipped into the dress—but in a classy way, not trashy. The gown made a definite statement about the woman who wore it. Shy Tahra would never have even tried it on, deeming it too...something. But the new, self-confident Tahra?

"How much is it?" she asked, craning her neck to try to locate the price tag.

When Angelina found it and told her, Tahra winced. Then she gazed at herself in the mirror once more, and knew that even if she had to eat peanut butter and jelly sandwiches for the rest of the year, Marek was going to see her in this dress.

* * *

Marek had plenty of time to regret his decision to see the king, to argue his case for telling Tahra everything planned for Saturday evening. He'd arrived extra early for his appointment—God forbid he should be late!—and was forced to wait almost half an hour in the outer office, thinking and rethinking his arguments.

"Captain Zale?" The king's appointments secretary stood in front of him. "The king will see you now."

The king was sitting behind his desk, talking with Major Lukas Branko—one of his two favorite bodyguards—but he stood to greet Marek when he walked in.

"That will be all, Lukas," the king said. He smiled his faint smile. "I think I am safe with Marek."

"Yes, Sire." The major rose and cast an assessing eye over Marek before heading for the door, as if he thought the captain was a potential threat...despite the king's assurance. Marek was one of very few men who could go armed in the king's presence—which he was—and he didn't blame Major Branko one bit for being extra cautious. Still, he couldn't help but be amused, even though he presented nothing but a serious, unsmiling, professional face to the major, and then to his sovereign when they were alone.

"Have a seat," the king invited as he reseated himself behind the desk. "What can I do for you?"

"I would prefer to stand, Sire, if it is all the same to you."

That drove the smile from the king's face. He leaned back in his chair with a slight creak of leather and said, "That sounds ominous."

Marek shook his head. "That is not my intention, Sire."

"I take it this has nothing to do with my son."

"No, Sire."

Marek drew a deep breath, but before he could speak the king said, "Then it must be about the plans for Saturday's reception—and my order regarding the secrecy around them." When Marek raised his eyebrows in surprise at the king's perspicacity, the king smiled again. "My cousin mentioned you were not happy about keeping your fiancée in the dark."

"She should be told, Sire. As should the queen." He hesitated. "Three years ago I would have agreed with you. Even two years ago. But Angelina—Captain Mateja-Jones—taught me a few things about women and their abilities, as I think you are well aware. Those lessons were hard-won, Sire—I will not deny it. But I cannot believe the king whose first proclamation upon ascending the throne granted women the right to serve in the military, the king who subsequently maneuvered the Privy Council into allowing women to serve in combat, thinks women cannot be trusted to keep a secret. His own wife among them."

The king steepled his fingers, then touched them to his lips as he considered this. Finally he said, "It is not that I think women cannot be trusted to keep a secret—Captain Mateja-Jones is proof of that. And it is not that I think my wife and your fiancée cannot act as if the reception is nothing more than a way to honor Miss Edwards—the queen especially. She was a brilliant actress, as you well know."

"If not that, then what, Sire?"

The king sighed. "Major Stesha reminded me we do

not know who is a member of the Zakharian Liberation Front and who is not."

"You cannot think—"

"Of course not. The queen would risk her life to save me…and has already done so. I would trust her with anything. As for your fiancée, her actions that day speak for themselves. No, Major Stesha's point is that traitors could exist inside my household, and we have no way of knowing…yet. Every person working inside the palace could be a member of the Zakharian Liberation Front. Even the bodyguards." The king's eyes were as cold as Marek had ever seen them. "Which is why we must limit knowledge of our plans on Saturday to a select few. Every person added to the secret is one more person who could accidentally slip up and say something that would mean nothing to someone who is innocent, but would betray us to someone looking for the smallest sign."

His argument was powerful, and one with which Marek was reluctantly forced to agree. Even if Tahra never forgave him for keeping this secret from her, he could not go against the king, could do nothing that would put any of the royal family in danger. "I understand, Sire."

"Good." The king's smile turned rueful, and the look he gave Marek was man-to-man. "If it is any consolation, I will have no easier time than you explaining my decision…after the fact."

He allowed himself to return the smile. "Small consolation, Sire."

"Yes, well…it is possible nothing will happen at the reception. We can but pray the attack will come when we are best prepared for it, but there are no guarantees.

And if nothing happens, there will be nothing for you to explain."

Marek shook his head slightly. "I see your point, Sire, but I have already kept too many secrets from my fiancée. I will not add to the list by availing myself of that excuse. Besides, Sir Walter Scott said it best when he wrote, 'Oh, what a tangled web we weave/When first we practice to deceive!' Trying to keep lies, half-truths and deceptions straight is too exhausting…and too demeaning to both Tahra and me. I have vowed there will be nothing but honesty between us from now on. Which means I will confess the truth…eventually."

The king's smile deepened, and he made a fencing gesture indicating a hit. "A good policy to follow, and one I learned myself…but only after paying a steep price."

Then his smile faded. "One more thing before you go," he said before Marek could leave. "I want your best, most trustworthy men guarding my son Saturday night. Lukas and Damon have convinced me I need them both on duty to watch over me," he said, referring to Majors Branko and Kostya. "I have already spoken to Captain Mateja-Jones about who I want guarding the queen, and she assures me that in addition to the two bodyguards on duty she will also be there. Ostensibly as a guest with her husband, the US embassy's RSO, but also to watch over the queen. Which relieves my mind of one great worry."

"Then I should also stay with the crown prince, in addition to his—"

The king shook his head. "Miss Edwards needs protection, too, and no one is better suited to that task than you. I would not buy my son's life by placing her life in jeopardy. But..." The king's face was implacable. "My son is the key. The Zakharian Liberation Front cannot succeed in seizing power without him to cloak their actions. Let nothing happen to him, Marek."

"No, Sire. You have my word."

Sergeant Thimo Vasska rode the train back to Drago, his thoughts in turmoil. On the one hand, he was glad he was being recalled to participate in what was being planned for Saturday. It meant a chance to redeem himself in Colonel Borka's eyes. On the other hand, he still couldn't shake the feeling he was being kept in the dark. That something was going on to which he wasn't privy. It shouldn't matter to a soldier—a good soldier didn't question the *reason* behind his orders. He merely followed them to the best of his ability. But still...

He sighed. He'd served his mandatory four years in the Zakharian National Forces and had left the military after working his way up to corporal and becoming something of a demolitions expert. Then he'd gone to work for a construction company and had made a decent living, until...

Until he'd lost his job to a refugee. And he'd been recruited into joining the Zakharian Liberation Front, which had promised to put a stop to the flood of immigrants taking jobs from hardworking Zakharians like himself.

In the first flush of zeal, he'd bought into everything he'd been told. He'd even come up with the idea for the bombs with the fléchettes in the knapsacks, an idea that had been seized upon with fervor. And he'd assembled the ten knapsacks that had been the Zakharian Liberation

Front's first blow for freedom, that had put the organization on the map, so to speak.

But since then he'd had plenty of time on the eastern border to think about exactly what he'd done. Too much time. And he realized he'd let his anger and desire for revenge against one man—the man who'd taken his job—cause him to do what would have been unthinkable a year ago.

But it was too late to turn back now, because he already had blood on his hands. All those who were dead or wounded because of the bombs he'd constructed—war or no—were on his conscience. Added to that, his deliberate attempt to kill the woman who'd seen his face the day he'd left the bomb at the preschool by bribing that nurse's aide meant he was guilty as hell. No, he hadn't been personally responsible for the aide's subsequent death in police custody—Colonel Borka had ordered that. But her death was on his conscience, too.

If he could turn back the clock—but he could not. So all he could do was carry out his new orders. Kidnap the crown prince and force the king to accede to the Zakharian Liberation Front's demands to close the borders, to let no more refugees enter and to expel those who were already here. That, at least, would be some small reparation to his fellow citizens for what he'd done.

Then and only then would he be free…to make his peace with God.

Chapter 19

"The queen sent you these to wear tonight," Ani told Tahra, holding out what couldn't be anything but a jewelry case, one that looked as if it came from a previous century. Ani opened the case and sighed in pure delight, delight that was transferred to Tahra when she saw the contents, too.

"Oh, my gosh. Those are gorgeous!"

"Let me, miss. It would be difficult with your cast." Ani reverently took the sapphire-and-diamond necklace from the case and slipped it around Tahra's neck, fastening it quickly. Then she picked up one matching earring and affixed it to Tahra's left ear before doing the same to the right. "Oh, miss, they are perfect with that dress." She tugged Tahra's arm to guide her to the old-fashioned cheval mirror in the corner of her bedroom so she could see for herself.

Ani is right, Tahra told herself as she turned from side to side. *They're perfect.* The necklace and earrings were just the finishing touch needed. The dress had a full back with a standing collar and three-quarter sleeves but was open-necked in the front. The necklace looked as if it had been made to match the dress, displayed to advantage by the artistically cut neckline and Tahra's pale skin. And the earrings—dangling clusters of sapphires and diamonds—caught the light every time she moved her head.

Ani had arranged Tahra's long, dark hair in an elegant, upswept hairdo Tahra would never have been able to do herself, even without the cast. And when she saw the final product—hair, dress and jewelry—she realized she really *did* resemble her older sister, Carly. The queen had been right about that after all.

A knock on the door to her suite caused Tahra's heart to skip a beat and had her gaze sliding to the clock on her nightstand. "It's Marek," she whispered to herself, but Ani heard her.

"You stay here, miss," Ani ordered. "I will let him in and put him in the sitting room. Then you can make a grand entrance." With that she bustled out.

Tahra took one last look at her reflection in the mirror, then placed her left hand over her pounding heart. "It's just dinner," she reminded herself. "Dinner with the king and queen. Followed by a reception with five hundred guests staring at me."

But Marek will be there, a comforting voice in the back of her mind reminded her. *You can do this.*

She raised her head and tried to channel Carly's supreme self-confidence. No question the dress helped. Not to mention the necklace and earrings represented a small fortune—assuming they were real. And they looked real. More than that, though, they added to the image she wanted to present. Elegant. Sophisticated. Assured.

She was still feeling all those things when she walked into the sitting room and saw Marek standing in front of the fireplace with his back to her, wearing what was obviously a dress uniform—navy blue with a silver belt around his waist—complete with a ceremonial sword at his side. She must have made a slight sound, because he turned at her entrance. And the expression on his face was worth the price she'd paid for the dress.

He whispered something in Zakharan she couldn't translate, and he appeared frozen in place. He breathed suddenly when she walked toward him, paused and slowly rotated so he could get the full effect. His reaction gave her renewed confidence.

"I think you like my dress," she teased.

"What dress?" At first she thought he was teasing her in return, but then he added in all seriousness, "I see the dress, yes. And it is stunning. A perfect foil for you. But it is the woman inside it who takes my breath away. A woman who knows she will be the most beautiful woman at the reception tonight."

"With the queen there?" Tahra asked skeptically, moving close enough so she could rest her hands on Marek's shoulders and look up into his eyes.

"There can be no comparison. Feature for feature, yes, Queen Juliana is more beautiful," he admitted with the honesty she wanted from him—although not, perhaps, at this very moment, when she needed his reaction to bolster her self-confidence. He didn't stop there, though. "But there is a beauty in you that will always outshine hers for me—because your beautiful soul is reflected in your face."

Tahra's eyes were suddenly swimming in tears that threatened to spoil the job Ani had done with her makeup. But before they could spill over, Marek quickly handed her a clean white hankie. "You are not to do that," he said, again without the slightest trace of anything but absolute seriousness in his voice. "You are not to cry when I tell you the truth."

Tahra choked on a laugh and dabbed at the corners of her eyes until she was able to safely blink away what remained of her tears. "I'll try," she said. "But no promises."

Dinner with the king and queen wasn't the ordeal Tahra had expected, for two reasons. First, the royal couple went out of their way to put her at ease with them. Second, Marek, who'd given her a little background as they'd walked from her suite to the private dining room where they were expected.

He'd known the king as far back as he could remember, he told her. "He was three when I was born, so we were never as close as he is to his first cousin, who is only a year older than he is. I knew them then as Andre and Zax, of course—young boys do not care about such things as royal titles. But now I am careful to address them correctly. Zax prefers his military title, Colonel Marianescu, over his royal title, Prince Xavier. And since he is my commanding officer—he is head of internal security, as I have already explained—he addresses me as Captain Zale or Captain. As for the king, I would never address him as Andre, although he still calls me

Marek. But I take that as a sign of affection, the way he calls Majors Branko and Kostya by their first names."

At Tahra's puzzled frown, he added, "They are the king's favorite bodyguards, and, in a way, his friends. I pity him in one sense. He has so few true friends, you see. Men he can trust enough to let down his guard. Zax, of course. Alec Jones. Princess Mara's husband, Trace McKinnon. And the majors—he served with them in Afghanistan when he was in the Zakharian National Forces. That created an unbreakable bond of friendship."

With that, Tahra was no longer apprehensive about having dinner with Zakhar's ruler. He went from being an august personage to a normal human being—one who couldn't afford to have many friends—and Tahra's heart went out to him. She knew what it was like to have an extremely small circle you could trust.

"As for the queen," Marek continued, unaware Tahra's thoughts had strayed. "I have known her longer than I have known her."

"That doesn't make sense."

His eyes twinkled at her. "Ahh, but it does, if you knew the king assigned me to surreptitiously watch over her when she was living in Hollywood. Before she returned to Zakhar to film *King's Ransom* and reunited with the king."

"You're kidding!"

He shook his head. "From the moment he ascended the throne, he sent me to command a team guarding her...without her knowledge or consent. Then he appointed me head of her security detail when they were married, which was when I was actually introduced to the queen."

"And I thought *you* were über-alpha," she murmured. "But compared to the king..."

Marek laughed. "Yes. He is somewhat...autocratic... where the queen is concerned. But he is a great king nevertheless."

For a moment it looked as if he was going to say something more, but he stopped himself, and Tahra was intrigued. But they arrived at their destination before she could ask him about it, and then it slipped her mind.

Tahra saw Juliana first. The queen was wearing a gorgeous gown in lavender blue, but the overall effect was muted, as if she was trying to fade into the background. Which could never happen, but Tahra was touched Juliana was making an effort to *not* be the center of attention at the reception in Tahra's honor. She was also quick to note the gown was cleverly designed to hide the queen's expectant condition from prying eyes. *"We haven't announced it yet—we wanted to wait until after I pass my first trimester,"* she remembered the queen saying at their luncheon, and realized, *she won't be able to hide it much longer.*

Then the king entered the room, wearing a dress uniform similar to Marek's. She tried to curtsy when Marek introduced her to him, but it was a little awkward. While her dress was a sheath, it wasn't so tight she couldn't move, but having her right wrist in a cast stymied her—she couldn't get proper purchase on the material.

But the king merely laughed—kindly—and said, "It is I who should be bending the knee to you, Miss Edwards. Bravery should always take precedence over an accident of birth."

"Oh. Well, I..." She fumbled for words to say after

that but couldn't think of anything. Then was secretly thrilled when the king gently raised her right hand to his lips and kissed the tips of her fingers, despite the cast on her wrist.

Tahra's enjoyment of dinner was assured when the king himself escorted her to the table, leaving Marek to accompany the queen. He entertained her with charming stories of her fiancé and his sisters and brothers when they were growing up—nothing embarrassing, just endearing. "He is the oldest of seven," the king explained. "I always envied him that. I only had the one sister."

"Whom you adore," the queen reminded him.

"Of course," the king replied, as if it went without saying. "But I would have loved being the oldest of so many, as Marek was. And he took that role very seriously."

"Is that where he gets his…umm…protective tendencies?" Tahra asked. "Especially toward women?"

"No, that comes from being Zakharian," the queen volunteered, throwing the king a saucy look. "Zakharian men are—"

"Quick learners," the king finished for her. He held his hand out to his wife, which she took with a tender, amused smile, and Tahra caught her breath in wonder at the unshielded love she saw in both sets of eyes. As if the world faded away when they gazed at each other.

"'Two hearts as one,'" Tahra whispered to herself, quoting from the queen's last movie, *King's Ransom*. "'Forever and a day.'" The epitaph carved in Latin upon the tomb of the first king and queen of Zakhar, a phrase that expressed the eternal love they'd shared. Which… apparently…also applied to Zakhar's current king and queen.

She glanced over at Marek and saw the same expression in his eyes when he looked at her that was in the king's eyes when he looked at the queen. Without even thinking about it, her lips parted and she mouthed, "I love you," to Marek. Words she hadn't said to him eight days ago when they'd made love for the first time. Words he deserved.

A fire was kindled in his bright blue eyes, and there was an urgency in his face that told Tahra if they were alone he would have taken her in his arms and kissed her until the world faded away for both of them. But they weren't alone. And they not only had to finish out this dinner, they also had to attend the reception in her honor. Which meant it would be hours before they could be alone.

Soon, she promised herself. All they had to do was get through the next four hours. *And then...*

From his vantage point a half mile away, Sergeant Vasska watched cars and limousines creep along the impressive drive leading up to the royal palace. The gates were thrown wide, but every vehicle was stopped at the gate, and two armed guards examined the invitation extended by the vehicles' occupants while names were checked off against a list held by a third man.

That wasn't the only gauntlet a guest had to face. Metal detectors were set up at the three entrances to the Great Hall—the main one, which was always used, and the two side gates that were used for such a large crowd as tonight's.

But the sergeant wasn't worried about the metal detectors. He and the two men with him weren't intending to enter the Great Hall. And they certainly weren't intending to enter the palace through the front gate. Once the gala reception was in full swing, he and his men would make their way through a back entrance and would be smuggled in disguised as palace maintenance men by two members of the Zakharian Liberation Front who truly *were* members of the maintenance crew. Once inside, one of the men with him would set off a diversionary bomb in another part of the palace—one the sergeant had constructed and had smuggled in earlier, a bomb that would make a lot of noise but would cause minimal damage...he hoped. The sound would cause panic in the Great Hall and draw off the guards...again, he hoped. While that was going on, he and the other three members of the Zakharian Liberation Front would make their way to the second floor and kidnap the crown prince.

Then escape the same way they arrived. Unnoticed.

"It is time, Sire," said the man Tahra recognized as Major Lukas Branko from when he'd accompanied her to her follow-up appointment at the hospital. Another man was with him, dressed exactly the same way—dark, formal suit, but with his jacket open, as if for quick access to a gun—and she wondered if this was the other major Marek had mentioned was one of the king's favorite bodyguards, Major Kostya.

Then two other men entered the room, similarly dressed, and they arranged themselves on either side of the queen. And for the first time Tahra realized just how dangerous was the life the queen lived...merely from being married to the king. The threat of assassination was always there. Not just for the king, but for herself.

And her son.

The thought popped unbidden into Tahra's head, and she couldn't fathom living like that day in and day out. *How does the queen do it?* she wondered. *How does she bear knowing her husband or her son could be assassinated in the blink of an eye? Or that she might be a target herself? How does she do it and still manage to be happy?*

She watched as the king took the queen's hand and tucked it securely in the crook of his arm. Then he murmured something to her in Zakharan, and the radiant smile that accompanied her response took Tahra's breath away.

Then it came to her. *They live each day as if it were their last. They must. That's the only way they can bear knowing what might happen.*

She turned her gaze to Marek, who was affixing something in his ear that matched the four bodyguards'—something she recognized as a wireless earpiece—and she realized once again how precarious *his* hold on life was, too. Because he would always interpose his body between danger and whoever he was guarding.

She also realized something else. *The relationship the queen has with the king...that's the kind of relationship I want with Marek.*

The job he did—he could be dead any minute. And she vowed then and there she would never weep bitter tears over lost chances, would never send Marek off to work not knowing he was loved more than anything in the world. And if he never came home, she would have no cause for regret. She would *grieve*...but she wouldn't regret.

* * *

Marek and Tahra stood just behind the king and queen at the top of the Grand Staircase leading into the Great Hall. They were silently joined by Colonel Marianescu, who took his place on Tahra's left, and Marek's eyes met the colonel's over her head. The two men didn't nod or acknowledge in any way what was about to take place, but the shared knowledge was in their eyes.

A hush had descended on the crowd assembled below when the king and queen appeared. Now the band, which had been playing soft background music, moved immediately into the Zakharian national anthem, and the Zakharians in the Great Hall began singing the stirring lyrics that accompanied the well-known music.

The five of them, especially the king, stood immobile at the top of the stairs while the anthem played. They were flanked by the royals' four bodyguards, but Marek knew if someone opened fire from below, they wouldn't stand a chance—no bodyguard alive was as fast as a bullet.

All they could hope for was that the highly publicized metal detectors had done their job, preventing anyone from smuggling a gun or guns into the reception. And if the Zakharian Liberation Front knew it couldn't accomplish its goal of assassinating the king, the queen and Colonel Marianescu that way…

It had gone against the grain for the king to absent himself from public appearances. The queen, too, for that matter. But they'd done it. They'd cancelled everything that might take them outside the palace this past week, and for the next three weeks, as a way of forcing the Zakharian Liberation Front to make a tough choice—attempt to storm the palace in order to carry out the assassinations. All three of their primary targets would be together in one room. And there was an added bonus from their perspective—Tahra would also be there. The woman who could identify one of the initial bombers and possibly bring down the whole organization like a house of cards.

The entire Privy Council had—as a matter of course—received an invitation to tonight's reception. And every councillor had accepted the invitation, including Colonel Lermontov. *He is down there somewhere*, Marek told himself. *He would not dare be absent—too suspicious otherwise.*

The band reached the end of the national anthem, and a huge cheer rose from the assemblage, which the king acknowledged with his faint smile and an upraised hand. Then the tight little group of nine began descending the Grand Staircase.

Two maintenance men approached one of the palace service doors, genially grumbling to the guard on duty about having to go outside to smoke. The first had already passed through the door when the second dropped his pack of cigarettes right at the guard's feet. He cursed and bent down to retrieve it, then came up swinging.

The guard never knew what hit him.

The two men had the guard bound and gagged in no time, and they dragged his body down the hallway to a closet containing cleaning supplies and other maintenance gear.

Then they exited the service door. Six minutes later five men entered through the same door. All were dressed as part of the maintenance crew—the three new ones indistinguishable from the first two—and their hands were bare.

The five paused and listened, but heard nothing to indicate anyone was aware the palace had been invaded. Then they moved purposefully down the hallway.

As soon as they were out of sight a man dressed as a waiter stepped out of the shadows. He touched his earpiece and said in an undertone, "Jay-three to Dee-two and Dee-one. One man down. Five men disguised as members of the maintenance crew are heading your way. If they are armed, it can only be light assault weapons hidden under their coveralls—no heavy firepower. Repeat, no heavy firepower. It has begun."

Chapter 20

Marek heard the warning, but it wasn't the one he was expecting. *Five* men? Only five to take down three primary targets and a secondary target? And no assault weapons? It didn't make sense. If his theory was correct, the Zakharian Liberation Front needed the king, the queen and Colonel Marianescu *dead*, not merely wounded. Yes, a man shot in the head or through the heart with a pistol was just as dead as a man shot with an assault rifle or a submachine gun. But a pistol would require closer range, something the Zakharian Liberation Front had to know was less likely with the bodyguards surrounding the royal family.

No, it didn't make sense…unless the five were a decoy of some kind.

He moved a little away from the receiving line—he wasn't there to shake hands, he was only there to watch over Tahra—and tapped his earpiece. "Say again, Jay-three. How many men?"

"Five men. Repeat, five total."

He barely waited for the response before saying, "Dee-two, can you confirm?"

"Confirm. Five men dressed as maintenance crew just entered the chapel. No, wait. One has peeled off, heading north. Repeat, four men entering the chapel."

"Dee-one here," said a low voice, almost in a whisper. "I am in the chapel and I have eyes on four targets. Repeat, I have eyes on four targets."

The chapel, in the older part of the palace. Not the Great Hall, where the reception was taking place. Marek tapped his earpiece again. "This is Captain Zale. Stay alert. This could be a decoy, not the main thrust of the attack. Repeat. Stay alert. Who has eyes on the fifth man?"

"This is Bee-five. The lone maintenance man has entered the kitchen. Repeat, one target has entered the kitchen."

"Marek." His name was spoken in a hushed undertone behind him. He swung around and saw Angelina, who, since she was also wearing an earpiece, had obviously heard everything that had just been broadcast.

"It makes no sense," he told her in a tight voice. "An all-out assassination attempt with only five men armed with just light weapons?"

"Agreed. But what if we are wrong? We dangled the bait, but what if they are not biting? What if they do not intend assassination tonight?"

Then it came to him. "The crown prince," he whispered. He whirled for the door, then halted abruptly, turning and gazing at Tahra standing beside the king and queen in the receiving line, torn by his competing duties.

"Go! I will guard Tahra!" Angelina ordered.

"You are guarding the queen."

"Not officially. Now go!"

He went. Not by way of the Grand Staircase, which would be obvious to everyone, but by the back stairs, the shortcut he usually took from his office to the second floor, where the crown prince's suite was located, next to his mother's. Marek was just about to announce the possible target to the security forces arrayed throughout the palace, when he heard Angelina's calm voice in his ear.

"All security units. This is Captain Mateja-Jones. The crown prince may be the target. Repeat, the crown prince may be the target. Captain Zale is on his way to the crown prince's suite. Units five and six move in to cover him. All other units remain in place. Repeat. All units except five and six remain in place. This could be a decoy or the leading edge of a two-pronged attack. All security units copy my orders."

Warmth speared through Marek as he heard nothing but "Unit one, copy, unit two, copy" and right down the line. Five years ago, a female officer giving orders to men would have occasioned at least a slight hesitation. But not anymore.

"Dee-one," Angelina continued. "Do you still have eyes on the targets in the chapel?"

"Yes, sir," came the somewhat hushed voice. "They appear to be waiting for something."

"Bee-five? Same question. Eyes on the target?"

"I do not have eyes on the target, sir, but he has not yet emerged from the kitchen."

Marek was almost to the crown prince's suite, and he could see units five and six converging on him, but he tapped his earpiece and said, "Bee-five, can you enter the kitchen unnoticed?"

"Negative, sir."

"Jay-three? You are disguised as a waiter."

"I'm on it, sir. ETA thirty seconds." They were the longest thirty seconds of Marek's life. Then he heard, "Jay-three in the kitchen. There is no maintenance man here. Repeat, no target here. But the service elevator appears to have gone to the fourth floor."

Marek cursed under his breath, and he knew Angelina would be doing the same. He pounded on the door to the crown prince's suite, knowing better than to just barge in—he had no intention of being shot by his own men. "It is Captain Zale," he barked. "Today's code word is *eucalyptus*. Open up."

Tahra was exhausted by the time the receiving line was finished. Her feet hurt, her left hand—which she'd been forced to substitute for the right one she couldn't use to shake hands with while her wrist was in a cast—was practically numb, and her smile felt glued to her face and just as fake.

"How do you do it?" she murmured to the queen at her side.

Juliana sighed softly. "I think about something else, if I can."

Tahra glanced around. She'd noticed when Marek had left her side, but she'd expected him to return eventually. He hadn't. And now she wondered where he was. Then Angelina was there, drawing Tahra a little to one side for a private word.

"Marek had to check on the crown prince," she said softly. "I promised him I would watch over you in his absence."

Tahra frowned. "Watch over me? Why does anyone need to watch over me?"

Angelina looked as if she'd like to say more…but couldn't. "That you will have to ask him. Suffice it to say it is necessary."

Tahra didn't like it. *More secrets*, she thought. *And after he promised me…*

Then she remembered her vow earlier this evening. She wasn't going to sweat the small stuff—and compared to what she and Marek shared, this *was* small stuff. If he was keeping a secret from her, he had a damned good reason; he'd given her his word and she was going to believe him.

"Well," she told Angelina, "if you're going to watch over me, I guess that means when I go to the ladies' room, you go. Which means you're going now because I have to go now."

Angelina looked torn. "I cannot leave the queen."

"You're not on duty," Tahra began, and then things started falling into place. "You *are*, aren't you? And so is Marek." Her voice was hushed. "That's why he had to leave, because something is going down." She put two and two together. "The Zakharian Liberation Front. And it has nothing to do with the refugees. Which means… assassination? Kidnapping? What?"

"I cannot tell you," Angelina insisted. "I *cannot*."

"I'll ask the queen," Tahra said, turning to look for her.

Angelina grabbed her arm. "She does not know, either."

A chill shivered through her. Whatever it was, it was bad. So bad not even the queen had been told. But that didn't remove her immediate problem, it only exacerbated it. "Angelina," she began, but then she spotted Marek wending his way toward her through the crowd. "Oh, thank God."

When Marek reached the two women, Angelina pulled him a little to one side and asked quietly, "The prince?"

He assured her just as quietly, "Safe. Units five and six arrived when I did. He has been moved to another location within the palace, and he has a dozen men surrounding him, with far more firepower than the five intruders we know are here."

"The four in the chapel are under observation, but—"

"Yes," he said. "One is unaccounted for. If we knew where he was…"

"Yes, if we knew where he was, we could nullify them all. But I am concerned about the missing man. And there is still—"

"Still the possibility this is a feint and the real attack will come when we least expect it," he finished for her. He couldn't keep the frustration out of his voice when he added, "I would give five years off my life to *know*."

Angelina's wry smile held nothing but understanding. "I feel the same. But that reminds me, I must return to the queen now that you are here to guard Tahra." She turned to where Tahra had been…but she was gone. "Where did she go? She was right here."

Marek swung around, then frantically scanned the crowded room, his heart clutching when he couldn't spot her. "Tahra," he mouthed as guilt swamped him. What kind of bodyguard was he, that he could let her out of his sight for even a moment?

"The ladies' room," Angelina said quickly. "She said she had to go, but I told her I could not leave the queen for that long, and then you showed up, and…"

"Stay with the queen," Marek told her. "I will find Tahra."

"Wait," Angelina cried after him. "You cannot go into the—" But he had already disappeared into the crowd.

Tahra had slipped away as soon as Marek and Angelina had begun talking. There was no way she was going to interfere with them doing their jobs, but her need was urgent. So she'd made her way through the packed room as best she could, heading for the nearest exit and what she hoped would be an obvious ladies' room. She was stopped several times by people who recognized her as the recipient of Zakhar's highest civilian honor—which the king had presented to her prior to the receiving line—but she thanked them shyly and quickly excused herself.

When she finally exited the main entrance into the Great Hall, she saw a long line of women leading out of a discreetly recessed doorway and correctly interpreted that as her destination. But the line was too long. Then she muttered, "Duh!" under her breath and headed for the staircase and her suite, which wasn't that far away.

Once her mission was finally accomplished, Tahra took a moment to check her hair and makeup and was just adding a little lip gloss when the palace was rocked by a loud explosion, emanating from somewhere overhead.

* * *

Panicked screams from the women in line by the ladies' room and the crowd inside the Great Hall didn't block out the sudden spate of reports coming in on Marek's earpiece.

"This is Bee-five. Jay-three is with me. We took the stairs to the fourth floor in pursuit of the target. We apprehended him, but not until he'd already set off a bomb in a small conference room. The bomb appears to have been a diversion tactic, because despite the noise there appears to be minimal damage. But we were too late to—"

Another voice cut in. "This is Dee-one in the chapel. The four targets are on the move. Repeat, the four targets are on the move, heading out of the chapel. Destination unknown."

Marek took a moment to push his way through the screaming women and thrust his head into the ladies' room. "Tahra?" he bellowed. When no answer was forthcoming, he quickly apologized to the women and made for the stairs. If she wasn't in the ladies' room, there was only one other place she could be.

He tapped his earpiece. "This is Captain Zale, heading to the second floor. Status on the royals?"

"The king is safe," said a voice he recognized as belonging to Major Kostya.

"So is the queen," Angelina chimed in. "And Colonel Marianescu."

Marek figured all three were together somewhere, under bodyguard protection, and he gave Angelina bonus points for not stating that over an encrypted military channel they hoped was secure…but couldn't be absolutely sure about.

As he raced up the staircase, praying Tahra was safely inside her room and not wandering around unprotected somewhere, he heard the unmistakable chatter of machine gunfire outside the palace. *I knew it! I knew the men inside the palace were just the leading edge of the attack.*

He frantically unbuttoned his dress uniform jacket and drew his SIG SAUER P320 from its shoulder holster. But he couldn't stop to investigate what was happening outside. He had to trust that the forces arrayed against the Zakharian Liberation Front they'd *hoped* would strike tonight were sufficient to handle whatever was thrown against them. His job was to protect Tahra. Not just because the king had ordered it, and Marek would never again—not while breath remained in his body—fail his king. But because Tahra was his world. If the members of the Zakharian Liberation Front who'd already infiltrated the palace saw her, they would have to silence her. And he couldn't let that happen.

At first Tahra waited in her suite after the explosion. She'd already figured out by what Angelina had said and what she *hadn't* said that something was going on. "They've set a trap for the Zakharian Liberation Front," she reasoned beneath her breath. "That's the only thing that makes sense."

And if the terrorists were taking the bait, as seemed likely, the true motive behind all the attacks didn't have anything to do with the refugees. What had Marek said in his office? *"It is nothing I can name, just a feeling there is something we are overlooking."*

"Oh, God," she whispered as the realization dawned. When you swept away all the extraneous clutter, all you were left with was the oldest motive in the world—a grab for power. And hadn't she just been thinking about this very thing after dinner? About the threat of assassination that hung over the royal family?

Including their son.

"Oh, no. No." Not an innocent little boy. They couldn't. They *couldn't*!

Then she heard Marek's voice in her head. *"Why are you surprised? If people would kill dozens of children in a schoolyard—which you prevented—why should one child be any different?"*

She had to find Marek. She had to *make* him tell her the crown prince was safe, that he'd already planned for this contingency. Because if not…

Tahra pressed her ear against the door and didn't hear anything, but the solid oak was something of a sound barrier. So she opened the door and peeked out. She didn't see anything, so she stepped cautiously out the door and turned in the direction that would take her back down the way she'd come up.

A sound behind her made her whirl around. Four men in coveralls she recognized as those worn by the palace staff were heading in the opposite direction, and her first reaction was to heave a sigh of relief. But then she realized the men were moving *away* from the explosion, not toward it as most people would have done—especially someone who worked in the palace. And the shock made her gasp.

One man heard her. Turned. And when their eyes met across the short distance, Tahra was suddenly rooted to the spot as her memory returned in waves. Those eyes. She knew those eyes. That face. And just as she had in the schoolyard, she knew why he was here. She *knew.*

But this time he didn't turn and walk away. This time his hand reached for something beneath the coverall he wore. He muttered to the three men with him, who all swung around, also reaching.

And Tahra knew it was too late to run.

Chapter 21

Marek turned the corner and saw Tahra standing in the hallway, her back to him. Apparently frozen. Beyond her stood four men, garbed as members of the palace maintenance crew. Their right hands were moving inside their dark blue coveralls, reaching for what he instinctively knew were guns.

Time slowed to a painful crawl. Desperately running, Marek reached Tahra and shouldered her to one side, then stood in front of her and squared up in perfect professional stance, with two hands on his weapon. Took careful aim. And squeezed the trigger. Again. And again.

Three of the shots the men got off went wide, but the fourth bullet whizzed so closely to Marek's left arm the fabric of his uniform was singed. Then four bodies thudded to the floor, one after the other, guns falling harmlessly from their hands onto the carpet runner. Marek moved on autopilot to kick their weapons away, his SIG SAUER still pointed at the men on the ground just in case any of them were still a threat. His breath rasped in his throat and his heart pounded as fear-induced adrenaline pumped through his body. All he could think of was *Almost too late. Almost too late.* A split second later, and Tahra would have been dead.

He went down on one knee and reached to check their pulses, then realized two of the men were still alive. He tapped his earpiece. "This is Captain Zale. I need an ambulance and emergency responders *now.* Second floor, outside Princess Mara's suite. The four targets from the chapel are down, but two are still alive. Repeat, four targets are down, but two are still alive, and I need assistance *now.*"

Then he heard a voice he recognized. "This is General Miroslav. Forces under my command have just intercepted two troop carriers attempting to crash the front gates, and a third troop carrier was intercepted at the rear gate. Shots were fired, but all attackers are either dead or in custody. Members of the Zakharian Liberation Front also attempted to seize control of the Drago airport, the train station and the main communications hubs—television, radio, telephone and internet. All attempts failed. Preliminary casualty reports for our forces are light. Enemy casualties are heavy."

Marek glanced up and saw Tahra clinging to the wall, her body shaking. He moved to her side, wrapping his left arm around her, but keeping his gun hand free and turning them so he could keep an eye on the four men on the ground.

"Shh," he whispered against her ear as she clung

to him, weeping softly. "You are not to cry in front of me, remember?"

"I remember," she said, her tears still flowing silently. "Oh, Marek, I remember. I *remember*."

He froze. "Say that again?"

"I remember. Everything. You. Me. The past eighteen months. I saw him and I remembered."

"Him?"

"The man from the schoolyard. He was one of the four maintenance men. He turned around and looked at me a minute ago, and it was the same way he looked at me then. His eyes. His face. And I knew…" She choked on a sob. "But I couldn't move. I *couldn't*. I thought I was going to die and you'd never know… I *remember* you. Oh, Marek."

He would have kissed her…if he'd dared. But until the terrorists were secured, he couldn't risk letting himself be distracted. His arm tightened on Tahra instead, holding her so close he was afraid he'd hurt her. "Hush now," he insisted. "Remembering is cause for rejoicing, not weeping."

A statement that made her choke again, but this time on laughter, not tears. "That's so like you," she replied. "Telling me what to do. Well, I have news for you—I'll cry if I want to, you hear me? You can't—"

Whatever else Tahra was going to say was lost as a dozen men rushed up to them, carrying stretchers… and guns.

Two days later Marek and Angelina identified themselves to the guards outside a hospital room, then walked inside. The man in the bed, though he had non-life-threatening injuries, had been positively identified by his fingerprints as a onetime corporal in the Zakharian National Forces.

They'd learned a lot about him in the day and a half the doctors had said he was too doped up to talk, and everything they'd learned had done nothing but add ammunition to their case against him. He'd been a demolitions expert in the military, then had gone to work in construction. He'd lost his job a year ago, and his neighbors claimed he'd blamed that loss on the immigrants moving into Zakhar. No one knew what he was doing now, but he'd come and gone at odd hours of the day and night. He'd been mysteriously absent from his home for more than a week recently, before showing up out of the blue and then disappearing again.

The prisoner had been questioned by Major Stesha's men more than once…and had refused to answer every time, not even to state his true name. Which was why Angelina and Marek had been called in. Now the man raised dull, listless eyes when they entered, then returned to gazing out the window. "I have nothing to say," he told them.

"That may well be," Marek told him. "But we have something to say to you."

The man didn't even bother to make eye contact again. "What?"

"Are you aware of the penalty for high treason?" Angelina said softly.

That got his attention. "High treason? What do you mean, high treason?" he demanded. "I—"

Marek knew his voice was hard and cold when he said, "Attempted regicide is high treason." He and Angelina had agreed he would play "bad cop" against her "good cop," but right now he wasn't acting. This was the man responsible for putting Tahra in the hospital. This was the man who'd bribed a nurse's aide to switch Tahra's IV bag, to murder her in cold blood. And this was the man who'd been heading for the crown prince's suite two days ago, intending to do what?

"Regicide?" The man seemed honestly horrified.

Angelina put a hand on Marek's arm. "That is not yet proved," she pretended to remind him.

"Do you think a jury would care? Every man in the Zakharian Liberation Front who goes on trial will be convicted of high treason. And the penalty is—"

"No, no," Angelina protested, covering her ears as if she were too sensitive to hear.

"An easy death will not be yours," Marek continued implacably. "You will be hanged. Drawn. Quartered. Disemboweled. Emasculated. Forced to watch parts of yourself burned before your eyes. *That* is the penalty for attempted regicide."

"No!" The man was practically shouting. "I know nothing of any attempt to kill the king!"

"Perhaps he is telling the truth," Angelina implored Marek, but he shook his head.

"He was heading for the crown prince's suite. When you combine that with the armed attempt to storm the palace, the insurrectionist attempts to take over the communications hubs, the airport and the train station, only one conclusion can be drawn. And attempting to assassinate *any* member of the royal family carries the same penalty as attempted regicide."

"No, I tell you. No! We did not intend to kill the crown prince. Kidnap him, yes. But only to force the king to accede to our demands. We would never have *harmed* the prince, no matter what—he is our future king!"

"If you could *prove* that," Angelina said swiftly, as if trying to get a word in before Marek could. "Perhaps the king could be persuaded to grant you clemency."

"There is still the assault on the palace to answer for," Marek insisted. "That can only be an assassination attempt. And for that someone must pay."

"I swear to you, I know nothing of any plot to kill the king. My assignment was to kidnap the crown prince. Hold him—safely!—until the king agreed to close the borders and expel the immigrants already here. That is all. How could the king do that if he was dead?" The honest bewilderment on his face was convincing to his listeners.

"There must be some way to prove your innocence," Angelina said. "At least where high treason is concerned. The king, he forgave the men who tried to kill him before, remember? He commuted their sentences to life in prison."

"It was Colonel Borka," the man blurted out. "That is not his real name, of course. No one used his real name in the Zakharian Liberation Front. Too dangerous. But I have met him. I am positive I could identify him. I knew there was something the rank and file was not being told, but I never imagined it involved assassinating the king."

Marek was hard-pressed not to smile at how guilelessly Angelina said, "Now, *that* is a good idea! If you could identify Colonel Borka…I would testify to how cooperative you were, how appalled you were to find out you had been duped."

"Yes," the onetime corporal said. "I was a sergeant

in the Zakharian Liberation Front. Sergeant Thimo Vasska. Colonel Damek Borka was the name he used. I do not know his real name, although from the beginning he reminded me of… That is…" He trailed off, casting an uncertain glance at his two inquisitors.

Marek drew a stack of photographs from his breast pocket. "I have some photos. Would you be willing to look through them, to see if anyone seems familiar?"

"Of course!"

Marek pulled a wheeled table across the bed, then began laying the pictures down one by one in front of the prisoner. The stack included the face of every man on the Privy Council, but the one he wanted confirmation on—Colonel Lermontov—was buried in the middle.

Face after face was laid on the table, and after the first dozen were rejected the man began to obviously despair. "No," he continued to say. "No. I am afraid… No."

Then Marek placed Colonel Lermontov's photo on the table.

"That is him!"

"Are you positive?" Angelina asked. "Look carefully. You do not want to accuse an innocent man."

"It is him, I tell you. It is him. He resembles the king's chief councillor, I know, but that is Colonel Damek Borka, the supreme commander of the Zakharian Liberation Front!"

Angelina darted a smile of triumph at Marek, then wiped the expression from her face before the man in the bed could see it. "Thank you, Corporal. Your cooperation is duly noted."

Marek nodded approvingly to himself when Angelina didn't mention the onetime corporal could still face the death penalty—no sense in reminding him while they still needed his cooperation. Someday he would tell the corporal...would take fierce pleasure in doing so...but not today.

"So once we received confirmation from the terrorist who set off the diversionary bomb and the other one who survived being shot," Marek told Alec as the four of them—Alec, Angelina, Tahra and Marek—relaxed in the Joneses' living room after dinner a week later, "we arrested Colonel Lermontov. And others."

Alec glanced down at Angelina, who was nestled against his shoulder, then back at Marek, who had his arm around Tahra. "Is that really the penalty for high treason in Zakhar? Don't take offense, but it sounds pretty barbaric."

Marek smiled. "No offense taken. No one has died that way in over three hundred years, but yes, it is still the law."

"Strong incentive not to commit high treason, I'd say."

"That is exactly the point," Angelina threw in before Marek could.

Marek frowned as he considered the issue for a moment, then he said slowly, "I will not say the king was wrong to acquiesce to the queen's plea for leniency for the five men—including his own cousin—who conspired to kill him a few years back. The queen is not Zakharian, and she could not bear the thought of any man dying in that fashion. But it is possible his decision in that case had some impact on the men who attempted to assassinate the crown prince eighteen months ago.

And on Colonel Lermontov's decision to try to seize power now."

"Especially on Colonel Lermontov," Angelina concurred.

"You agree with that law?" Alec asked her, surprised.

"This is my king," she explained, as if it should be obvious. "His wife. His child. The royal *family*."

Tahra caught Marek's eyes. "You agree with the law, too, don't you?"

He couldn't lie to her. "Yes. And yes, it is barbaric. But it had been an effective deterrent for three hundred years…until the queen begged the king not to impose the penalty. If he had—" Marek shrugged. "Who can say? All I know is no one attempts to assassinate my king or his family and gets away with it. No one. I would call down the wrath of God if I could on any man who so dares."

Tahra looked across at Alec, who still appeared upset. "It's not our country," she said softly. "You and I, we're Americans. So from our perspective, it seems… barbaric. But let me ask you this. How would you feel if someone tried to kill Drew? Or Angelina? Wouldn't you want him prosecuted to the fullest extent of the law? And maybe…even beyond it?"

Alec opened his mouth, then closed it again, words unsaid. But Tahra wasn't finished. "My sister shot the man who was trying to kill her fiancé. Angelina shot and killed a man defending you. You shot and killed two men in self-defense before you ever came to Zakhar. And Marek…" She turned to smile at him in a way that made his heart turn over. "Marek shot four men who were going to shoot me. Two of them died. Am I sorry they died? Yes, of course. But I'd rather it was them than me."

Alec nodded slowly. "When you put it that way, I guess it's all a matter of degree."

They talked of other things for a few minutes, then Alec said to Tahra, "So now that your memory has returned, when should I expect you back at work?"

"Monday," she replied promptly. She held up her right hand. "My computer skills won't be up to par until this cast comes off. But other than that..."

"That's great news. I can hardly wait."

Tahra made a face. "Umm, there *is* one thing, though. I'll need a week of vacation in about three weeks."

Alec laughed. "Yeah, I figured. Won't be a problem because I won't be here, either."

"I keep forgetting," Tahra said. "My sister's marrying your brother." When everyone turned startled eyes on her, she said, "What?" Then she seemed to get it. "This is *not* amnesia," she asserted. "This is just your average, ordinary kind of forgetting." She smiled up at Marek, a smile that drove every thought out of his head except one—Tahra was his. Truly his. "I might forget that in three weeks I'm going to be related to my boss by marriage. But there are some things I'll *never* forget. Ever again."

Epilogue

"You've changed," Carly told Tahra with a little note of gladness in her voice as she put the finishing touches to her wedding day makeup while eyeing her younger sister in the mirror at the same time. "You're a lot stronger than I ever gave you credit for." A shoeless Tahra was sitting cross-legged on the bed the way she used to when she was a nine-year-old girl watching her sixteen-year-old sister get ready for dates all those years ago.

This time, though, Tahra wasn't wearing jeans and a T-shirt. She'd already donned the maid of honor dress she'd bought in Zakhar and brought home with her—a dress that made a definite statement without in any way detracting from the bride—and the frothy, rose-colored layers of her chiffon skirt were fluffed around her so they wouldn't get crushed. When Carly was finished, she came to sit next to Tahra on the bed, taking her sister's hands in hers.

"After Mom and Dad died, I was so afraid the state would try to separate us," she explained in a low voice. "Fortunately, Mom and Dad's will made sure that didn't happen. Naming Dad's attorney as our guardian until I was old enough to assume guardianship of you was a smart move, and the money we inherited made it possible for us to stay together. But I was always afraid the state would step in if I wasn't the perfect guardian... which meant I couldn't let anything happen to you—one mistake on my part could have been all the excuse they were looking for. I honestly didn't realize how overprotective and bossy I was being."

"Not bossy. But yes, overprotective. I didn't realize it, either, until a little while ago, until I saw Marek doing the same thing."

Carly sighed softly. "Then when Jack...died...it was even worse. I couldn't lose someone else I loved, especially after losing Mom and Dad. I just *couldn't*."

"I know you only wanted what was best for me," Tahra began, but Carly shook her head decisively.

"I didn't see I was hurting you, not helping you. It wasn't until I met Shane...and fell in love with him, that I realized you can't live someone else's life for them. You can't stop them from making choices and taking risks they *need* to take...because of who they are. Even if it means you end up with a broken heart. You have to let them be the person they are and let them grow into the person they want to be. Not the person *you* want them to be."

She leaned over and kissed Tahra's check. "I'm so glad I didn't…well…cause any damage you couldn't overcome."

"You didn't," Tahra rushed to assure her, squeezing her sister's hands. "Part of it was my fault—you were so good at it that it was always easier to let you make the decisions and fight my battles for me. Until I finally had to grow up and fight my own battles. Until I had to make my own difficult decisions about what I wanted for my life." After a moment she said diffidently, "So it's okay if I don't want a career after all? If I want to be just a wife and mother like Mom was?"

"Oh, honey, you don't need me to tell you that. You already know the answer…in your heart. And besides, there's nothing 'just' about being a wife…or a mother." Carly laughed a little self-consciously. "In fact, Shane and I have already discussed it, and…"

"Children? You and Shane?" Tahra couldn't keep the eagerness out of her voice.

Carly scrunched her face. "I'm a little old for a first-time mother, but…we're going to be trying…starting with our honeymoon."

"Oh, Carly, really?"

Unusually for her sister, warm color touched Carly's cheeks. "Really."

"You'll be a terrific mom," Tahra stated with assurance. "I know from experience."

"Thanks for the vote of confidence…but I'm far from perfect. I hope to do better this time around, though, not be such a 'helicopter' mom." The sisters shared a soft laugh. "And I'll have Shane to remind me if I forget."

Tahra blinked back sudden tears. "You really love him, don't you?" Her sister nodded. "I'm so glad for you. All these years you sacrificed for me. No, don't pretend you didn't," Tahra said when her sister started to protest. "I know how much you gave up to be there for me, always, and I can never repay you. So you deserve to be happy. I can't think of anyone who deserves it more."

"I can—you. You deserve it, honey. You're so good, through and through. You don't have a mean bone in your body. You deserve a happily-ever-after ending." Carly touched Tahra's cheek. "Are you sure he's the one you want? Are you sure he's the one who'll make you happy?"

Tahra shook her head. "You have it all wrong. Marek doesn't *make* me happy—I have to make my own happiness. But that's the thing, Carly. I'm happy when I'm with him. He makes me smile. He makes me laugh, even when I don't feel like laughing sometimes. I'm even happy when he's *not* there—although a little ache begins the minute he leaves that doesn't go away until he returns—because I know he loves me." She drew a deep breath and let it out slowly. "And he tries so hard to love me the way I need to be loved. It sounds so simple, but it's really not. Especially for him, because he wasn't raised that way. But he tries so hard. And that's how I know he's The One."

A knock on the closed bedroom door made Tahra quickly knuckle the tears from the corners of her eyes, so as not to mar her makeup. "Come in."

The door cracked open, and Carly's future sister-in-law—Keira Jones Walker—stuck her head in. "I hate to intrude, but Shane is going to have a nervous breakdown, Carly, if you don't come out soon."

She smiled in a conspiratorial manner. "Cody, of course, is getting a huge kick out of this," she said, referring to her husband. "You would *not* believe the grief Shane gave him at our wedding. Well," she amended, "not just Shane. All my brothers, actually. But you don't have to worry. Alec and Liam wouldn't dare do anything to Shane, not with their wives here to keep them in line, not to mention the babies they have to set a good example for. And besides, my mother laid down the law this time around—even best man Niall is trembling in his boots."

"We'll be right there," Carly assured her.

When Keira closed the door, Tahra said, "You're marrying into such a large family. Does it scare you…even a little?" She couldn't help thinking about Marek's family. Parents, grandmother, four younger brothers and two younger sisters—not to mention aunts, uncles and cousins galore, including those royal second cousins. She'd finally met his immediate family two weeks ago. All of whom—especially Marek's parents—had given the happy couple their wholehearted blessings. Kind of old-fashioned, but Tahra liked it…a lot. Because a woman didn't just marry a man, she married his family, too. And anyone who thought differently was fooling herself.

Carly shook her head. "No, it doesn't scare me, but then I don't scare easily. And besides, all the Joneses have welcomed me into the family, including Shane's mother. She and I have a lot in common, and I already love her. She reminds me of Mom…and that's the highest compliment I can pay her."

Another knock on the door had Tahra calling, "Come in," again.

This time the door opened all the way to admit Marek. "Alec sent me to tell you, Carly, that if you do not wish to find your future husband a…" He searched for the exact wording. "Oh, yes, a basket case—" He gave them a puzzled look when the two women laughed. "I am not quite sure what that means, but apparently you know."

Carly leaned over and kissed Tahra's cheek one last time. "I'd better go settle Shane down," she murmured, standing up and straightening the off-white cocktail-length lace sheath she'd chosen for her wedding dress. Her gaze slid to Marek, then back to Tahra, and only Tahra could see the wicked light in her sister's blue eyes. "Don't be long—the wedding starts in fifteen minutes. And don't let him muss your hair…much. You don't want everyone knowing what you've been up to."

Marek held the door for Carly and closed it behind her. Then he leaned back against the door and just stared at Tahra, who'd scrambled off the bed, smoothed down the skirt of her tea-length dress and slipped her shoes on.

"Your sister is wrong," he said softly, his gaze sliding over her like a caress. "I dare not touch you the way you look now…for I could never stop."

She laughed a little at that, but the heat in his eyes scorched her, kindling a corresponding flame. She could feel warmth steadily rising in her cheeks, but she tried to ignore it. "Do you like my dress?" she asked, twirling around, then glancing at his face. Her breath fluttered in her throat at the suddenly hungry expression she saw there.

"You are beautiful in anything, *mariskya*. But no dress—not even one that makes you look like a rose, as this one does—is as beautiful on you as it is off." He moved so swiftly Tahra was taken by surprise. His arms were iron bands as they pulled her into a crushing embrace, and his lips devoured hers. When he finally raised his head, there was a satisfied light in his eyes and his voice was very deep when he said, "I could not resist, but you are not immune, either. That is good. Very good."

"You already knew I wasn't…immune."

"Yes, but if I must behave, it is good to know it is no easier for you than it is for me." She laughed again—the laughter she'd told her sister he could always evoke. "Let us be married soon, Tahra," he said, pressing his body all along the length of hers, emphasizing—as if she needed the emphasis—exactly what he meant. "Very soon."

"Yes." She smiled up at him, an invitation in her eyes. An invitation that shy Tahra would never have dared to extend. "But we don't have to wait for that, you know."

"Yes, we do. I have sworn not to touch you that way again until we are man and wife—and a Zale never breaks a vow."

"Hmm." She considered this for a moment. "What if I'm doing all the touching? And what if I say 'please'?"

A wolfish smile slashed across his face, the kind of smile that promised everything her heart desired. Not to mention her body. Multiple times. "Now, *that* is a different situation entirely." His expression morphed into what she called his über-alpha, intently male look—a man with only one thing on his mind. "Exactly how long will your sister's wedding take?"

Tahra laughed softly, then sighed with happiness, her heart full to bursting. She loved that Marek was a man of his word…but she also loved that he wasn't *too* inflexible. That he would find a way to compromise, because that was a must in any long-term relationship. And they had a lot of years ahead of them between now and forever.

No, wait, what was the phrase from that movie *King's Ransom*? The phrase referring to the love shared by the first king and queen of Zakhar…the phrase that meant so much to all Zakharians? Not just forever, but "forever and a day." That was it. That was the bond they shared. Forever and a day.

"'Two hearts as one,'" she began, barely above a whisper. Marek was such a romantic, would he…?

She caught her breath at the naked look of love that flashed into his eyes. Then his smile softened, and his voice was deep and low as he murmured, "Yes, *mariskya*. 'Two hearts as one, forever and a day.'" He drew her left hand up and pressed three slow kisses into her palm, melting her insides and making her shiver with longing. Then he held her palm against his chest so she could feel his heart pounding in unison with hers. "Oh, yes. Your heart and mine, *mariskya*. Together. Always."

* * * * *

COMING NEXT MONTH FROM

HARLEQUIN®

ROMANTIC suspense

Available December 6, 2016

#1923 COLTON CHRISTMAS PROTECTOR

The Coltons of Texas • by Beth Cornelison

Investigating the Colton family's lawyer puts ex-cop Reid Colton and Penelope Barrington Clark, his partner's widow, in a shooter's crosshairs—and rekindles a forbidden attraction that puts their hearts on the line.

#1924 TAMING DEPUTY HARLOW

Cold Case Detectives • by Jennifer Morey

When Deputy Reese Harlow went looking for her birth father, she didn't expect to also find Jamie Knox, the sexy head of security at Dark Alley Investigations. Despite the chemistry, he's all wrong for her. But Jamie knows Reese is the woman for him, and as they work on a dangerous case, he's on a mission to tame the beautiful deputy.

#1925 HER SECRET CHRISTMAS AGENT

Silver Valley P.D. • by Geri Krotow

Undercover Silver Valley police officer Nika doesn't need anyone's help investigating a cult, not even from a former Special Forces operative turned hottest chemistry teacher in Silver Valley. Until the stakes turn lethal, and Mitch becomes her lover...

#1926 NIGHTS WITH A THIEF

by Marilyn Pappano

Lisette Malone has one goal: steal back a priceless heirloom. But to gain access to the island on which it is kept, she must seduce the dashing Jack Sinclair. It was never supposed to be real. Now Lisette is forced to answer one question: What's a thief to do when she falls for her mark?

YOU CAN FIND MORE INFORMATION ON UPCOMING HARLEQUIN® TITLES, FREE EXCERPTS AND MORE AT WWW.HARLEQUIN.COM.

HRSCNM1116

Widow Penelope Barrington never thought she'd speak to Reid Colton again, as he's the man she holds responsible for her husband's death. But when she finds evidence incriminating her father in his *father's disappearance, she's forced to team up with her teen crush to find the truth...before it's too late.*

Read on for a sneak preview of Beth Cornelison's COLTON CHRISTMAS PROTECTOR, the final book in ***THE COLTONS OF TEXAS*** *miniseries.*

"Reid..." she rasped.

He raised his head to look deeply into her eyes. "I want you, Pen. I won't pretend otherwise any longer. But if this isn't what you want, you can tell me to go to hell, and I'll respect your feelings."

She opened her mouth to reply, but so many thoughts and emotions battled inside her, she could only stare at him mutely.

When she didn't reply, his expression darkened. He levered farther away from her as if to leave, and she tightened her grip on his shirt.

"Pen?" He angled his head, clearly trying to read her.

"I...need more time." Her heart thrashed in her chest like a wild animal tangled in a snare. She felt trapped, caught between loyalty to Andrew and a years-old lust for Reid. Factoring in the mind-numbing twists her life had taken, her father's deceit and the foggy road that was her future, how could she know what was right? For both her and Nicholas, because she had to put her son's needs at the top of her considerations.

Reid bowed his head briefly, his disappointment plain. "More time. Right. Because we've only known each other for fifteen some years. Been friends for seven."

"Andrew—"

"Has been gone for over a year," he finished for her, his voice noticeably tighter. Pain flashed in his eyes, and he shoved away from her. "All right. I promised to respect your choice, and I will."

Freed of his weight and warmth, a stark chill sliced through her. Confusion or not, she didn't want to be without him. She did desire him, value the protection he offered, appreciate his friendship.

"Wait!" she cried before he could rise from the couch. She sat up, shifting her legs under her to kneel on the cushion beside him. "Reid, I'm still sorting out my feelings, but I want…" Her throat tightened. "I need…"

He arched an eyebrow to indicate he was listening, waiting.

She drew a slow breath, her body quivering from the inside out. She threaded her fingers through the hair near his ear before cupping the back of his head and drawing him close. "This…" she whispered as she slanted her mouth over his.

HRSEXP1116

HARLEQUIN®
A Romance FOR EVERY MOOD™